"I should not have touched you." *Or almost kissed you*, he added silently.

"Why?" Mairi said softly. "It is not as though you are really a servant, are you, Lucas? You were a soldier."

This was his chance to tell her who he really was, but the gunfire sounded again.

"I was a soldier, but I grew up in a great house." Let her believe he was John Lucas. "In any event, I should not have behaved as I did toward you. It was wrong of me."

She let go of him and walked a little faster, putting herself a step or two ahead of him. He caught up to her.

"I know you are right," she said, but her tone was sharp.

Had she wanted the kiss? He'd thought so. He'd been too familiar with her. In his father's house he would not dream of becoming so involved with— say—one of the maids. But she was not a maid, and he was not really a butler. How had this become so complicated?

Author Note

Readers like to ask where we romance authors get our ideas and often I am unable to answer such a question. This time, though, I know exactly where this story idea came from. *The Lord's Highland Temptation* was inspired by a Hollywood movie. Two, actually.

My Man Godfrey, in both versions, is a comedy in which a wealthy man is mistaken for a homeless person and winds up becoming the butler to an eccentric family. In the end he winds up with the quirky younger sister. In both versions, though, I thought the moviemakers missed a better story. The oldest daughter, the serious one, would have made a much better romantic heroine. She had so much more room to grow.

Of course, my story is not a comedy and Mairi and Lucas must endure some dark places before they find their happy ending. But while you read their story, look for glimmers of *My Man Godfrey*. They are in there!

PS—The settings in *The Lord's Highland Temptation* were loosely based on Auchinleck House in Ayrshire and Blair Castle in Pitlochry, two of my favorite places from my 2018 visit to Scotland with Number One London Tours.

DIANE GASTON

———

*The Lord's Highland
Temptation*

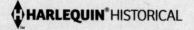

HARLEQUIN® HISTORICAL

Recycling programs
for this product may
not exist in your area.

ISBN-13: 978-1-335-63533-4

The Lord's Highland Temptation

Copyright © 2019 by Diane Perkins

Printed in U.S.A.

Diane Gaston's dream job was always to write romance novels. One day she dared to pursue that dream and has never looked back. Her books have won romance's highest honors: the RITA® Award, the National Readers' Choice Award, the HOLT Medallion, the Golden Quill and the Golden Heart® Award. She lives in Virginia with her husband and three very ordinary house cats. Diane loves to hear from readers and friends. Visit her website at dianegaston.com.

Books by Diane Gaston

Harlequin Historical

The Lord's Highland Temptation

The Governess Swap

A Lady Becomes a Governess
Shipwrecked with the Captain

The Society of Wicked Gentlemen

A Pregnant Courtesan for the Rake

The Scandalous Summerfields

Bound by Duty
Bound by One Scandalous Night
Bound by a Scandalous Secret
Bound by Their Secret Passion

Visit the Author Profile page
at Harlequin.com for more titles.

To Henriette and Liz, my wonderful friends
and former coworkers

Chapter One

Scotland—September 1816

The thundering of a thousand horses' hooves, the roar of the charge, the screams of the injured pounded across Lucas Johns-Ives's brain. He slashed at the French soldiers, so many caught off guard by the British cavalry, easy prey for their sabres. The charge had begun in glory, but now it was slaughter—blood everywhere, men crying out in agony, horses falling.

Dimly, the sound of a bugle reached Lucas's ears. *Ta-ta-ta. Ta-ta-ta.* Over and over. The signal to retreat. They'd ridden far enough. Done enough. Killed enough. Time to retreat.

Where was Bradleigh?

Lucas searched for his brother and spied him still waving his sword, his eyes bulging, a maniacal grimace on his face. He'd been so angry at Bradleigh, angry enough to refuse to ride next to him. Let his brother fight on his own for once.

But now Lucas shouted in a voice thick with panic, 'Bradleigh! Bradleigh! Retreat! We've ridden too far. Bradleigh!'

From the corner of his eye, Lucas saw a thousand French cavalry on fresh horses galloping closer, swords drawn.

His brother took no heed.

'Bradleigh! Bradleigh!'

Bradleigh impaled a blue-coated French soldier through the neck, pulled back his sword, dripping with the man's blood. He laughed like a madman.

Lucas spurred his horse to catch up to him. He'd pull his brother out of danger, just as he'd promised their father. Drag him back to the Allied lines. He'd save Bradleigh from himself.

He was almost there, almost at his brother's side, but then suddenly a French cuirassier on a huge black horse roared between them. Lucas pulled on his horse's reins to avoid crashing into the man and beast. The cuirassier charged to his brother, raised his sword and ran it through his brother's chest.

'No!' Lucas cried as his brother's blood spurted and his body fell from his horse. 'No!'

'I love the stone circle.' The melodic voice of a young girl broke into Lucas's reverie, melting away the sounds and sights of the battle.

The girlish voice laughed. 'Remember how we played here?'

Lucas shook his head. It could not be. This was Belgium, was it not? Where was the battle? Where was his brother?

Suddenly the air smelled of wet grass and a breeze cooled his burning skin. He'd been walking, he remembered. He'd felt light-headed and queasy—nothing another bottle of fine Scottish whisky couldn't cure. Had the drink caused the dream? Was *this* a dream? If so, which was the dream: the battle or the melodic voice?

'That was when we were mere children,' another voice

answered. A boy's voice this time. 'Or at least when I was a child. You still are one.'

'I am not,' the girl protested. 'Fourteen is not a child.'

'Ha!' the boy responded. 'Wait until you are sixteen. Then you will know fourteen is a child.'

The girl harrumphed. 'Oh, yes. You are so grown up.' Her voice changed. 'Niven, look! There is a man in the circle.'

'Where?' he answered.

'There. On the ground beneath one of the larger stones.'

Lucas heard them move closer.

'Who is it?' the boy asked.

'I do not know,' the girl replied. 'He's a stranger.'

'Stuff!' the boy said. 'There are no strangers hereabouts. Not on our land, anyway. We know everybody.'

Their land? Where was he, if not Belgium? Where had the stench of blood and gunpowder gone?

Lucas struggled to open his eyes, but the light stung them. He braced himself against the stone at his back and tried to rise. 'Bradleigh.'

His legs wouldn't hold him. He collapsed, scraping his head as he fell.

Their footsteps scrambled towards him and he forced his eyes open a slit. Two young people, a girl and a boy, floated into view, like apparitions.

'Sir! Sir! Are you hurt?' The girl leaned down to him, but she was just a blur.

Lucas tried to speak, but the darkness overtook him.

Mairi Wallace shook the dirt from her apron and lifted the basket of beets, carrots and radishes that she'd gathered from the kitchen garden. What a scolding she'd receive if her mother knew she'd been digging in the dirt.

'Now, Mairi,' her mother would say in her most patient but disapproving voice. 'It is not fitting for a baron's daughter to gather vegetables. If you must put yourself out in the sun, cut flowers. You are not a kitchen maid, after all.'

Except that all the kitchen maids except Evie had left. So many of their servants had bolted for positions that actually paid their wages that the household was woefully understaffed. Only two housemaids remained and two footmen. Mairi did not mind taking on some of their work. She rather liked the sun and fresh air on such a fine Scottish day.

She turned and gazed over the wall and caught sight of her younger brother, Niven, running down the hill as if the devil himself was after him.

Mairi frowned. Had he not gone for a walk with Davina? Mairi's heart beat faster. Where was Davina?

She dropped the basket and ran through the gate.

'Mairi! Mairi!' Niven called. 'Come quick! I need you!'

Mairi rushed to his side. 'What is it? Is it Davina?'

'No. Well, a little.' He fought to catch his breath. 'Oh, just come with me. Now.'

Niven, at sixteen, was old enough to have some sense, but he was as impulsive and impractical as their father. This would not be the first time Mairi had had to pull him out of a scrape. But Davina, their younger sister, was typically more prudent. Slightly.

What did he mean, *a little*? Was she hurt? If something had happened to Davina, she could not bear it!

Mairi followed Niven over the hill and to a part of their land that remained rustic and wild. They rushed too fast for talking. Niven led her to the stone circle, a place of danger, magic and mystery, according to family lore. She saw Davina silhouetted against the sky, the stones framing her. The ache in Mairi's throat eased a little.

Davina ran to meet them. 'Mairi! I am so glad you are here. We did not know what to do.'

Mairi wanted to embrace her in relief, but held back. 'Do? About what?'

Davina gestured for her to follow, leading her into the circle where a man—a stranger—was slumped against one of the stones, no hat on his head, his grey topcoat open and his clothing underneath rumpled and stained.

Two empty whisky bottles lay at his side.

Mairi's skin grew cold.

'He's passed out,' Davina said. 'I believe he is sick.'

Drunk, more like.

Mairi seized her by the shoulder. 'Did he hurt you?'

'Hurt me?' Davina pulled away. 'What a silly question. We found him leaning against the stone. When we called out, he tried to rise, but he collapsed again. I sent Niven for help.' She knelt at the man's side. 'I think he is feverish.'

Mairi wanted to drag Davina away from him. Her sister had no idea how dangerous a man—a drunkard—could be.

But the stranger was senseless at the moment, so there was no immediate threat. Mairi leaned down close.

Davina touched the stranger's forehead. 'He feels hot to me.'

The man was pale, but fine-looking. Fair-haired. A chiselled chin, strong nose, and lips befitting a Greek statue.

'Is he dead?' Niven asked.

Mairi forced herself to press her fingers against the side of his neck. She felt a pulse. 'He is alive.' She placed her palm against his brow. 'He is feverish, though.'

'Do you suppose the Druids got him? Mayhap he came here at midnight.' Niven spoke in all seriousness.

Tales of the Druids had abounded for generations. It was said their spirits would rise to attack anyone disturbing their midnight frolic amid the stones.

His clothes were damp.

'More likely he was caught in last night's rain,' Mairi said. What had he been doing on these hills in the middle of their land? The dampness of his clothing indicated he might have been there all night.

Davina's voice rose. 'We must be like the Good Samaritan.'

Davina had heard the sermon on Sunday? Mairi had thought she'd been too besotted with Laird Buchan's youngest son to heed Vicar Hill.

'We cannot leave him here,' Davina went on.

Leave him was precisely what Mairi wished to do. She wanted to run from him and take her brother and sister with her.

'No, we cannot leave him,' she said instead. He was ill, even if he was also drunk. He was in need.

And he could pose no danger in the state he was in. Could he?

She reached out her hand, but almost took it back again. She made herself shake the man's shoulder. 'Sir! Sir! Wake up.'

His eyes opened—blue eyes, vivid blue eyes—but they immediately rolled back in his head. They would never get him on his feet. And he was too big for them to carry.

Mairi turned to her sister. 'Davina, run back to the stables. Tell MacKay or John to come and bring a wagon.'

MacKay, older than their father, had stayed on as their stableman, and John was his only stable worker. In better times they'd had five or six men keeping the horses and carriages in fine order.

'Me?' Davina protested. 'I want to stay. Have Niven go.'

'I'll go,' Niven said.

Mairi didn't want Davina anywhere near this stranger, but nor did she wish to explain why.

'Very well,' she conceded. 'Niven, you go get the wagon.'
He dashed off.

It would take a long time for a wagon to wind its way around the hills to the stone circle. They would have to wait with him all that time.

'We will take him to our house, won't we, Mairi?' Davina asked. 'Not to the village, surely.'

Why not the village? Mairi thought.

'Who would care for him in the village?' Davina went on. 'We can nurse him until he gets better.'

Mairi did not want this man under their roof, but it made better sense to take him to their house. The village was further away and there was no guarantee someone would agree to care for him.

'We should summon the doctor, too,' Davina said.

How would they pay the doctor, then? This man would have to pay. If he had money. And if he had money, why had he been caught out wandering in the hills and not in some snug and dry inn?

'Should I run to the village for the doctor?' Davina asked.

Davina go alone to the village? Mairi hated it when Davina walked alone to the village, although no one but she knew to worry about it. On the other hand, she certainly did not wish to leave Davina alone with this strange man. Mairi trembled at the thought.

And at the memory of when she'd encountered a stranger while alone, a man who'd also been full of drink. Mairi did not want to be alone with another stranger.

But this man was obviously very sick. How would she feel if he died for lack of a doctor's care? Her heart pounded.

What if the man died before help arrived? And what if Mairi left Davina alone to care for him? Davina was too young for such a burden.

'Yes.' Mairi nodded. 'Excellent idea. I will stay here and wait for Niven to come with the wagon. We will meet you back at the house.'

'I will run like the wind,' Davina said dramatically.

Mairi watched her run down the hill where she'd meet the road and still have another three miles to go until she reached the village.

Mairi sat on the still-damp grass next to the man. 'At least you are no threat to me,' she murmured.

His eyes opened again and he suddenly lurched forward, seizing her by the shoulders.

She shrieked.

'My brother,' he rasped, his eyes wild. 'Bradleigh.'

He tried to stand and she scrambled away from his grasp.

He staggered, touching the stone to steady himself. He looked around, staring in her direction, but she had the notion he did not see her. He was somewhere else in his delirium.

'Must find Bradleigh,' he said again.

Mairi could not breathe.

He took a step towards her, but swayed and reached for the stone again. 'Must... Bradleigh...' He slid down the stone, insensible once more.

Mairi sat with her hands pressed against her face. He didn't move.

Was he dead? She was not so heartless that she wanted him dead. But she was still afraid of him. She remembered a man's fingers around her neck, forcing her to the ground...

She made herself stare at the stranger until she could see his chest rise and fall. He was still alive. She approached him once more and manoeuvred him so that the stone shaded him from the sun. Then she sat on the ground again.

At a safe distance.

* * *

The shade of the stone lengthened as Mairi waited for Niven to return with the wagon. After what must have been more than two hours, she finally heard the horse's hooves and the creak of the wagon wheels. There was only MacKay, the elderly stableman, to help, and the three of them had a struggle to get the man in the wagon.

By the time they reached the house, Davina was already there. 'I left word for the doctor. He was out.'

He was the only doctor for three villages. It could be hours or days before he'd come.

'Did you tell Mama and Papa about the man?' Mairi asked.

'No,' Davina answered. 'They have not returned from calling on Laird and Lady Buchan, Mrs Cross said.'

It was a wonder Mrs Cross, the housekeeper, knew the whereabouts of their parents. With only maids Betsy and Agnes to tend to the whole house, she spent a great deal of her time working along with them, cleaning and polishing and cleaning some more.

'We can tell Mama and Papa later,' Mairi told them.

Niven jumped down from the wagon box. 'What now? Where do we put him?'

Mairi climbed out more carefully. She certainly was not going to place him in a guest room. 'In the butler's room.' Their butler had left the family's employ over a month ago.

One of their two remaining footmen helped carry the man into the house and into the butler's room, far enough from the rest of the house not to give their parents any bother. Mairi would wait until dinner to tell them of the stranger.

'We must get him out of his wet clothes.' Mairi looked from Niven to the footman. Both avoided her gaze. She put her hands on her hips. 'You two must do it. You cannot expect me to. Or Davina. We will find some dry clothes for him.'

'Oh, very well,' Niven grumbled.

Mairi left the room and closed the door behind her.

Mrs Cross charged down the hallway. 'What is this, Miss Mairi?'

'Davina and Niven found a stranger at the standing stones. He is feverish. We could not leave him.' Though she dearly wished they could have.

'We cannot care for a sick man,' Mrs Cross protested. 'We are barely able to do the work that needs to be done as it is. What if he makes us all sick?' She sounded at the end of her tether.

'You and the maids will not have to go near him,' Davina piped up. 'We will take care of him.'

Mairi swung to her. 'Not you, Davina. You must not.'

'Why not?' her sister huffed.

Because he could be dangerous, she wanted to say.

'Because you are too young,' she said instead. 'And it isn't proper.'

Mairi would have to take charge of him. Her insides turned to stone at the thought.

That night at dinner, Mairi told her parents about the sick man in their butler's room.

Davina piped up, 'We were being Good Samaritans, were we not, Mama?'

Their mother smiled indulgently. 'Very Good Samaritans, Davina. Of course we must care for the poor man. I hope you told Mrs Cross to care for him as if he were a member of the family,' her mother added.

'I spoke to Mrs Cross about the man's care, yes,' Mairi responded.

She shot warning glances to Davina and Niven to say no more about it. Her mother and father would be thrown into a tizzy if they knew Mrs Cross could not handle one additional task. And her parents could so easily be thrown into a tizzy, like when Mairi tried to talk to them about economising, or suggest they sell something to at least pay the servants. Surely selling just one of her mother's necklaces could pay the servants and perhaps hire new ones.

Later that night, when she was certain that her mother and father had retired, Mairi crossed the hall to Niven's room.

'Come with me, Niven,' she insisted. 'We must check on the man.'

'Why do I have to go?' Niven protested.

'Because I said so!' He would be her safeguard.

She led him to the servants' stairs. They climbed down to the ground floor, where both the butler and Mrs Cross had their rooms.

They entered the butler's room.

Davina rose from a chair by the man's bedside. 'I tried to spoon him some broth, but it was no use.'

Mairi gasped. 'Davina! What are you doing here? You shouldn't be here.'

Davina tossed her a defiant look. 'We told Mrs Cross that we would care for the man.'

'I said not you.' Davina should be nowhere near this man. 'You go to bed. Niven and I will remain with him.'

She'd meant only to check on the man, not stay, but now she feared if she did not, Davina would sneak back down.

Besides, he looked deathly ill.

'I don't want to stay the whole night,' grumbled Niven.

Mairi whirled on him. 'Well, you must.'

Davina tossed her head haughtily as she walked to the door. 'Try to get him to take some broth.'

Niven settled in the upholstered chair that had once sat in their library before their mother had decided on a whim to redecorate. Niven promptly closed his eyes. Mairi moved the wooden chair away from the bed. She stared at the stranger and felt her cheeks grow hot.

He'd thrown off the covers and was naked above his waist. The nightshirt Mairi had sneaked from their father's room lay folded on a nearby chest.

'Niven! Why did you not dress him?'

'He started fighting us,' her brother replied without opening his eyes. 'Do not fret. He's wearing drawers.'

The man looked even more formidable bare-chested with every muscle in stark relief. Even more disturbing were the scars criss-crossing his chest, a dozen random cuts. Mairi made herself approach the bed and pull the blankets over him. He stirred and flung the covers off again.

'Niven!' she whispered.

But her brother had fallen asleep and she did not have the heart to wake him.

Her gaze returned to the stranger and she saw that his breathing was ragged. She reached over and felt his forehead. It was still hot with fever.

She must do something for him. She rose to the chest of drawers and poured water from the pitcher into the basin. She grabbed a towel and brought the basin to the bed. Dipping the towel in the water, she bathed his head. When she touched the scrape on his forehead, he groaned. His eyes opened and fixed on her.

She gasped.

He stared at her. 'Are you an angel?' His speech was slurred.

She recoiled. 'An angel? No.'

His brow furrowed. 'Not heaven?'

'No. Not heaven.' She glanced towards Niven. He was still asleep. No help to her.

'No,' the man rasped. 'Wouldn't go to heaven.' He swallowed and the effort seemed painful. 'Bradleigh. Where is he?' He tried to rise.

'Bradleigh?' Was it possible there was another man out there? 'You were alone.'

'Alone.' His ramblings were very close to madness. He lay back down and closed his eyes. 'Yes. Yes. I am alone.'

His accent was English.

Her attacker had been English.

Reluctantly she pulled her chair closer. 'You should drink some broth. Sit up.'

'Want whisky.' His eyes opened again, but for a mere moment. 'To forget.'

She bristled at the word *whisky*. The memory of its pungent odour struck so vividly she thought she could smell it all over again, even though it had been five years ago. This man did not smell of whisky, even though there had been bottles at his side. This man smelled of fever.

'No whisky,' she stated firmly. 'Broth.'

It took Mairi several minutes to compose herself enough to assist him. He could not sit on his own. She needed to put her arm around his bare shoulders to help him. His skin was damp with sweat, but still very hot. His muscles were rock-hard. No wonder his grip had been vice-like when he'd lunged at her. How easily he could overpower her.

Holding her breath to still her trembling, she brought the bowl of broth to his lips.

Her head was inches from his and her hand shook at how close and vulnerable she was. His face was deathly pale and the bristles of his unshaven jaw made him appear rakish. Still, she could not deny how fine his features were.

His handsome looks did not reassure her, though. Not all ogres had warts and pointed teeth.

He drank only a few sips before slumping against her arm. His body was too heavy for her to hold and she had to release him. He returned to his fitful sleep.

She moved her chair a bit further away. When she glanced at him, she saw that he still tossed and turned and mumbled in his sleep. Had they helped him at all? What would happen if he died?

What would happen if he lived?

Of one thing she was certain. She would not allow him to hurt her family.

As she had once been hurt.

Chapter Two

As the night stretched on, the man's condition worsened. His breathing turned raspy and he often seemed in the throes of some delirium. He kept calling for Bradleigh, reliving something dreadful over and over. There in the middle of the night, all alone, deprived of sleep, Mairi, too, relived something dreadful. Rescuing this man—this *Englishman*—had cracked open memories she always tried to keep at bay. Now those memories assaulted her and she relived that day when a strange man—another Englishman—had seized her arm, dragged her out of sight of the village road and ruined her life for ever.

Sometimes she could go for days without thinking of it. Then a sound, a word, even a smell, would put her right back in that shrubbery, that horrid man on top of her—

She pressed her fingers into her forehead.

Stop! Do not think of it.

It had been five years ago. It was over. No one knew and she could keep pretending it had never happened.

Mairi turned to the sick man in the bed. He was still. Quiet. Her heartbeat quickened. No. No. He could not die!

She glanced over at Niven, who was still sound asleep. She wanted desperately to wake him so she would not be alone with a dying man, but how cruel would it be to put her brother through what she feared to endure herself?

Finally, the man took a deep, rasping breath and sat up, startling her so much she almost tipped over in her chair.

His feverish eyes fixed on her, but without indication he really saw her. 'Let me die,' he begged. 'Me, not him. My fault.'

His tone was bereft. Mournful. A wave of incredible sadness washed over her. She shook herself. She did not wish to feel sympathy for this man, this stranger. This Englishman.

But she also did not want to witness him dying. She stood and gently pushed on his bare shoulders. 'Lie down. No talk of dying now. You must rest.'

He lay back against the pillows, breathing hard. 'No. Better to die.'

The pain in that statement washed through her again. She remembered wishing she could die. After what had been done to her, she'd felt too ashamed to live. She'd once stood on the red sandstone cliff, determined to throw herself over the edge, but then she'd thought of Davina and Niven, and her mother and father. They needed her. No matter her unhappiness, she would not desert them. Gradually, she'd learned to live with what had happened to her.

The stranger rolled on to his side, facing away from her. She strained to see that his chest still moved. She shifted her chair to a better vantage point and tried to stay awake.

She did not succeed.

She woke to Niven shaking her. 'Wake up, Mairi! The doctor is here.'

She straightened in the chair and her gaze shot to the stranger. Still breathing, thank God!

He lay on his back, the bedcovers flung off, revealing his undressed state.

Mr Grassie, the doctor, a stocky man who seemed perpetually in a rush, strode into the room, stopping abruptly at the sight of her dishevelled appearance and the half-naked man in the bed nearby.

'Miss Wallace!' He eyed her disapprovingly. 'You are tending to this man?'

She stood and lifted her chin. 'Niven and I watched over him during the night.' At least the doctor would not presume she'd been alone with the man.

Mr Grassie's gaze swept over the stranger as he approached the bed. He felt the man's pulse, then opened his black bag and pulled out a glass tube. He pressed one end of the tube to the man's bare chest and the other to his ear, moving it to various spots. He frowned. He put the tube away and opened the man's eyes with his thumb and looked inside his mouth. The Englishman did not rouse.

Finally Mr Grassie stepped back. 'His chest is not clear. He is gravely ill. How did he come to be here?'

'Niven and Davina found him at the standing stones,' Mairi told him. 'He's not been sensible enough to tell us anything more.'

Mr Grassie gestured to the scars on the man's chest. 'He was a soldier, I'd wager. Those are sabre cuts. I've seen the like before.' Mr Grassie had once been an army surgeon.

'A soldier!' Niven's eyes kindled with interest.

Mairi's brows knitted. 'What was an English soldier doing on our property?'

Mr Grassie looked up at her. 'English, is he?'

'In his ravings, he spoke with an English accent.' He'd called for whisky and wished he would die. 'What are we to do? Is there some medicine for him?'

The doctor shrugged. 'I'll have the apothecary mix up something. It might help his breathing.'

'*Might* help?' This was not very encouraging.

He gave her a direct look. 'If the fever doesn't break soon, well, there is no hope for him.'

'Do you mean he could die?' cried Niven. 'He must not die.'

Mr Grassie patted Niven's shoulder. 'Only time will tell, son.' He picked up his bag. 'Give him broth or tea. He'll need the fluids to flush out the fever. And limit who tends to him. I've seen this grippe in the village. It is highly contagious.'

That did it. Mairi would tend to him alone and no one besides Niven would enter the room.

'Shall I stop above stairs and report this to your father or mother?' the doctor asked.

She knew he was in a hurry. 'I will tell them.' Or some version of the doctor's report. She did not wish her parents to fret. In any event, they were likely still abed. The morning was not yet very advanced.

'I will come tomorrow if I can.' Mr Grassie shook his head. 'But there is a lot of this sickness about.'

'Come when you can, sir.' She walked him to the door. 'I'll have Niven or one of the footmen collect the medicine from the apothecary this afternoon.'

The doctor nodded and took one more glance at the patient. 'I wish I had more to offer.'

So did Mairi.

As he was crossing the threshold, Davina appeared in the hallway. 'Good morning, Mr Grassie,' she said brightly. 'How is he?'

Mr Grassie hesitated to answer her.

Mairi broke in. 'Let Mr Grassie be on his way, Davina. I'll fill you in.'

The doctor nodded gratefully and hurried away.

Niven came up behind Mairi. 'He said the man could die, Davina!'

'Oh, no!' Davina cried.

Niven couldn't keep his mouth shut. Why alarm Davina that way?

'We will not let him die,' Mairi assured her, although the truth was more uncertain. 'We will take care of him.'

Davina gave her an earnest look. 'I will help. What can I do?'

Mairi certainly would not risk Davina becoming ill. 'The doctor said he is very contagious and that we must limit who is in contact with him, so I do not want you in his room.' Even if there was no chance of contagion, she did not want Davina in the presence of a half-naked Englishman. 'I've already been exposed, so I will continue to care for him.'

'I can help, too,' Niven said. 'I've also been exposed.'

'Yes, you can help,' she agreed. 'But I must be the only one who touches him. No sense you getting sick.'

'I must do something, too!' Davina insisted.

'Help Mrs Cross. She really needs help and I won't be able to assist her,' Mairi said. 'Or go with Niven to pick up the medicine.'

Davina pursed her lips. 'Oh, very well.'

She stormed off, and Mairi, still very weary, returned to the bedside of their patient.

After the doctor left, Mairi sent MacKay and John out to look for this other man the Englishman kept raving about. Had he called him his brother? No one was found, but they did retrieve a satchel she presumed belonged to the Englishman. She and Niven searched through it and discovered a purse full of money, but nothing that told them anything about the owner. At least there would be money to pay Mr Grassie, which was one worry off Mairi's shoulders.

* * *

The Englishman remained feverish for two days straight. Mairi fed him the medicine the doctor had ordered. She pushed him to drink broth and tea. She bathed his skin with cool cloths and remained by his side with only short breaks to eat and change clothes. She no longer insisted Niven stay with her. The man was no threat to anyone in his state and she was long past any limit propriety would dictate. She did ask Niven to fetch things for her and to sit with the man while she caught a little sleep, but that was all.

The doctor returned on the second day and declared it a hopeful sign that their patient was still alive, but he also cautioned that the fever needed to break soon.

The hours of care Mairi devoted to the man played havoc with her emotions. He was still a stranger, an Englishman—a whisky drinker—young and strong enough to be an object of fear, but, at the same time, he was so very ill. His life depended on her care. She swung from feeling great compassion for his suffering to wishing he had never entered their property. His ravings both disturbed her and piqued her curiosity. What had he done that tormented him so?

She discovered the Englishman's ravings dissipated if she talked to him. So, even though he lay insensible, his breathing still laboured, she rattled on to him, about how they'd found him and brought him to the house, about how they'd found his satchel, about how they did not know who he was or where he belonged.

She also scolded him for wanting to die.

'You must not die, you know,' she told him. 'Not after Niven and Davina saved you. It would hurt them greatly to think their good deed had such a terrible result. They are so very young, you see. Too young to know how difficult living can be. It would hurt them badly. So you must not die.'

He shook his head back and forth, as if he'd heard her.

'Do not disagree with me, sir!' she went on. 'If they had not come upon you, you would have got your wish.' She yawned. Talking helped her stay awake as well. 'You owe them your life.'

To her surprise he turned towards her and opened his eyes. They still looked as feverish as ever.

'Should have left me,' he murmured.

'And have your death on their consciences?' she countered. 'You cannot wish that on them.'

His expression turned even more bleak. 'Should be me to die,' he rasped. 'Do not want to live.'

She leaned closer. 'Listen to me! Such a feeling passes. I know. You must live for Niven's and Davina's sakes. Mr Grassie thinks you are some sort of soldier. If so, you should fight now to live, just as you would do in battle.'

Whether he heard her, she could not say. 'Thought you were an angel. Thought I was already dead.'

No. She was definitely not an angel, not despoiled as she was. 'You must fight to stay alive.' As she had. She'd fought her attacker, but he'd overpowered her. She'd also fought her own death wish. And won.

'Fight,' he said so softly she was uncertain she'd heard him.

She went on, trying to push away those despairing times. 'You are not the only one, you know, who must fight to live. Or the only one who has regrets.'

'Regret,' he repeated.

She went on. 'You may not realise it, but there will be ways you are still needed. There are people who will suffer if not for your help. You must simply endure and persevere.'

She was sitting close so he could hear her. He reached over and grasped her hand. Her impulse was to pull away, but if he needed that small comfort, who was she to deny it to him?

'Angel,' he murmured.

His eyes closed again and soon he slept as fitfully as before.

That third night it seemed as if the Englishman's fever worsened. Mairi despaired. She'd done all she could, but he thrashed even harder in the bed, calling always for Bradleigh. Bradleigh. She was exhausted and near tears when he finally quieted. He would die, she knew it. Now she needed to stay awake so he would not be alone when that moment came.

But in spite of her resolve, her eyelids drooped.

When she woke herself, she had no idea how long she'd slept. How could she have dozed off at such an important time? One of the lamps had burned out, and in the dim light of the one remaining lamp, the man looked very still. Was he breathing? She could not tell.

Tentatively she extended her hand, preparing herself to find him cold to the touch. She pressed her hand to his forehead.

Not cold. Not hot, either!

She touched her own forehead. Same temperature. She touched him again. The fever had broken!

'Oh!' she cried aloud. 'Thank God. Thank God.'

Lucas opened his eyes at the sound of the voice that had echoed through his dreams, that entrancing voice that was the lifeline he'd grasped on to. Next to him sat a dark-haired young woman whose pale skin and blue eyes seemed ethereal in the lamplight.

She broke into a smile. 'You are awake!'

He had just enough energy to nod.

She jumped up from her seat and came even closer.

'You should drink something. Are you able to sit? Let me help you.'

She placed her hands, so warm and gentle, on his bare skin and helped him pull himself up. Where were his clothes? Why was he half-naked in front of this exquisite creature? He couldn't speak.

She turned to a table and picked up a cup, bringing it to his lips. One sip convinced him he was very thirsty. He drank all of it.

And could finally speak. 'I don't remember—'

'What happened to you?' she finished for him. 'You have been very ill with a fever, but it has broken now. You'll soon get well.' She sounded very relieved.

He remembered now. Remembered fevered dreams. Dreams of Bradleigh, impaled by the French cuirassier. Dreams of an angel. 'You.' His voice rasped. 'Do I know you?'

'No. You are not from here,' she responded. 'My brother and sister found you. We brought you here.'

'Here?'

'Scotland. Ayrshire.'

That was right. He'd wanted to get as far away from Fox-grove as he could and he'd not cared where. He'd headed north into Scotland and ridden from inn to inn, drinking enough whisky to keep him so constantly in his cups he didn't have to think about…anything.

'Village?' Not that it mattered.

'You are not in a village,' she explained. 'You are in the home of my father, the Baron of Dunburn.'

She was a baron's daughter? Not a tavern maid? He'd assumed this was an inn. 'How did I get here?'

She sat again. 'My brother and sister found you on our land, insensible from fever. We have taken care of you.'

He had a glimmer of a memory. Of leaving an inn where

the stranger with whom he'd shared a room had coughed and hacked the night through. Of somewhere losing his horse and climbing hill after hill in the rain.

He opened his mouth to speak, but his words caught. 'More. Drink,' he finally managed to gasp.

She rose and poured more tea into the cup and brought it to his lips again. This time he wrapped his hands around hers and held on while he drank.

'How long have I been here?' he asked.

'Three days,' she said.

Three days?

He stared at her, the angel whose voice had called him back. She'd stayed by his side for three days? A baron's daughter?

She poured him another cup of tea. 'You were very feverish.' She handed him the cup this time.

He drank gratefully.

'You kept calling out for Bradleigh.' Her lovely brow knitted. 'Was he with you? We searched, but could not find him.'

He glanced away from her. 'My brother. He was not with me.'

'Thank goodness.' She sighed. 'I was quite worried.'

No need. Bradleigh was beyond worry.

Lucas wished there was whisky in that cup. He slid back down in the bed.

'Sleep now,' she said and lifted his blankets to cover him up like his mother used to do when he was in leading strings. 'Now that your fever is gone, I'll leave you to sleep. But I'll be back in the morning.'

She extinguished the lamp and the only light in the room came from the glowing coals in the fireplace.

When she reached the door she turned back to him. 'Goodnight. Sleep well.'

Chapter Three

Lucas woke to daylight and a strange room. It took a moment to remember. He was in the house of a Scottish baron and had been cared for by his angel of a daughter— or had that merely been another fevered dream? His head pounded, his mouth tasted foul and his throat felt parched.

He sat up in bed, waiting for a moment until his head stopped spinning, then swung his legs over the side of the bed. When his bare feet touched the cool slate tiles of the floor, he looked down at himself. He wore only his drawers. Where were his clothes? Where was his satchel? His money?

Folded on a nearby chest was a nightshirt. Lucas tossed it aside and opened the chest. There were some clothes in there, but not his own. He rummaged through the chest and found a shirt and breeches that had been made for a more corpulent man. They would fit, especially with the set of braces at the bottom of the chest. Still seated on the bed, he put them on, having to rest at intervals from the exertion. When he gathered strength again he rose and took a step towards the door. His legs wouldn't hold him and he collapsed on to the bed again.

Voices sounded from outside the room. One voice came closer. A woman. A familiar voice. 'He is in here.'

The door opened and the lovely creature of his dreams entered the room. Lucas expelled a grateful breath. She was real. In the daylight from the window he could clearly see she was taller than most women, elegantly so. Her mahogany hair was coming loose from its pins, framing her face with its arched brows, nearly perfect nose and lips and an unmistakable look of intelligence.

He managed to stand.

'You are awake.' She sounded surprised. 'And dressed.'

He gestured to the chest. 'I found some clothes.'

With her was an older man in a black suit, carrying a black-leather bag. 'This is the doctor, Mr Grassie.' She turned to the doctor. 'As you can see, he is much better.'

The doctor had seen him before? Of that he had no memory.

His legs weakened and he grasped the bedpost to keep from falling. 'Forgive me. My strength fails.'

'No need for apology,' the doctor answered. 'Please do sit on the bed and let me examine you.'

The doctor opened his bag and took out a glass tube, which he placed against Lucas's chest. 'Breathe in and out.' He moved the tube to various spots on Lucas's chest before putting it down. 'Your lungs are much improved. Almost no congestion. How do you feel?'

'My head aches and my throat feels dry.' Lucas stole a glance at the young woman, who waited by the door with her arms crossed. There was a warmth in her expression that loosened one of the knots inside him.

'Open your mouth,' the doctor ordered.

Lucas complied.

After looking inside Lucas's mouth, the doctor stepped back. 'Your throat is better, too. A little red still, but that might be from lack of fluids. You've had a bad case of the grippe. There is too much of it going around. It can be very contagious, you know. Your fever has broken, so that is a good sign, although it will return if you exert yourself and you might not be able to throw it off next time. You need rest.'

The baron's daughter frowned.

Lucas turned back to the doctor. 'Mr Grassie, I presume I am imposing on this family's hospitality. Perhaps I should gather my belongings and retire to an inn somewhere.'

The doctor shook his head. 'No, no. That you must not do. You could spread this all over the county. Rest here. At least ten days. If your symptoms continue to abate, you will not be contagious by then.' He turned to the young woman. 'He must rest. You can accommodate him, can you not?'

A worry line creased her brow. 'I suppose so.'

Had Lucas misread her earlier warmth?

Lucas directed his gaze to her. 'I will not stay if I am imposing.'

The doctor packed his bag again and shut it. He glared at the young woman. 'Miss Wallace, shall I speak to your father or mother about whether this man may recuperate here?'

So her name was Miss Wallace. Not married, then. An eldest daughter.

Her face coloured. 'You need not trouble Papa or Mama, Doctor,' she retorted in as sharp a tone. 'We will not turn away a sick man.'

'Excellent.' The doctor picked up his bag.

'About payment?' Miss Wallace sounded uncertain as the doctor walked towards the door.

Lucas spoke up. 'I am well able to pay. Assuming my purse is with my clothing.'

'I will send a bill,' the doctor said. He hurried out of the door without once asking Lucas's name.

Lucas's gaze met Miss Wallace's and held, but before either spoke, two young people burst into the room.

'You are awake!' The girl appeared to be a younger version of the beautiful Miss Wallace, this one on the verge of womanhood rather than in its finest bloom.

With her was a youth, a brother by the family looks they shared. He, also, was younger than Miss Wallace. He reminded Lucas of the young ensigns sent to war when barely breeched.

'How are you, sir?' the boy asked. 'Mairi said your fever broke during the night. What did Mr Grassie say?'

Her name was Mairi.

Mairi Wallace ignored her brother's question and shooed them back to the doorway. 'You two must leave at once. Wait for me. I will be right out.' She closed the door and turned back to Lucas. 'My brother and sister. Your rescuers.'

'I hope I might thank them,' he said, although he wasn't yet sure whether he was glad he had not perished.

He tried to stand, this time bracing himself against the side of the bed. 'Miss Wallace, no matter what the doctor said, if you prefer I leave—'

Her expression softened again. 'No. No. We will not turn you out. You must forgive me if that is what you thought.'

He looked around the room, which seemed plainly furnished and devoid of decoration. 'Whose room am I in? I gather this is not a guest room.'

She nodded, but her expression seemed…uneasy. 'This is our butler's room. He…he left our employ recently, so this room was not occupied. The silver is kept in another room, not here. And, for now, the housekeeper holds the keys.'

Why mention the silver? Did she think he might pinch it?

He looked down at himself. 'Are these the butler's clothes I am wearing?'

'They were in the chest? We did not realise he'd left anything behind.'

Had the man left in haste? Lucas wondered. 'And my clothing? My satchel?'

'They were washed and brushed,' she replied. 'Possibly they are dry now. I will check. I charged Niven with keeping your purse.'

'Niven?'

'My brother.'

The intruding youth, no doubt.

She turned to leave.

He stopped her. 'Miss Wallace, wait.'

She turned back.

'You should know who I am.' It was on the tip of his tongue to introduce himself as Lucas Johns-Ives, son of the Earl of Foxgrove, but was he not now Viscount Bradleigh—his father's heir—his brother's title? He could not bear to be that person, could not bear taking his brother's name and rightful place. Disappointing his father. He wanted none of it.

'I am… Lucas. John Lucas.'

That was who he would be, plain John Lucas.

She nodded and smiled, albeit sadly. 'I will bring you something to eat, Mr Lucas. You must be hungry.'

He smiled back and fancied his smile a reflection of hers. 'I am ravenous, Miss Wallace.'

Mairi's heart raced as she stepped into the hallway. In daylight, without the pallor of illness, he was quite the handsomest man she'd ever seen, even with three days' worth of beard. Even more disturbing was the connection she felt with him, as if nursing him through his fever had somehow linked him to her in a way she did not understand. She shivered, trying to shake the feeling away.

Davina and Niven accosted her.

'Is he recovered?' Davina asked. 'What did Mr Grassie say?'

Niven chimed in. 'What was wrong with him?'

What was wrong was that he was a stranger—an Englishman—who would now be a guest in their house for at least ten days.

She pushed past them. 'I need to speak with Cook. He needs food and water.'

They followed her to the kitchen.

'At least answer us!' Davina cried.

Mairi held up a finger to warn them to give her a moment.

Cook was busy stirring something in a pot over the fire.

'Mrs MacNeal, our patient is hungry. What might I bring him?'

Mrs MacNeal's wrinkles creased into a sympathetic look. 'Oh, the poor lad. I take it he is feeling better?' Cook had kept her supplied with broth and tea for him the last three days.

'He is much better,' she replied. 'His fever has broken.'

Cook winced as she tottered over to a shelf where the servants' dishes were stacked. The poor woman's arthritis must be paining her. She ought to be given a nice pension and a little cottage on the estate, not running the kitchen with only one kitchen maid to help.

'Let me help you,' Mairi said, hurrying to her side.

'Thank you, Miss Mairi.' The old woman pointed to a high shelf. 'One of those bowls and a plate will do. The soup is ready. I'm keeping it warm for dinner. And there is fresh bread.'

'I'll cut some bread,' Davina offered. She skipped over to the bread box and took out a loaf.

'He'll want some ale, I expect,' Niven added. 'Shall I get him some?'

Mairi nodded.

'I'll slice some cheese for him, as well,' Davina said. She carried some cheese to the worktable.

Cook, Davina and Niven arranged a very generous tray for the Englishman.

'Now tell us about him,' Davina demanded. 'Who is he? What did the doctor say?'

Of course they would be curious about the man she'd rescued.

Mairi replied, 'His name is John Lucas.'

'But what is his regiment?' Niven asked. 'I thought he was a soldier.'

'I did not ask him about being a soldier. He has only this morning been out of danger.' Mairi glanced from Niven to Davina. 'Mr Grassie believes he is much improved, but he must rest. And he still may be contagious, so you must stay away from his room.'

'I do not mind helping,' Davina said.

Mairi frowned. 'Better it be Niven. It would not be proper for you to be in his room.'

Davina's chin lifted. 'Then it is not proper for you either, Mairi. But you were in his room day and night, were you not?'

Mairi could see that Cook listened to their every word. 'Only because he had the fever and we had to limit how many were exposed to it. In any event, now that the fever is gone, it should be Niven who attends him.'

'But I won't be here!' Niven protested. 'Not tomorrow. I am off to Crawfurd's tomorrow.'

William Crawfurd was Niven's childhood friend, about to embark on a Grand Tour abroad—something out of the question for Niven since both his tutor and Davina's governess had left for positions that would actually pay them.

'Well, attend him today.' Mairi would worry about tomorrow, tomorrow.

She followed Niven down the hallway, knocked on the butler's door and opened it, stepping inside long enough to see Mr Lucas rise.

'Miss Wallace.' He nodded.

Again she felt that pull towards him.

She stepped aside so Niven could enter. 'My brother. Niven.'

The Englishman's eyes left hers only briefly to acknowledge Niven.

'He brought you food,' she said unnecessarily.

Before the man could say another word, she left the room.

The youth carrying the food tray grinned at Lucas. 'You'll have to forgive Mairi. She has a bee in her bonnet about something, I'll give you that.'

'I understand she tended to me these last three days,' Lucas responded. 'She must be quite fatigued.'

'Well, I helped some,' the boy said. He lifted the tray slightly. 'I've brought you some food. Shall I set the tray on the table or would you like to eat on the bed?'

'The table.' After the doctor had left, Lucas had forced himself not to crawl back under the bedcovers, but he'd not progressed beyond sitting on the bed's edge.

He rose, holding on to the bedpost until he knew his legs would support him. He marshalled enough energy to walk the few steps to the chair by the table. He nearly collapsed into it.

'Mairi said your name is Lucas.' Niven set the tray in front of him.

He ought to have introduced himself. 'That is so.'

The boy flopped down on a second wooden chair at the table. 'Mr Grassie said you were in the army, because of the scars on your chest. Is that so?'

They'd seen his scars? Of course they had. He'd been nearly naked.

'Not any more,' he replied, wishing the boy would probe no further. He tore off a piece of bread and swallowed a small bite. 'Tell me what you know of how I came to be here,' he said instead. 'Your sister said very little of it.'

The boy was eager to answer. 'Davina and I found you. Davina is my other sister. You saw her before when we came in.'

He told the story in great detail with emphasis on the speed of his running to seek help from his older sister and again to send for the wagon that had carried Lucas back from one of the hills on their property, a hill that possessed a stone circle. Flashes of memory returned. The rain. Staggering to a stone that kept the cold wind from his back. Voices—Niven's and Davina's voices, he now surmised.

Mairi Wallace had waited with him until the wagon came. It seemed she'd been at his side right from the beginning.

'How was it your sister was the one to care for me?' Why not a servant? Or their mother?

'Mairi? She wouldn't let anybody else,' the boy responded. 'Except for me. I sat with you when she had to eat or rest or something, but she wouldn't let me touch you. Said nobody else should get close.'

Because they could become ill? What about her? She had risked illness tending to him.

Lucas took a long gulp of ale. 'Were there no servants who could help?'

'Mairi would not hear of it,' Niven replied. 'We don't have that many servants, anyway. Several have left us recently.' Niven leaned back, balancing on the back legs of the chair. 'So Mairi thinks she has to do everything to make up for it.' The chair slipped, but he caught it in time to right it again. 'If Mama knew it, she'd be very cross.' He grinned mischievously. 'Mama thinks the servants are still doing all the work. I tease Mairi that I'll tell Mama she's doing it. Or making Davina and me do it. Mairi becomes too iron-handed at times. She can be the most insufferable nag.'

Mairi sounded incredibly burdened. More so now with him barely able to stand.

'Why did your servants leave?' Lucas asked.

'I think they wanted to get paid,' Niven replied. 'Things are a little tight for us at the moment.'

That was quite an admission. Lucas had apparently wound up in a household that could not afford one extra mouth.

The boy chattered on as Lucas finished the soup. An hour passed pleasantly enough and Lucas learned more about the family than he suspected Niven's older sister would have wished.

There was a rap on the door and Niven called out, 'Come in.'

Miss Wallace—Mairi—entered. Lucas stood, but braced himself on the table.

'Niven!' She glared at her brother. 'I've been searching for you. What are you doing in here? You should not be bothering this man.'

Niven looked petulant. 'We were conversing. Conversing isn't bothering.'

'It is when he's unwell,' she retorted. 'Take the dishes

back to the kitchen, then wait for me. I need your help.'
She turned to Lucas. 'I've brought your purse, Mr Lucas.'
She handed it to him.

'Thank you, Miss Wallace.' His hand brushed hers as
he took it from her. 'I appreciate that.'

Niven glanced towards Lucas and rolled his eyes. 'I suppose I must do her bidding. Good day, Lucas.'

'Thank you for bringing the food.'

'Mairi made me do it.' The boy grinned. 'But I did not
mind.'

'Go!' Miss Wallace commanded.

Niven slowly slid off the chair and ambled from the room.

Miss Wallace turned her lovely blue eyes on Lucas. 'I
am terribly sorry. He wasn't supposed to stay.'

'He was no bother,' Lucas assured her. 'Thank you for
the food, Miss Wallace. I am much restored.'

She shrugged. 'Cook had the soup already made.'

Her gaze caught his and held. Her presence soothed him.
He did not want her to leave.

She glanced towards the door and back. 'Do you require
anything else?'

He would not hold her there, much as he wished to.

He rubbed his chin. 'My satchel? My razor should be
in it.'

She nodded. 'Your satchel was also hung to dry. That
night you spent out on the hill, it rained quite heavily.' She
started for the door. 'I will have Niven bring it to you.'

Not her?

'I will leave you now.' Their gazes caught again, but she
turned towards the door.

'Miss Wallace?'

She looked back at him.

'I am grateful to you. More than I can say.'

She lifted the latch on the door and walked out.

Lucas was left alone with only his memories and regrets. He closed his eyes, wishing he had the company of a bottle of whisky. Or two.

Chapter Four

Mairi again left his room with her heart racing. When the Englishman looked at her with those vivid blue eyes all she could see was pain. Not physical pain, but the kind that reaches down into one's soul, the kind of pain with which she was acutely familiar. It felt like a bond with him.

What nonsense, though.

She shook off the feeling and hurried to the kitchen, where Niven was happily munching on some biscuits Cook had given him.

'Niven, I need you to bring Mr Lucas his clothing and satchel and everything that was in it. They are in the footmen's room.'

Her brother looked up at her. 'Zounds, Mairi. No need to bark orders at me. I want to help.'

She walked over to him and ruffled his hair, which always annoyed him. 'I am sorry, Niven. I do not know what I would do without you.'

He ran a testy hand through his hair, but looked up at her with serious eyes. 'Do you need me to forgo my visit with Crawfurd?'

Niven knew their family was in financial difficulty, but Mairi did not have the heart to tell him precisely how serious she suspected it was and how she feared it might result in him losing his birthright.

'No, dear Brother.' She kissed him on his head, another gesture that irked him. 'You deserve some enjoyment.'

He waved her away, but grinned at her.

She made her way up the stairs to the hall. Papa and Mama would be up by now and they should be informed about what the doctor had said.

Davina stood at the foot of the staircase. 'I just saw Niven in the kitchen. He said he'd be taking care of Mr Lucas today. I do not see why he gets to do it. Why can I not help?'

Mairi opened her mouth to answer, but Davina interrupted.

'Never mind saying it isn't proper. You have to help, so I should be able to help as well.'

Mairi put her arm around Davina's shoulders. 'There is plenty to do here besides seeing to Mr Lucas, Davina, as you well know.'

'But I wanted to be the Good Samaritan.' Davina's lip trembled.

'You have already been the Good Samaritan,' Mairi assured her. 'By finding Mr Lucas and seeing he was helped.'

'Niven is telling everyone he found him,' she protested. 'But it was me. I saw him first.'

'And you could have walked by him. That makes you like the Good Samaritan.'

Davina's eyes widened. 'I could never have walked by him!'

Mairi's younger sister possessed a pure, kind heart. She was sweet. And unspoiled.

Mairi gave her a hug. 'Let us find Mama and Papa and tell them that Mr Lucas is much improved.'

* * *

Their parents were in the morning room finishing a leisurely breakfast with one of the footmen, Robert, to attend them.

Davina entered the room first, rushing up to her mother. 'Good morning, Mama. Good morning, Papa.' She kissed both on the cheek.

Mairi poured herself a cup of tea and sat at the table. 'The sick man is much better. His fever broke at last. Mr Grassie was here earlier.' Her father lowered his newspaper to listen.

'Oh, yes, the sick man.' Her mother spoke as if she'd forgotten about him. 'What did the good doctor say?'

'Mr Grassie has prescribed rest. The man must stay here for a week or so.' Mairi softened the time frame and omitted the part about him being contagious, both matters guaranteed to rattle her mother. And, of course, Mairi neglected to mention that she had been the one caring for Mr Lucas.

Her father turned back to his paper. 'Good man, Grassie.'

Her mother smiled approvingly at her husband's pronouncement. 'Indeed he is.' She glanced back at Mairi. 'See that the servants give our patient good care, will you, Mairi?'

Robert glanced at Mairi, his bland expression turning to one of worry.

She nodded to him so he'd know she noticed, before answering her mother. 'I will see to it, Mama. His name is Mr Lucas, by the way.'

'Lucas?' Her mother looked up in thought. 'I do not believe we know any Lucases.'

'He is an Englishman, Mama.'

'An Englishman?' Her father dropped his paper again. 'I do not fancy an Englishman in our house.' Her father prided himself on being a full-blooded Scottish patriot.

'It will only be a few days.' She changed the subject. 'What plans have you for today?'

Her mother leaned forward with bright eyes. 'Mrs Webster will be calling.' Mrs Webster was the local dressmaker. 'She is in possession of some new muslins and fashion prints, so don't you run off somewhere.' She gave severe looks to both Mairi and Davina. 'We must measure you both for new gowns.'

'No, Mama!' Mairi protested. 'We do not need to spend more money on gowns!'

Her mother tapped Mairi's hand. 'We must! For the house party at Lord Oxmont's. You must look your best.'

It was no secret that her mother had great hopes that this house party would result in a proposal of marriage for Mairi, but how could she marry? She was not a virgin. A man would be able to tell, she'd heard the maids say.

In any event, they could not afford to pay Mrs Webster for new dresses. 'Mrs Webster might alter our old dresses,' she said. 'That would certainly cost less.'

Davina's brow furrowed. 'Do we not have enough money for new dresses?'

Their father took Davina's hand and squeezed it. 'It is not as bad as all that, my wee one.'

But it was every bit as bad as all that. And more.

Her father returned to his paper. Mairi could expect no support from him.

She sighed. 'What about you, Papa? What are your plans?'

He put down his newspaper again. 'I am off to look at a horse. Laird Buchan put me on to a pretty mare for sale.'

'Papa!' Mairi could keep quiet no longer. 'We do not need another horse!' They'd lost most of their grooms already, those who wanted to be paid for their work in coin, not promises. 'We cannot afford it!'

Her father's face turned red. 'I'll not have you speak to me in that tone of voice, lass.' He lifted his paper again. 'Besides, a steed like this one comes around once in a lifetime. Or so I'm told.'

Mairi had tried every way she knew to convince her parents to economise. She'd begged them to stop buying things. She'd suggested they sell what they no longer needed. Her mother had gone into palpitations when Mairi had said they should sell some of the jewellery her father was so fond of buying for her.

If her father and mother did not change their ways soon they'd lose the *caput*—their land and with it her father's title. In Scotland, a baron could sell both. What future would Niven and Davina have then?

Mairi rose. If she remained another minute, she was likely to lose her temper completely and she knew from experience it only made matters worse.

'I must go,' she said. 'If I have your leave, Papa?'

'Yes, lass.' Her father's good humour returned as it always did. 'Do not forget about the dressmaker.'

Mairi strode out of the room.

Robert followed her. 'Does your da not have enough money?' the footman asked worriedly.

Robert was twenty, Mairi's age, and a simple young man, the son of one of the crofters. He had not been a footman for very long.

'Money is tight, Robert.' She would not lie to him. 'That is why you have not been paid, but we have enough to keep a roof over our heads and food in our mouths, so there is that.'

Robert's parents had died of fever a year ago and he'd been their only son. Her father had generously offered to make him a footman. At the time, it had seemed an extravagance to Mairi, but now she did not know what the family would do without him and Erwin, their only other footman.

'And don't think I will ask you to care for Mr Lucas, the sick man,' she added. 'I know you are overworked and I do not want you to catch the fever.'

His face relaxed. 'I can help some, miss,' he said earnestly. 'I already brushed out his clothes and polished his boots. They should be dry by now.'

'I saw that you did that, Robert,' she responded. 'They were quite wet and dirty. It was a big job. I do appreciate it so very much.'

His face turned red at the compliment. He glanced towards the door. 'I best return to my duties.'

'Yes,' she said.

He bowed and re-entered the morning room.

Mairi turned away. She'd promised the housekeeper she would tidy her parents' rooms and she needed to hurry before they finished their breakfast.

That afternoon Mairi helped Mrs Cross close down the guest bedrooms. They were rarely used and it would save the two maids much work to take down the curtains and cover the furniture with dust covers.

Davina came to tell her the dressmaker had arrived. 'Mama wants us to come straight away.'

'Very well.' Mairi closed her eyes for a moment to calm herself before removing her apron and cap and brushing off her dress.

As they walked to their mother's dressing room, Davina asked, 'Can we really not afford new dresses, Mairi?'

At fourteen, Davina was old enough to know the reality of their situation. 'We should not order new clothes,' Mairi responded. 'Papa has been unable to pay our servants for some time. That is why so many have left. He has many unpaid bills. He will not be able to pay Mrs Webster for anything we buy.'

Davina turned her head away and did not speak for a few moments. Finally she said, 'Then I will say I dislike all of the new fabrics and the fashion prints. Mama will not make me order a dress I do not like. And I will try to convince Mama that the fabrics and designs will not do for her either.'

Mairi put her arm around her sister. 'Very clever, Davina. Mama will not like to be embarrassed that way. We can show Mrs Webster some of our old dresses. I believe Mama will be satisfied if we have something that looks new.'

Lucas took another sip of tea as young Niven peppered him with questions about himself—about his time in the army.

'What regiment were you in?' Niven asked.

'The First Royal Dragoons,' he replied.

The boy's eyes brightened. 'The First Royals? Were you in the charge with the Scots Greys at Waterloo?'

The memory of it came back. The thundering of the horses, their screams, the contorted faces of the French soldiers, the blood.

His brother.

By Jupiter, he needed whisky.

'Yes,' he replied. 'I was.'

'Wait until my father hears about that!' Niven beamed. 'He is excessively proud of the Scots Greys. To hear him, you'd think they won the battle for the Allies.'

The Scots Greys were brave, no question, but they also had been untried in battle. They'd ridden too far ahead of the main charge and, as a result, too many had been cut down.

Like Bradleigh.

'Were you in the Peninsula, too?' Niven asked. 'What other battles did you fight? Was it glorious? I cannot imagine such a sight. A cavalry charge!'

Lucas's answers were terse and he hoped the boy did not notice the trembling of his hands, the stiffening of his shoulders. It was the anguish of remembering. Enough of this. He wanted out of this place. The boy forced him to remember and the sister made him care when all he wanted was to shut off his emotions and be alone.

There was a knock at the door.

'Come in,' Niven called as if this was his room, not Lucas's.

Miss Wallace peeked in, her gaze riveting on her brother. 'Niven! I was afraid you were here.'

Lucas rose to his feet, but braced his hands on the table. She gestured for him to sit down. He wanted to remain standing, but his legs threatened not to hold him. He sank back into the chair.

Niven lifted his chin. 'I brought Lucas some tea and biscuits. I'm keeping him company.'

'He is still ill, Niven,' she scolded. 'You should leave him in peace.'

Niven seemed to ignore what she said. 'Did you know? He was in the First Royals! Fought at Waterloo. That's a cavalry regiment, you see. He was in the charge with the Scots Greys.'

Her gaze caught Lucas's briefly and he fancied she could somehow see the pain he wanted to hide. From himself as well as everyone else.

'You should not trouble him, Niven.' She peered at Lucas even more closely and crossed the room to him. 'Are you feverish again, Mr Lucas?'

He felt hot and perspiration dampened his face.

She placed her bare hand on his forehead. 'You are a little warm.'

Her touch filled him with yearning, but he did not wish anyone to care about him—or to care about anybody himself. Obviously seeing to his care merely added one more burden to her slim shoulders.

'I am well enough,' he insisted.

Her brows knitted. 'You should rest.' She turned to her brother. 'Let us leave Mr Lucas now. I need your help in the garden. Cook wants some turnips and onions.'

Niven stood. 'How delightful! Digging in the dirt.' He smiled at Lucas. 'I'll bring your dinner later, Mr Lucas. Do not be surprised if it includes turnips and onions.'

Lucas's stomach revolted at the thought.

'Thank you.' Lucas rose. 'I will rest a while.'

Miss Wallace gave him a worried look before she and her brother walked out of the room.

When Niven had returned some time later with the dinner tray, Lucas had simply told him to leave it on the table, but he fell asleep before touching it.

He woke again when the clock in the room struck eleven. The door opened and, through slitted eyes, Lucas watched Miss Wallace enter, her face illuminated by a candle. Her brother was behind her.

'See, he is still abed,' Niven said to her. 'I do not think he ate any of his dinner.'

Miss Wallace approached and gingerly placed her palm on his forehead. Her hand felt soft and cool and he was taken aback with how much he desired her touch.

He opened his eyes and she jumped back with a cry.

'Miss Wallace?' He sat up.

'Niven was concerned. You did not eat dinner,' she said.

'I was not hungry.' He'd made up his mind. He'd leave in the morning.

'You still feel warm.' Her brows knitted.

He refused to worry her. 'I just need sleep.' Their gazes caught as before. She needed sleep as much as he did. 'Please. Return to your beds.'

She stared at him a while longer. 'Are you certain?'

'Go to bed, Miss Wallace,' he murmured. 'Do not trouble yourself with me.'

The next morning, Lucas woke as dawn was just breaking. His fever continued, but he was clear-headed. All he needed to do was walk to the nearest village and seek a room in an inn. Then he need not impose on this family—on Miss Wallace—any further.

He'd slept in the clothes he'd borrowed from the departed butler, so he rose and bathed his face in the cool water from the room's pitcher and basin and shaved his face. Wiping his face again, he searched for his toothbrush and brushed his teeth, rinsing the foul taste of illness from his mouth.

As he turned away from the basin, he noticed his untouched evening meal still on the table. His stomach was no better than the night before, but he knew he must eat and drink something. He buttered the bread and drank the ale. It would have to be enough until he could purchase a meal from an inn.

If his appetite ever returned.

He dressed in his own clothes and repacked his satchel, then picked up the tray so he would not leave extra work for Miss Wallace. He carried the tray to the door and managed to open it. In the hallway, he could hear sounds from what he presumed was the kitchen. Butlers' quarters were typically near the kitchen. He followed the sounds and entered a large room where the odours of cooking meat and bread made him nauseous.

'I beg your pardon,' he said.

A red-faced, grey-haired woman turned from the pot she was tending on the fire. She smiled kindly. 'Ah, you must be our patient, Mr Lucas.' The woman bustled over to him. 'Here, let me take the tray.' She turned away and called, 'Evie!'

A very young kitchen maid emerged from what must have been the scullery. 'Mrs MacNeal?' The girl blinked when she spied Lucas.

Mrs MacNeal handed the girl the tray. 'Here.'

The girl carried the tray back to the scullery.

The cook gave Lucas a scolding look. 'You did not eat much of your dinner.'

'I slept through it, I'm afraid,' he responded.

'Then will you be wanting breakfast?' The woman began to look stressed. 'I am not quite ready for cooking breakfast.'

Lucas's father's kitchen would have been bustling with kitchen maids and footmen at this hour. He saw only the cook and one helper.

'I am quite satisfied with what I ate from the dinner plate this morning,' he assured her. 'I merely wished to return the tray.'

'That was good of you, sir.' She returned to tending her pot.

He left the kitchen and met a footman in the hallway.

'You must be the visitor,' the young man said.

'I am.'

The footman eyed him up and down. 'I hope your clothes are satisfactory. I brushed them off best I could.'

'I am very grateful.' Lucas reached into his pocket and pulled out a coin. He handed it to the footman.

The young man's eyes lit up. 'Thank you, sir!'

It had been a very small coin, not worth so much appreciation.

Lucas should ask the footman his name, but it was better for him not to know anybody. Already Miss Wallace and her brother threatened his desire for isolation.

'I'll be leaving in a few minutes,' Lucas said.

The footman peered at him. 'Leaving? You were to stay at least a week, Miss Mairi said.'

'I am recovered,' he responded. 'No need to stay.'

Lucas returned to the butler's room, but had to sit down to rest. When he gathered his strength again, he took more coins from his purse and left them on the table, enough, he hoped, to pay for the doctor, his food and for the trouble he had caused. Forcing himself to stand, he donned his topcoat, picked up the satchel and slung it over his shoulder. He strode out of the room and followed the hallway to a door to the outside. He began making his way towards the road that he hoped would eventually lead him to the nearest village inn.

Chapter Five

Mairi woke early, as she was accustomed to doing since some of the housemaids had left and Nellie was the only one left with time to act as lady's maid to her mother, Davina and herself. Mairi made certain she did not need a great deal of Nellie's help, merely tying the laces of her stays and her dress.

She next went in search of Mrs Cross to see what assistance the housekeeper required that day, but first she knocked on Niven's door.

'Who is it?' he responded testily. And sleepily.

'You know it is me, Mairi,' she replied. 'I'm going to send Erwin to you to help you dress, then come straight to the kitchen to bring Mr Lucas his breakfast.'

'Oh. Yes.' Niven's voice brightened. 'Mr Lucas. I'll be ready. Have Erwin come right away.'

Erwin was slightly more experienced as a footman than Robert, so he was tasked with acting as valet to Niven. Wilfred, their father's valet, was over seventy, and it was taxing enough for him to serve their father, but he had provided Erwin some rudimentary training.

Mairi descended the stairs to the hall and entered the morning room, where Erwin was setting the table for breakfast.

'Good morning!' She made her tone cheerful. It kept her spirits up and, she hoped, the spirits of their overworked servants.

Erwin stopped his work and bowed. 'Good morning, miss.'

'When you are done here, would you tend to Niven?' she asked. 'He has much to do today before he goes out.' Of all the times for him to visit his friend.

'Yes, miss.' Erwin placed the cutlery next to the breakfast plate with less precision than their butler would have done.

'Thank you, Erwin,' she said breezily, using the servants' door to lead her to the ground floor, where she found Mrs Cross, the housekeeper, in an intense conversation with Betsy, one of their two maids, while Cook looked on from the worktable where she was rolling out dough for biscuits for the afternoon tea.

'Good morning,' Mairi said again in a cheerful tone. 'I came to see how I can help today.'

Mrs Cross rubbed her brow. 'Let me think. Your mother will not want to see you polishing furniture, but you could tidy up her room and your father's like yesterday.'

'I will see to it.' It did not seem like enough to do. Mairi turned to Cook. 'Mrs MacNeal, Nevin will be down directly to bring Mr Lucas his breakfast. Shall I put together a plate for him?'

Mrs MacNeal shook flour from her hands. 'Miss Mairi, the fellow left already. Robert told us.'

'Left?' But he was still ill! 'When?'

'A while ago, miss,' the cook responded. 'Robert told me right when I took the loaves out of the oven.'

Mairi touched one of the loaves. It had cooled considerably.

Still, Robert might have been mistaken.

Mairi hurried out of the kitchen and ran to the footmen's room, but Robert was not there. She hastened to the butler's room, opening the door without knocking. It was empty. There was a stack of coins on the table. She picked them up and counted. Enough for the doctor's bill and more. She sank into a chair and fingered the coins.

Things were back to rights again, then, were they not? As if he'd never been there. They could all go on as they had done before…

Except he'd been ill the night before; she was certain of it. His forehead had glistened with sweat and his skin had been hot. The fever certainly had returned, just as the doctor said it might.

She placed her hand over her mouth. Goodness, what if he collapsed again? What if he were not found until he was dead? How would Davina and Niven feel then?

How would she feel?

She glanced at the clock. There was time before she'd need to tidy her parents' rooms. She could go in search of him and reassure herself that he would not die on his way to wherever he was going. She had enough on her conscience; she did not need to feel responsible for a man's death.

She rose and resolutely walked out of the room. On her way past the kitchen, she called out, 'I am going out. I will be back soon.' Without waiting for an answer, she grabbed her old cloak, which hung on a hook by the garden door. She swung it around her shoulders and went outside.

He had probably followed the track that the wagons used to deliver goods to the back door of the house. She walked briskly down it.

Before it met the main road, she called to John, the stable worker, who was exercising an unfamiliar horse in a paddock. Her father's latest purchase, no doubt. 'Did you see a stranger walk by here?'

He nodded. 'He asked directions to the village.'

'Thank you!' That, at least, was a more sensible plan than traipsing over the hills as he must have done before.

Mairi walked as quickly as she could down to the main road that led to the village. If he was as ill as she feared, she would catch up to him.

Over a quarter of an hour later, she saw a figure seated at the side of the road.

The Englishman. Head bowed. Elbows resting on his knees.

She quickened her pace. 'Mr Lucas!'

He raised his head, apparently with some effort. 'Miss Wallace.'

He was certainly still ill.

She stood in front of him. 'What are you about? Your fever is back, is it not?'

He rose to his feet.

She continued her scold. 'The doctor said you must rest. For ten days at least. Now look. You are sick again.'

'Do not concern yourself, Miss Wallace.' He swayed.

She glared at him. 'You can barely stand up.'

He straightened. 'I am well enough to make it to the village.'

But the village was three more miles from here. At this rate it would take him all day to reach it. 'Are you? You looked fatigued enough after walking this short distance. How long have you been walking? An hour? It will only get harder the further you go. I am persuaded that someone might very well find you in a ditch. Imagine how my brother and sister will feel when they hear you are dead, after they went to such exertions to save you.'

'None of you should think of me at all,' he protested.

She crossed her arms over her chest. 'Davina and Niven

will, though. You owe them your life. You should consider their feelings in this matter.' And hers.

He glanced away. 'Tell your brother and sister I reached the village.'

If he did make it to the village, Mr Grassie would undoubtedly learn of it. Perhaps people would say her father had turned out a sick man. The last thing they needed was more talk about their family.

'Come back with me,' she insisted. 'Come back and remain the ten days. Or more if necessary. Stay and make Davina and Niven feel they've done something that counts.'

And because she could not bear it if he died.

Lucas could make it to the village. He was not that ill. The tower of the church was visible on the horizon, as were some village rooftops. It wasn't far. He'd endured worse hardships than this. He'd withstood long marches through Spain. He'd fought on when stabbed by enemy swords. He'd come close to death, but pushed through to keep his brother from being killed.

Except at Waterloo. At Waterloo he'd abandoned Bradleigh.

How could he explain to the lovely Miss Wallace that he did not deserve to live? All he wanted was to forget; to numb the pain.

She ought to have let him die. She should not have pulled him back with her entreaties to live. She should leave him now and, if he were lucky, he would die in a ditch, like she had warned him against.

Suddenly weary again, he sank back to the ground.

She stood above him, hands on her hips. 'Is this where you would like Davina and Niven to find you dead?'

The fresh, earnest faces of those two young people flashed

through his mind. Would he indeed be injuring them if he simply let go of life, here at the side of the road?

Miss Wallace lowered herself to sit next to him, hugging her knees. As she did so, Lucas suffered a spasm of coughing. She lifted an eyebrow as if to say, *See? You are sick.*

When he could talk again he looked her in the eye. 'Why do you want me to return with you, Miss Wallace? Your family is in straitened circumstances, I understand. I am only a burden to you.'

Her eyes widened in surprise, then narrowed. 'I should throttle Niven. You could not have learned that from anyone else.'

Not that he would tell on the boy.

She blew out a pained breath. 'My father's finances are...' she paused '...a bit challenging at the moment, a fact we certainly do not wish the world to know.'

He held up his palm. 'My word. I will not tell.'

She shook her head. 'I can see it plainly. If you make it to the inn—or are found in this ditch—our family will be the talk of the village. *The Baron of Dunburn turned out a fevered traveller.*' Her voice was mocking. 'We do not deserve that sort of gossip.'

No, they did not. Families experiencing financial difficulties never desired the speculation of others.

It was one thing to toss away his worthless life, quite another to hurt the people who'd rescued him.

And this woman who'd nursed him back to life.

He dropped his head in his hands. 'Very well. I will return with you.'

He felt her straighten her spine. 'And you will stay the ten days the doctor ordered? Longer if you are still ill?'

He did not answer her right away. 'On one condition.'

'What condition?' Her voice turned wary.

He lifted his head and faced her. 'No one waits on me.'

Not her. Not her brother. 'I take care of myself. Your cook can fix me a plate for meals, but I will walk down to the kitchen and carry it back myself. I'll take care of my clothes as well. And anything else.'

Her clear blue eyes searched his. He fought an impulse to look away.

Finally she nodded. 'Very well.'

'Let us go, then.' He attempted to stand, but his legs threatened to buckle. She bounced to her feet and held his arm, helping him up.

He lifted her hand away. 'I am able to walk.'

She fell in step with him, walking close enough, he suspected, to grab him if he became unsteady. After a few steps he wiped his brow.

'You still have a fever, do you not?' she accused.

'Possibly,' he admitted.

It was some effort to walk at a normal pace, but he had enough pride left to prove to this lady that he could have made it to the village.

She broke the silence between them. 'Why are you in Scotland, Mr Lucas? Why were you wandering in the hills on my father's land?'

'I do not know why I was on your father's land,' he told her. 'I do not remember much about that day.' He'd begun to feel feverish when he'd left that last inn. He'd medicated himself with whisky, he recalled. A lot of whisky.

'Where were you before that?' she asked.

'What town, do you mean?'

She nodded.

The towns and villages were all the same to him. 'I do not recall the name.'

'Why are you in Scotland?' she pressed.

'Travelling.' If you called running from life travelling.

She stopped and gazed at him a long time before starting

to walk again. The silence between them returned and he was grateful she did not force him to say more about himself. He wanted to forget himself. Even these few questions brought back the turmoil inside him, but, just as when he'd been delirious with fever and her voice had been the one thing he could cling to, her presence next to him held him together even better than a bottle of whisky.

They finally reached the gate of the property, marked by a wrought-iron arch made out to spell *Wallace*. Lucas's legs were aching with fatigue, but he pressed on.

When they came to the door, he opened it for her. She glanced at him as if surprised he could do such a gentlemanly thing.

As they stepped into the hallway, she turned to him. 'Do you need anything?'

He raised a finger. 'Remember our agreement. I take care of myself.'

'I could tell Cook to fix you breakfast,' she persisted.

'I will do it.' Later. After he'd rested. 'Go on to your other tasks.' He suspected there were many.

'I will say goodbye, then,' she said.

He was reluctant to part from her, but bowed and walked directly to the butler's room. Once there he removed his topcoat and sank into the upholstered chair, placing his feet up on the nearby stool.

He closed his eyes and felt a fog in his head from the fever and the exertion. He did not need her company. He did not deserve it.

He shifted in the chair. He'd keep to himself. He could do that. It was only ten days.

Lucas rested that day and the next. All traces of his fever had gone by that second day and there was nothing reminding Lucas of being unwell but an occasional cough. He'd been blessed with a strong constitution and always bounced back quickly from any illness or injury.

As agreed, Lucas had been left to care for himself, merely needing to visit the kitchen when hungry and carry his food back to the butler's room. He would have done very well in the village inn—Miss Wallace's sacrifice had been totally unnecessary, but he'd made his bargain with her and, unless she freed him from it, he would honour her wishes.

Upon waking this third day, Lucas felt restless. The four walls of the butler's room were closing in on him and the prospect of further inactivity was intolerable. His window looked out on to the yard and, from what he could tell, it seemed to be a fine sunny day. It almost made him believe in hope.

He picked up his breakfast tray and carried it back to the kitchen.

Cook looked up as he appeared in the doorway.

'Another excellent meal, Mrs MacNeal.' The woman always looked so harried. He felt sorry for her. 'Where shall I put the tray?'

'Ah, Mr Lucas.' She gave him a tense smile as she chopped bright orange carrots, tossing the pieces into a brass pot. She inclined her head. 'In the scullery.'

He carried the tray to the scullery, which was laden with dishes needing to be washed. He returned to the kitchen and asked, 'Where is the scullery maid?' He'd become used to seeing the young girl there.

'Evie is helping Mrs Cross today.' The cook wiped her brow with the back of her hand. 'Mrs Cross told me I must wash the dishes today, but I dinnae ken how or when!'

Lucas shrugged. 'I'll wash your dishes for you.'

He might as well do something useful.

Mrs MacNeal gaped at him. 'You, sir?'

'Why not?' He felt too well to still be contagious.

'Do you know how?' she asked sceptically.

'I've been around kitchens before, Mrs MacNeal.' As a boy he'd loved to hang around the kitchen—all the better to be given extra treats. 'I can manage it.'

She waved a hand. 'Well, put on an apron and go to it, then.'

Lucas washed, dried and put away every dish. As soon as he finished, the footman who'd cleaned his clothes brought more from the family's breakfast.

The young man stumbled back a step on seeing Lucas in his apron.

Lucas could not help but be amused. 'I thought I might help.' He smiled.

The footman blinked. 'Are you not fevered, then?'

'Well recovered,' Lucas assured him. 'I must stay for another week, so I might as well work.' He nodded to the man. 'I am John Lucas.'

The young man's forehead furrowed. 'I know that, sir.'

Cook called over to them, 'He wants to know your name, Robert.' She shook her head in dismay.

'Aye.' The footman turned back to Lucas. 'I am Robert.'

Lucas nodded again.

'Back to work, Robert,' Mrs MacNeal cried, 'before Mrs Cross finds you still.'

Robert hurried out.

Lucas finished this latest round of dishes and Cook thanked him profusely. He returned to the butler's room, but it felt more confining than ever. He stood at the window and put on the butler's battered hat. The sun still shone and the sky was a clear azure. He spun around and walked out of the room again.

He stopped by the kitchen. 'Mrs MacNeal, if Miss Wallace thinks I've absconded again, explain that I am merely taking a turn in the garden.'

'I will. I will.' Cook looked up. 'Do not make yourself ill again, Mr Lucas.'

He knew himself. The fever would not return. 'No fear of that.'

He made his way to the servants' door and stepped outside, lifting his face to the sun and filling his lungs with the clean, fresh air. Off to the right was the kitchen garden, where one of the maids appeared to be tending the plants. He walked towards her.

As he came near, the maid looked up.

'Miss Wallace!' he said in surprise.

She wore an apron over her dress and a wide-brimmed straw hat. She held a hoe in her hands.

'Mr Lucas, what are you doing?' Her tone was suspicious.

He walked closer, holding up his hands. 'I assure you, I am well. Completely recovered. But do not fear. I am not escaping. I simply wished to take a walk.'

She peered at him a long time as if assessing his health for herself.

He'd not seen her since his attempted departure. She looked like a vision from some bucolic painting, tilling the soil.

'What are you doing?' he asked. But what he really meant was, *Why are you working in the garden like a labourer?*

She lowered her gaze and stabbed the earth with her hoe. 'Oh, I am turning the earth to ready it for autumn planting.'

A baron's daughter? 'Why you, Miss Wallace? Do you have no gardeners?'

She blinked and could not quite meet his eyes. 'There

is only Kinley, but he cannot do it all.' She raised her head and lifted her chin. 'And we must have food, must we not?'

'What about your footmen? Can they not help?' Robert was a strong young man.

She attacked the ground again. 'Robert and Erwin are proud of being footmen. It would be beneath them to work in the garden.'

He tilted his head. 'But not beneath the baron's daughter?'

Her face flushed. 'I do not mind the work.'

'Your brother, then.' Niven had seemed an energetic youth.

'Niven is not at home. He is visiting a friend.'

That seemed quite frivolous when there was so much to be done at home—most of it falling to Miss Wallace. Or, rather, most she took upon herself. It bothered Lucas to see her performing such hard labour. And it bothered him that her plight affected him at all.

It was none of his affair, he told himself.

'I will leave you to it, then.' He turned away and walked a few steps, but turned back to her, inclining his head towards a pond he'd glimpsed in the distance. 'I thought I might walk to that pond.'

She stopped hoeing. 'Are you certain you feel well enough?'

'You need not worry about me, Miss Wallace.'

She had enough worries on her shoulders.

Chapter Six

Lucas walked around the pond, completely convinced now his illness was gone. His limbs were fatigued, but the previous days' inactivity could account for that. He rounded the last bend and came face-to-face with a well-dressed older gentleman.

'You, sir!' The man's tone was instantly bellicose. 'What is your business here on my property?'

This must be Miss Wallace's father, the Baron of Dunburn, Lucas supposed. Lucas bowed. 'Forgive me if I have intruded where I ought not to have been. I hope you would have heard of me. I am Mr John Lucas, the one indebted to you for the care I've received while ill.'

'Oh!' The man's expression brightened. 'You are the Englishman my children brought home! I quite forgot. I am Dunburn, you see. Well. Well. You look very fit for a man supposed to be at death's door.'

'I believe I might credit your household for that,' he responded. 'I was very unwell when they found me, I've been told.'

'Indeed. Indeed.' The man clapped him on the shoulder. 'Good that you are well now, isn't it?'

'Yes, I shall not have to prevail on your hospitality for

much longer.' Lucas had the feeling that Dunburn knew very little of his situation. 'If you wish me to leave today—'

The Baron lifted his hand. 'No need for that. Stay as long as you wish.' He eyed Lucas up and down. 'My son told me you are a cavalryman. Rode in the charge at Waterloo.'

Lucas's spirits plummeted. He had no wish to talk of Waterloo. 'I *was* in the cavalry. No longer,' Lucas responded.

Dunburn did not seem to notice he'd not mentioned Waterloo. 'What was your regiment again?' he asked.

'First Royals,' Lucas managed to say.

'Yes, yes. That was what Niven told me!' Dunburn's excitement escalated. 'I knew it. You were at Waterloo. Part of the glorious charge with the Scots Greys!'

Hardly glorious, Lucas would have said. Not when it killed his brother.

The man fell in step with him. 'Come sit with me and tell me all about it. Do you not think the Scots Greys' bravery secured the victory?'

Lucas opened his mouth to refuse, even though it would be churlish to do so, but Dunburn reached inside his coat and took out a flask, raising his brows and smiling.

Perhaps Lucas could talk about the Scots Greys, if he were fortified by whisky.

Dunburn led him to a nearby bench and passed him the flask when they sat down. Lucas lifted it to his lips and took a long sip, savouring the familiar aroma, taste and the warmth spreading through his chest.

'The Greys did their part,' Lucas said.

He spoke of the tactics, the successes of the Greys, the sort of account that would appear in a newspaper. As he spoke, memories returned of the blood, the rage and fear on the soldiers' faces, the wild eyes of the horses, the mud, the screams, the horror of seeing his brother cut down. Lucas drank most of the contents of Dunburn's flask.

As he sat with the older man, who clearly had no short-age of Scottish pride, he spied Miss Wallace on the path near the kitchen garden. She stood a long time watching her father converse with him. He had not a clue what she might be thinking. After some time she turned and walked away.

The sun rose high in the sky and warmed the air even more. Finally, Dunburn stood. 'My head's mince! I promised I would call upon Laird Buchan and now I'm a wee bit late.'

Lucas rose with him.

Dunburn clapped him on the shoulder again. 'It would be grand if we could invite you to dinner, Mr Lucas.' He raised his arms helplessly.

'No, sir. I would not presume.' He did not wish to be treated as a house guest, not when he was an actual burden.

The Baron nodded agreeably. 'For a Sassenach, you are a right fine fellow.'

Lucas bowed. 'Thank you, sir.'

Mairi left the kitchen garden to help Mrs Cross with cleaning the drawing room, the sitting rooms and the library while her parents were calling upon Laird Buchan. She wished she'd been able to do more. Truth was, she was not very good at hoeing the earth.

As soon as she and the maids were done with the rooms, she hurried to the anteroom of the kitchen entrance and put on the apron and hat she'd worn outside before. There would be a little time left to work in the garden before her parents returned home.

She hurried outside, but stopped short. Mr Lucas stood in the plot, hoeing the ground. She quickened her step and came quite close before he saw her.

He stopped his work. 'Miss Wallace.'

Most of ground she'd left undone had been turned over already. 'You are working in the garden!'

He leaned on the hoe. 'I thought I might as well be useful.'

'It is almost ready for planting.' She felt like weeping. She'd not known how she would get everything done.

'I should finish today.' He seemed to be breathing heavily.

She began to worry. 'Are you certain you feel well enough?'

He smiled and his handsome features transformed into something wondrous that made her heart beat faster. 'I feel very well, Miss Wallace.'

She could hardly speak. 'How can I thank you?' she managed.

'No thanks required.' He stabbed at the ground with the hoe. 'If I am to stay another week, I should work. I will do the planting tomorrow, if you like.'

'Do you know how?' she asked, although she should have merely thanked him again.

He glanced up at her. 'I grew up on a farm.'

'Well, that will be helpful indeed.' She blinked away tears. It would have taken her at least a whole other day to do the work he'd done so far. With the planting done, she would not have to worry about food. There was no way she could convey to him what this meant to her.

For the next two days Lucas worked in the garden, planting coleworts, broccoli and leeks, among a half-dozen other vegetables and herbs. He'd hoed turnips, weeded onions and pricked cauliflowers. Kinley, the head gardener, was delighted to see the kitchen garden tended. The poor man was grizzled and stooped and apologised to Lucas that he'd been neglectful.

He reminded Lucas of the head gardener at Foxgrove Hall, his father's country house. His brother, Bradleigh, had often had more important things to do besides playing with his younger brother, and Lucas had had plenty of spare time to bother old Barlow in the garden. Barlow loved his plants. He'd loved teaching Lucas about them, and as a boy he had been an interested pupil.

At least Lucas had learned enough to satisfy Kinley that he was a competent worker.

Lucas walked back from the garden as the sun was low in the sky. He removed his boots before entering the house and headed for the footmen's room, where his boots could be properly cleaned and his coat and trousers brushed off.

Erwin, one of the two footmen, approached, carrying a tray full of dishes, apparently from the family's dinner. He looked Lucas up and down. 'You look as if you have been digging in dirt.'

'I have,' Lucas replied. 'I need to clean my clothes.'

Erwin inclined his head in the direction of the footmen's room. 'Leave them. Robert can tend to them.'

By Lucas's estimation, all of the servants were overworked, but, of all of them, Erwin worked the least.

'I'll clean them,' he responded. 'I do not mind.'

'Suit yourself.' Erwin continued on his way.

Lucas cleaned and polished his boots and brushed the dirt from his coat and trousers. Still in stockinged feet, he returned to his room and washed his face and hands. The day before he'd started eating meals with the other servants, which was at about nine o'clock once the family had no need of them. They sat at a long table in the servants' hall and it was clear there were many empty seats.

But he would not be expected for over an hour, so he sat to rest. The labour of the day had felt good. It was strangely satisfying to exert oneself physically, then afterwards to survey the results: rows and rows of plantings, baskets of onions, turnips and cauliflower.

He leaned back in the chair and closed his eyes. In his stillness, though, the memories returned. And the regrets.

He shook them off. Tomorrow he hoped to find other chores to perform. Surely Kinley had need of him somewhere in the gardens. He might as well help this family while finishing out his ten days.

He'd only caught glimpses of Miss Wallace these last couple of days, although her younger sister seemed to find time each day to stop by and complain about being worked to a frazzle.

There was a knock at the door.

'Come in,' Lucas called.

Erwin opened the door. 'The Baron wishes to see you in the library.'

This was a novel occurrence. Lucas had not spoken to Dunburn since that walk around the pond.

He reached for his boots and pulled them on. 'Did he say why?'

'Not to me.' Erwin turned to leave.

'Where is the library?' Lucas asked. He'd not been above stairs in this house.

'Main floor.' Erwin left before he might have been more helpful.

Lucas stood and ran a hand through his hair. How odd to feel even this mild unease at being summoned by a Scottish baron, as if he were a mere gardener's helper. Perhaps he was finally succeeding at losing himself.

He found his way to the hall and from the hall to the library, where Dunburn sat in a comfortable chair facing the fireplace.

Lucas knocked on the open door. 'You wished to see me, sir?'

'Ah, there you are.' Dunburn swivelled in his chair and signalled for Lucas to enter.

Lucas walked over to him and stood deferentially.

The Baron gestured to the chair adjacent to his. 'Come, sit. Have a whisky with me and tell me again about the charge of the Scots Greys.'

No, Lucas wanted to protest. *Not again.* Already the images of the battle flew through his mind. The sounds and smells would certainly follow.

He straightened. 'Sir, surely it is not proper for me to share a drink with you.'

'I know. I know.' The older man smiled as he poured a glass of whisky. 'But I am in need of company and I did so enjoy hearing an account of the charge from someone who was there.'

He extended the glass to Lucas, who accepted it gratefully.

Was there no other excuse he could give to avoid revisiting the memory that was so painful to him? Or did he owe it to the man? After all, Dunburn had allowed him to recuperate under his own roof, even though he could ill afford feeding another mouth.

Dunburn leaned forward in his chair, eagerness filling his expression. Lucas gulped the whisky and let it burn its way down his throat.

Dunburn poured him another. 'Start at the moment the order to charge came.'

The tension before the charge rushed through Lucas's body. He took another sip. 'Ponsonby ordered the Inniskillings, the First Royals and the Scots Greys to prepare to charge.' The whisky was blunting his emotions. He continued as if by rote. 'The cavalry were behind the slope so could not see what they would be facing. Before the order was given, the Scots Greys shouted "Scotland for ever" and De Lacy Evans waved his hat—'

Dunburn closed his eyes and sighed. 'Scotland for ever.' He turned to Lucas again and twirled his finger. 'Go on.'

Lucas tried to quiet the memories assaulting him. He finished his second glass of whisky. 'De Lacy Evans waved his hat—' Lucas saw it all again. How he'd glared at his brother. How his brother had smirked back at him. 'We started up the slope.' He was detached no more, instead in the throes of the memories again. 'We surprised the French.' And the blood began to flow and the screams filled the air while Lucas slashed at men with his sabre, seeing their shocked faces when his weapon struck, feeling the blood spatter his face before they fell.

His heart beat faster and beads of sweat dampened his forehead. He seized the whisky bottle, poured himself another drink and drained the contents of his glass.

'And then what happened?' Dunburn poured a drink for himself.

Lucas forced himself to speak again. 'Then the fighting was thick, but the French had no chance. Some tried to run. Some fought.'

The sound of hoofbeats reached his ears and Lucas was uncertain whether it was memory or real. He lifted his glass to his lips and drank some more. Before he could start talking again, someone pounded on the outside door. He turned his head towards the sound.

'Erwin will see to it.' Dunburn twirled his fingers. 'Continue. Tell me about the Greys.'

The French had been helpless at this point, but Lucas could find no glory in recounting their fear and their deaths. He tried to think of what to say that would appease this man.

'The Greys were in the thick of things,' he said, although

at the time he'd taken no notice of anything except what was around him—and finally of his brother. 'They gave a good accounting of themselves, even though this was their first battle.'

'I knew it.' The older man gave a pleased look.

Erwin rapped on the library door. 'Beg pardon, sir, but a messenger just arrived. He gave me this letter for you.'

Dunburn looked annoyed, but he gestured the footman over and took the letter from his hand, opened it and read.

Erwin's brows rose when he saw Lucas in the chair next to the Baron, a whisky in his hand.

'Oh, dear!' Dunburn shot to his feet.

Lucas stood as well. 'Bad news, sir?'

'Oh, dear. Oh, dear. I must speak with Lady Dunburn right away.' Dunburn gave Lucas no heed and simply left the room. 'Jane! Jane!' Lucas heard him call.

He and Erwin followed Dunburn into the hall.

Lady Dunburn, followed by Miss Wallace and Davina, came rushing down from the floor above. Miss Wallace locked gazes with Lucas and frowned.

'What is it, Rory?' her mother asked. 'What has happened?'

'A messenger from Lord Crawfurd—' Dunburn said.

'Oh, no!' she cried. 'Has something happened to Niven? My poor Niven?'

'No. No. Nothing like that.' Her husband gulped. 'They're bringing Niven home tomorrow and Niven has invited them to spend the night rather than stop at an inn on their way to Lord Oxmont's.'

'Spend the night?' Lady Dunburn cried. 'Who is coming to spend the night?'

'Lord and Lady Crawfurd,' her husband said in exasperation. 'And their son.'

'We cannot take guests.' Miss Wallace, still standing on the stairs, spoke with finality.

Her parents ignored her.

'What will we do?' wailed her mother. 'They will certainly see how it is here. Everyone will know.'

'We must contrive something,' Dunburn said.

They seemed heedless to their audience—their daughters, their footman and Lucas, a virtual stranger to them.

Miss Wallace raised her voice. 'Send a return message that we cannot accommodate them.'

Lady Dunburn glared at her husband. 'I told you to hire more servants! I told you we must have a butler. What will they think that we do not have a butler?'

'I have tried,' Dunburn shot back. 'The agency writes that they have no one to send.'

In these times of high unemployment? That seemed unlikely.

'Please do not quarrel!' Davina cried.

Lady Dunburn paid no attention to her either. 'You ought to have insisted,' she said to her husband. 'At least to hire a butler.'

Miss Wallace broke in. 'The agency did not send a butler because we cannot pay for one.'

Both her parents whirled on her.

Her mother's eyes shot daggers. 'Mairi!'

'Hold your tongue, girl!' her father scolded.

Davina whimpered. Miss Wallace flushed and her hand gripped the banister. Lucas hated seeing her distress.

He stepped forward. 'I could help.'

Miss Wallace's eyes darted to him.

He glanced back to her. 'I could masquerade as your butler. I have knowledge enough of the role to pass muster.' He'd grown up with Burton as his family's butler. He knew enough of what a butler must do.

Miss Wallace's eyes widened. Her parents turned to him as if he'd plucked them from the very gates of hell. Erwin's brows rose.

'Could you do that, Lucas?' Dunburn had already fallen into calling him by what they supposed was his family name, which was how a butler would be addressed.

'I can try,' he replied.

'You are the Englishman, are you not?' Lady Dunburn had not appeared to take notice of him before this. 'You would take the position of butler for us?'

'While you have guests.' He preferred the manual labour, the physical exertion that seemed like a fitting penance, but he could do this for the people who had saved his wretched life.

Davina clapped her hands. 'This is wonderful!'

Lady Dunburn tapped her finger on her cheek. 'You will need clothes.'

He wore his oldest country clothes, made shabbier by his weeks of dissipation. He had no doubt they thought him a man of simple means.

'Of course he will need clothes!' Dunburn's voice turned cheerful.

Lady Dunburn turned to her eldest daughter. 'Mairi, you will find some clothes for...for...' She did not recall his name.

'Call me Lucas, ma'am.' He spoke in tones like Burton might have done.

'Lucas!' She beamed.

Both the Baron and Lady Dunburn seemed to have forgotten their sharp words to their daughter a minute before. Now they assumed she would solve the problem of his clothes.

Miss Wallace descended the stairs and turned to Erwin. 'Do you or Robert have any clothes that will do?'

Erwin shook his head. 'We can look to see what was left in the butler's room.'

'There were the breeches I wore before,' Lucas offered.

She turned to her father. 'Do you have anything?'

Her father winced. 'I cannot give up any of my coats—'

'Papa!' Miss Wallace cried. 'You can sacrifice one old coat! We all have to sacrifice if we are to work our way out of this mess. You and Mama must grasp how serious this is!'

Her father scowled at her again. 'I do not need my daughter to lecture me!' He sighed. 'Very well. I will give up the clothes off my back. See Wilfred. He will know which coat I might spare.'

Lucas had met Wilfred, Dunburn's valet, at the servants' dinner the night before. Wilfred was another old retainer who, like Cook and Kinley, the gardener, was of an age to be pensioned off.

Miss Wallace pressed her fingers against her temple. 'I cannot believe I am agreeing to this folly.' She glanced towards Lucas. 'Follow me, Mr Lucas.'

'I'll come, too.' Davina started up the stairs with them.

'Oh, Davina, you must not go,' her mother said. 'I need you to play cards with me. If I don't have some distraction, I'll suffer more palpitations.'

'But, Mama,' Davina protested, 'I want to help.'

Miss Wallace put a kind hand on her sister's arm. 'I'll find you later. I will very much need your help with the sewing. We must be done by morning.'

Davina appeared a bit mollified. 'I can help sew.'

Miss Wallace glanced towards Lucas and they continued up the stairs. Lucas was wafting in an all-too-familiar dreamlike fog from downing three glasses of whisky. Perhaps that was why he had volunteered for this—what had Miss Wallace called it?—this folly.

Or had he volunteered because Miss Wallace's parents had spoken so harshly to her?

They reached the first floor and walked past a large drawing room to her father's bedchamber.

She opened the door. 'Wilfred? Are you here?'

They stepped inside a lavishly decorated bedchamber, done in the latest style, with a huge walnut bed.

Wilfred emerged from what Lucas suspected was Dunburn's dressing room. 'Miss Mairi?' The old valet's wrinkled face looked surprised. 'What is it? What may I do for you?'

She took a deep breath as if gathering courage. 'I will let Papa explain the details to you, but we need to find decent clothes to fit Mr Lucas.' She glanced towards him with a look of apology. 'We are to have guests tomorrow and Mr Lucas will act as our butler. He needs something fitting to wear.'

'Of the Baron's?' Wilfred asked.

Lucas could not blame him for not immediately grasping the situation.

'Papa said you might know what clothes would do,' Miss Wallace responded. 'He will need a coat and waistcoat and neckcloth—'

'And shoes?' Wilfred added.

'Shoes.' Miss Wallace's face fell. 'Where are we to find shoes?' She waved a hand. 'Never mind. We will address that problem later.'

'A coat, waistcoat and trousers...' Wilfred walked around Lucas as if measuring his size. 'You are taller than the Baron, sir, but he is rounder. His coats might fit, but his trousers will be much too short.'

'The butler left a pair of breeches that could be altered,' Lucas said. 'They are loose in the waist.'

'Mr MacLeish was a bit rotund.' The valet looked up at him. 'What colour?'

'Black,' he responded.

'Excellent. Black will do quite well.' The old man frowned. 'It would help to have them here to match with a coat.'

Miss Wallace spoke up. 'I will get them. Where will I find them, Mr Lucas?'

He felt he should spare her the trip, but she was already at the door. 'In the chest by the bed.'

As she left, Wilfred extended his arm towards the dressing room. 'Come with me, Lucas.'

Chapter Seven

Mairi took the servants' stairs to the lower floor.

How could any of this work? This whole scheme was a terrible idea. It would merely be one more way her parents could avoid tackling their real problems. They needed to economise. They needed to take stock of their possessions and sell everything they did not absolutely need. They needed to stop spending money on anything but necessities. How many times had she begged them to economise this way? Pay off their debt? They should pay the poor servants and workers who toiled on their behalf, receiving nothing for themselves. They certainly should not—and could not—hire more help until they had the money to pay them. Having a pretend butler would not accomplish any of those things.

She'd been stunned that Mr Lucas had volunteered to act as their butler. It was so very kind of him to want to help, but they all would be acting out a lie, would they not?

She feared her family was on the brink of financial collapse, although she could not know for certain since her father refused to show her his ledgers. She had no idea how close they were to her father having to sell his title and land, but she feared the worst.

It did not seem fair that an English baron could not sell his entailed land or his title, even if he were forced into bankruptcy. In England the title of baron was attached to the person, not to the land. Whoever carried the title owned the land. In Scotland, though, the title of baron was attached to the property, the *caput*. Whoever owned the *caput* carried the title. A Scottish barony, the property and the title, could be bought and sold.

She encountered Robert in the hallway on her way to Mr Lucas's room.

She stopped him. 'Robert, did Erwin tell you what is happening?'

'That Mr Lucas will be our new butler, do ye mean?' he replied.

'That he will act as our butler while our guests are here,' she clarified. 'We are finding him some clothes. We need shoes, though. Do you know of anyone who might have some suitable for a butler? That would fit him, that is.'

Robert looked down at his own shoes. 'Mine, maybe?'

She touched his arm. 'Oh, no, Robert. You need those. Never mind. Something will turn up.' She started for Lucas's room again, but turned back. 'Would you tell the others? About Mr Lucas acting as our butler?'

His face relaxed. 'Oh, everyone knows, miss.'

She nodded. How efficient of Erwin.

She entered Lucas's room. In her mind it had become his room, not the butler's room. It smelled of his soap and of...him.

She hurried over to the chest by the bed and quickly found the breeches. Folding them over her arm, she hurried back to the stairs. When she reached the floor for her father's room, she paused. Best she also bring her sewing basket. She ran to her bedchamber and back down the main stairs to her father's room.

When she entered the room, Wilfred was just coming out of the dressing room, Mr Lucas behind him.

'What do you think of this? Will it do?'

He'd put the soldier in one of her father's coats, black as the night, contrasting with the waistcoat and neckcloth, which were white. The knot of the neckcloth was tied very simply.

Mr Lucas, in civilised clothes, was quite transformed. Mairi could not quite look at him, he affected her so. But she also could not quite look away. Her gaze locked with his.

She quickly blinked and glanced away. 'I've brought the breeches.'

She handed them to Wilfred, who brought them over to Mr Lucas and held them against the black coat. 'The cloth is not as fine, but I think these will do nicely. If we can make them fit.'

She glanced at Mr Lucas again. His lips stretched into a half-smile.

Wilfred tossed the breeches aside and pulled at the coat's shoulders and sleeves. 'The fit is all wrong, but some alterations should improve the look.'

Mairi lifted her sewing basket. 'I've brought pins.'

'Let us take off the coat and turn it inside out.' Wilfred assisted in the coat's removal and putting it back on. 'Bring the pins,' he told Mairi.

She stepped forward with her pincushion, a silver dish with a green-velvet cushion stuffed with sawdust to hold the pins.

At the shoulders Wilfred pinched the fabric of the coat between his fingers. 'Pin here.'

Mairi faced Mr Lucas with only inches between them. She rose on tiptoe to put the pins where Wilfred directed.

She was close enough to feel his heat and to catch his scent in her nostrils. Her heartbeat accelerated.

Since her assault, anxiety flooded her any time she thought she might be closer than arm's length to a man, but it was not anxiety she felt now. Though she did not know this Englishman, not really, she was not afraid of him. Not after enduring his fevered delirium. Something haunted him, like her assault haunted her. Was that why she felt connected to him?

He smelled of bergamot and lime, like the soap in his room. Her fingers tingled wherever she touched him to place the pins.

His gaze lowered to her face with a soft expression in his eyes that made her feel as if she would melt. She stuck the pins through the cloth, making herself focus on the task, not the man.

Wilfred moved over to the other shoulder and she put the pins where he indicated. Next, he asked Mr Lucas to raise his arms and showed Mairi what modifications were needed there. He adjusted the back seams so the coat fit more closely to Mr Lucas's body. Mairi was acutely aware she was touching Lucas all over.

Finally, Wilfred pronounced, 'There. That should do.' He helped Mr Lucas off with the coat. 'Let us try the breeches next.'

They disappeared into the dressing room and came out a few minutes later with the Englishman in the breeches. Mairi tried her best to attend only to pinning the cloth and not to the turbulence of emotions inside her. Apparently oblivious to her disordered emotions, the old valet seemed energised by this project, keeping a running account of his thoughts on how the final costume would appear and of how he would pull out some white stockings and gloves for Mr Lucas after they were done.

When he walked back into the dressing room for the additional items, Mairi and Mr Lucas remained where they were, still standing close, still gazing at each other.

Lucas gazed into Miss Wallace's captivating eyes. The drink was putting all sorts of notions in his mind. Like wanting to wrap his arms around her. Wanting to kiss her.

Cursed whisky. It was supposed to numb his feelings, not crack them open, not make him care about this brave young woman. Not make him desire her.

He forced himself to speak. Better to talk than act on his emotions. 'You think this plan foolhardy, do you not, Miss Wallace?'

She stepped back and glanced away. 'Not foolhardy. But my parents ought to be seeking a solution, not engaging in contortions to pretend our problems do not exist.'

'Is it as bad as that?'

'I do not know precisely,' she said, but the elderly valet re-entered the room.

'I have found you stockings and gloves, and an extra shirt and neckcloth.' Wilfred lifted them so they could see. 'When the sewing is complete you should be all set.'

Except for shoes, he thought.

'Thank you, Wilfred,' she said. 'You have been an enormous help.'

Lucas was impressed by the elderly man. He'd not expected to find such a skilled tailor in the wilds of Scotland.

Of course, he'd not expected to find anything in Scotland. He'd run away from his troubles, not towards any particular place.

Wilfred folded the clothes and handed them to Lucas. He and Miss Wallace stepped out into the hallway.

'Where would you like these?' Lucas asked.

She turned to him. 'Oh, give them to me.'

Their arms brushed as he placed the clothes in her hands. He gazed into her face just as she looked up into his.

His voice turned low. 'You are good to take on all this sewing, Miss Wallace.'

Hers was slightly facetious. 'I should say you are good to volunteer to be our butler.'

'But,' he concluded for her, 'you believe it is foolhardy.'

A smile flitted across her face, making her look even lovelier, but it was gone too quickly.

She turned to walk away, but turned back. 'The whole scheme will fall apart unless we can find you some shoes.'

He raised his brows. 'Is there a cobbler in the village?'

'Yes, but there isn't time to have shoes made and I do not want my father to owe money to the cobbler as well. Who knows how many other merchants he owes?'

He could pay for shoes. He had not drunk away his funds yet. Perhaps the cobbler had shoes already made that would fit him. It was worth a try.

'Try not to worry, Miss Wallace,' he told her. 'Something will turn up.'

'Well, I hope it is made of black leather and has soles.' She spun away and walked down the hallway.

Lucas watched her until she reached the stairs they'd walked up. He started to follow her, but caught himself. If he wished to forget he was the son and now heir to an earl, he shouldn't act like one. He turned in the opposite direction and found the servants' staircase.

Early the next morning, Mairi brought down the altered garments and laid them outside the door to the butler's room. As she did so, the door opened.

She jumped.

Lucas, dressed only in shirt and trousers, looked surprised as well.

'Miss Wallace!' He paused a moment before bowing.

'The clothes are finished.' She stepped back. 'I do hope they fit.'

He looked down at her with a concerned expression. 'You did not sleep, did you? You look pale.'

Her hand went reflexively to her face. She must look a fright. 'I am quite well.'

He picked up the clothes. 'But without rest.'

It had taken most of the night to finish the alterations. Davina had fallen asleep in Mairi's bed after an hour or two and Mairi had finished her sewing for her. Mairi's eyes still hurt from the strain of stitching by lamplight and from only three hours' sleep.

'I slept enough,' she said.

'You do too much.' He lifted the clothes. 'Even though you do not approve this scheme.'

His voice and words were kind and, in her weariness, she felt tears stinging her eyes. She blinked. 'Well, do try the clothes on and send word to me if they need work.'

He nodded. 'I will do so.'

She peered at him. 'You look different, Mr Lucas.' She could not place her finger on it, but, she had to admit, he looked even more dashing than before, even in his state of undress.

Or because of it?

He smiled. 'You have not seen me cleaned up properly. I took a bath last night.'

A bath? A vision of him naked flashed through her mind. She pushed it away. A bath usually caused the servants a great deal of work. Heating the water. Filling the tub. Draining it again.

His expression sobered. 'Do not fear. I prepared the bath for myself. The others have enough to do.'

How kind of him. Perhaps that was why she did not fear him like other men. His kindness.

But she did not want to think of this Englishman as handsome and kind. She did not want him to sense what she was thinking. He seemed to do that much too often.

'Well, that is all right, then.' She turned to go.

'A butler must not look like he's been planting vegetables,' he said.

She did not know what to say, so she simply walked away. Before she entered the kitchen, she glanced back and glimpsed him turning to re-enter his room.

Cook took one look at her and told her to sit at the table. 'You look dead on your feet, miss.'

'I am well enough,' protested Mairi. 'I only came to ask Mrs Cross what needs to be done to make the guest rooms ready.'

'You need to eat,' Cook insisted.

Mrs Cross walked into the room at that moment. 'Goodness, yes, child. Eat something!' She brought Mairi a napkin and a spoon.

From a big pot on the fire, Cook filled a bowl with porridge and set it in front of her. She poured some cream in the bowl and a dollop of jam. 'There. You eat all of it, mind.'

Mairi had been fussed over by these two dear women her whole life and, before that, they'd done the same for her father. They deserved a pension and a little cottage on the estate and some rest. 'You both are too good to me.' Tears stung her eyes again, but she blinked them away and dipped her spoon into the porridge.

'I cannot find Robert anywhere,' Mrs Cross said.

Cook brought Mairi a pot of tea, some milk and sugar. 'He's gone to the village to find some shoes for Mr Lucas.'

'Oh, yes. I forgot.' Mrs Cross rubbed her forehead. 'But who is going to clean the family's shoes before they rise?'

Mr Lucas entered the kitchen, this time wearing his coat. 'I could do that, Mrs Cross.'

The older woman looked relieved. 'Thank you, Mr Lucas. That would be very good of you.'

'I do not know which rooms to deliver them to, though.' He glanced at Mairi and nodded.

Mrs Cross pressed her cheeks. 'Goodness! You do not know the house, do you? We cannot have you play a butler without knowing the house. I shall have to give you a tour as soon as the family are up.' She smiled at Mairi. 'All those except Miss Mairi. She is our early riser.'

How dearly Mairi would have liked to sleep until ten today like her parents, but there was too much to do. She should eat her porridge as quickly as possible, but it was hot and warmed her so soothingly when she ate it slowly. And when had she last relaxed over a cup of tea?

'I'll be off to polish shoes,' Mr Lucas said.

Another kindness, Mairi thought.

Polishing the shoes turned out to be an easy job. Dunburn's were not particularly soiled and the ladies' shoes were nearly spotless. All but Miss Wallace's. Lucas could tell instantly which pair of walking boots were hers. They were the only shoes that looked as if any work had been done in them.

Glimpsing her seated at the kitchen worktable eating a bowl of porridge took him back to his own childhood, doing much the same thing.

Seated next to his brother.

He whisked the brush over Dunburn's boot, removing every speck of dust, then chose a brown bottle from the shelf and pulled out its cork. Its scent was sharp and strong. He dampened a cloth with the liquid, wiped the leather with the cloth and followed with a polishing brush. At the end, Dunburn's gleamed and Miss Wallace's, too.

That was some achievement, he supposed. It actually felt good to accomplish even this menial task.

There was a rap on the door and the door opened.

Miss Wallace stepped in. 'I can take the shoes upstairs.'

He wiped the brush over the leather again, although it was not at all necessary. Why did it sting that she did not even greet him?

'I will come with you,' he responded, although he knew she would not like it. 'You can point out which room is which in case Mrs Cross does not have a chance to give me a tour.'

'As you wish.'

When he finished he put the shoes in a basket and waited for her to leave before him. Lucas followed a little behind her, even though it felt odd. It was how a servant would behave, however. Shedding his aristocratic sensibilities was more difficult than he'd thought, but he wanted to shed everything about his aristocratic self. It suited him very well to play the role of butler. He'd model himself after Burton, his father's butler, a man who'd extricated Lucas from many a scrape. Happy memories for a change.

Miss Wallace led him up the servants' staircase to the bedchambers.

She stopped by the first door. 'My father's, as you know,' she said quietly.

Lucas placed his boots outside the door.

She showed him the other rooms, all in the same wing, and Lucas delivered the shoes. She stopped in front of one. 'This room is mine.'

She next led him to another wing to show him the guest rooms. She opened the door to the first one and frowned. 'I suppose this should be readied for Lord Crawfurd.'

Miss Wallace entered the room and sighed.

'Is there a problem?' he asked from the doorway.

She blinked. 'Oh, no. It is simply that the maids and I just closed off this room so we would not have to clean it as often. We closed off all the guest rooms. Now we will have to start over again. We'll have to undo two more.'

He followed her inside. 'Shall I remove the dust covers?' The furniture was covered in white linen sheets, looking like misshapen ghosts in the dim light.

'I suppose.' She strode over to one of the windows and opened the sash.

The breeze from the window was cool, but welcome. Lucas carefully folded over the linen cloth, revealing a comfortable red chair beneath. He continued through the room.

'At least it has not been closed up so long that we will have to beat the carpets.' Miss Wallace seemed to be speaking more to herself than to him.

'I am at liberty, Miss Wallace,' he told her. 'Put me to work.'

'Mr Lucas, I cannot ask you—'

'You did not ask me,' he interrupted. 'I offered. Take me to the other rooms and we may get started.'

They took the dust covers off in two other guest rooms and carried them down to the storage closet below stairs.

Robert appeared in the hallway. The shoes, Mairi thought suddenly. She'd forgotten all about the shoes.

'Mr Lucas!' Robert cried when spying them.

The Englishman quickened his step. 'Do tell me, Robert. Do you have shoes?'

Robert grinned and lifted up a pair of leather shoes with side buckles. 'I took your measure and the cobbler had one pair he'd finished. I paid him double, like ye said.'

Mairi stopped mid-stride. 'Double! Who paid double?'

'I did,' Mr Lucas said.

'Why would you pay?' She was dumbfounded. 'You are doing us a favour. And double. For shoes you cannot want.'

He shrugged. 'I am certain I will use them some time.'

She still did not understand it. 'How is it you have so much money you can throw it away?'

'I do not have a great deal of money,' he protested.

She looked sceptical. 'Where did it come from?'

'My soldier's pay.'

But why use good money on shoes he did not need?

Mr Lucas leaned against the wall and pulled off one of his boots. He tried on a shoe and stood again. 'It fits well enough.' He looked at Robert. 'I believe you have saved the day for your baron and his family. Well done, Robert.'

Robert beamed. The young man was always so hungry for a kind word from anyone. It had been thoughtful of Mr Lucas to give him credit.

But the Englishman's generosity in this instance unsettled her. It made no sense.

His expression remained unconcerned, though. 'Shall we finish getting the guest rooms ready, Miss Wallace?'

She did not have time to puzzle over the Englishman's vagaries. There was work to be done.

Chapter Eight

Lucas's tasks were to rehang the curtains in the guest rooms and to move any furniture that needed rearranging while Miss Wallace dusted and made up the beds with fresh linens. He felt content working beside Miss Wallace, although she said little to him beyond basic instructions. In any event, he was pleased to ease her burdens a little.

When they were finished he went in search of the housekeeper for his tour of the house. He found her in the dining room, where she and the maids were cleaning. The dining table was large enough to accommodate at least twenty. On the walls hung portraits—Wallace ancestors, Lucas supposed. Perhaps one of the bearded, helmeted ones was William Wallace himself.

After giving the two maids some instructions, Mrs Cross took him on a room-by-room tour of the house.

Foxgrove Hall, where he had grown up, was twice as big as this house and with many more rooms, but it still was a lot to remember. With any luck, he would not direct the guests to the wrong places.

As Lucas and the housekeeper toured the house, he asked her, 'Is there anything else I should know to be the butler? Anything about the family?'

Mrs Cross halted and turned to him. 'I will tell you this in great confidence, although I have no doubt you would discern it on your own eventually. The Baron of Dunburn and Lady Dunburn are too frivolous for their own good. The family is in some financial straits—I cannot pretend to know the details—but the Baron is unequal to the task of solving the problems and her ladyship has no notion how to economise. I do not know what will happen to us all. So many of the servants have left. The Baron has not paid us, you see.' She gave him a pointed stare. 'So if you think he will pay you, you have another think coming.'

'I surmised as much,' he responded.

She started walking again. 'The only one with any sense is Miss Mairi, you know. Although Davina and Niven are dear ones, they are still very young. I suspect they do not grasp the seriousness of the family's predicament. Miss Mairi has figured it out.'

'Is that why she is so serious?' He meant why she was so unhappy, but felt he was not yet on such terms with the housekeeper that he could indulge in that kind of gossip.

Mrs Cross sighed. 'I suppose it is. She was once as gay as Miss Davina, but she had a bout of melancholy when she was Davina's age.' She paused as if in thought. 'I do hope Miss Davina never experiences such a thing. All the others are cheerful sorts, I'll give them that. Anyway, Miss Mairi is the only one who sees things as they are. She has helped us immensely.'

A bout of melancholy, Lucas thought. Had something happened to change her? He certainly had been changed by his brother's death. Irrevocably so.

It took only the thought of his brother... Again, he heard the sounds of the battle. Smelled the blood. Watched the French cuirassier impale his brother over and over.

'Mr Lucas?'

Lucas blinked and saw Mrs Cross gaping at him.

'Forgive me,' he said. 'I was wool-gathering.'

She gave him a sceptical look.

Later that afternoon, Mairi had put herself together, wearing one of her good dresses and fixing her hair properly. She'd also helped Davina to look her best. The Crawfurds would not know from their appearance that anything was amiss.

Mairi made her way down to the servants' floor. This plan for an out-of-work itinerant Englishman to pretend to be their butler seemed doomed to fail. How would he know what to do? Footmen trained for years to take such a position in a house.

Had anyone even asked him why he thought he could manage this?

There was no answer to her knock at the butler's room, so she followed the sound of voices coming from the servants' hall.

They were all there. Mrs Cross, Mrs MacNeal, Betsy, Agnes, Robert and Erwin. Even Wilfred and Nellie, the lady's maid, were there, as were John and MacKay, their stablemen, and Kinley, the gardener. And at the head of the table sat Mr Lucas, leading an animated discussion of the tasks that were to be performed.

Mr Lucas saw her in the doorway and rose. Conversation stopped and the others stood as well.

'Please sit,' Mairi said. 'I came to see how we are progressing.'

None of the servants sat.

Wilfred came over to her. 'Come. Come, Miss Mairi. See your handiwork.' He led her over to Mr Lucas.

He faced her, standing very erect, chin raised, gaze carefully averted from hers.

'Is the costume not sublime?' Wilfred brushed his hand over Mr Lucas's arms, ending in a little flourish in front of the snow-white neckcloth.

What was more, Mr Lucas's hair had been trimmed and his expression was suitably bland.

'Miss Wallace.' He spoke in haughty tones, still not meeting her eye. 'Does my appearance meet with your approval?'

He looked magnificent, enough to take her breath away, but she certainly had no intention of telling him so. 'Well, you look the part, Mr Lucas.'

Betsy, one of the maids, tittered. 'Is that nae so?'

His gaze slid to her briefly and his eyes twinkled in amusement. 'Ah, but you must call me Lucas, Miss Wallace. We must follow the conventions.'

Yes. The other servants would call him Mr Lucas. To the family and their guests he would be Lucas.

'Lucas,' she repeated.

He even sounded the part.

'Yes. So.' She turned to them all. 'Have you been discussing plans of how to endure this?'

Mrs Cross spoke. 'We are accepting the challenge.'

The others nodded their assent.

'My family could not be more grateful,' Mairi said. 'I vow I will do my best to see you all rewarded.'

Cook patted her hand. 'Now do not worry over that, miss. Take matters day by day.'

Her gaze spanned them all. 'You are all too good.'

They lowered their gazes.

Mr Lucas—Lucas, she meant—broke the silence. 'We do have one question.'

She turned back to him, but it was Mrs Cross who spoke. 'Should Mr Lucas be given the key to the silver and the wine? I did not feel I had the authority to decide this. Shall we ask your father?'

'No, no need to bother my father.' He would say yes without giving it any thought. Lucas was a stranger and there was no reason to trust him, but she did. 'Yes, of course. The butler must have the keys.' She simply could not imagine him taking their silver, not with all he'd done for them already. She turned to him again. 'Will you be able to select the wine?' She did not know of anyone else who would be up to that task.

He answered her in a butler's voice. 'Every butler is knowledgeable about wine, miss. I will endeavour not to disappoint your family.'

The maids giggled.

Mairi did not see the humour, though. She wanted to snap at him to stop talking like that, to talk like himself. Like the kind man he was. But she had to admit that his tone suited a butler.

She took a deep breath. 'Well, I do hope you are ready. The guests should arrive any moment now.'

'You must not worry, miss,' Mrs Cross said. 'Mr Lucas's suggestions of how we should go on will keep us well sorted.'

He'd organised them? Assigned them duties as if he were a real butler? She prayed their faith in him was not misplaced.

True to Miss Wallace's word, an hour had not gone by before the carriage passed through the gate. Lucas had sent John ahead to watch out for it so they could be warned as quickly as possible. As the carriage approached the door, the family was all present to greet the guests and Lucas had lined up all the servants to receive them. Lucas had often stood in such a formation growing up, but never in the line with the servants.

Good God, what was he about? This scheme was probably rife with pitfalls and depended too entirely on him.

Perhaps he should have walked away, let the cards Dunburn had played fall where they may. Lucas did not have a good record of protecting those he cared about.

He glanced at the Baron and Lady Dunburn. Both were all nerves. Miss Wallace was composed, but solemn, and Lucas had an impulse to reassure her all would work out in the end. If he played a convincing butler, that was. Davina was merely eager and excited, but Lucas suspected she did not comprehend the stakes of this game.

When the carriage was slowing to a stop, Miss Wallace's hand pressed against her temple. 'We forgot about Niven! Niven does not know Lucas is the butler!'

Niven and his friend rode on the top of the carriage.

Dunburn began to sputter. Lady Dunburn looked about to weep.

Davina spoke up. 'Leave Niven to me. I'll pull him aside as soon as he climbs off the carriage. They will think I am glad to see him.'

'Tell him he must not confide in anyone, not even his friend William,' Miss Wallace warned.

It seemed less and less likely this would succeed.

The carriage stopped and Erwin was quick to put down the steps and open the door. Lady Crawfurd emerged first. Lucas stepped forward to assist her from the carriage.

Dunburn bowed. 'Lady Crawfurd, how good to see you.'

'Welcome.' Lady Dunburn smiled nervously, landing a light peck on Lady Crawfurd's cheek.

Next Lord Crawfurd exited the carriage and received their greetings. Niven and his friend climbed down from riding outside and Davina ran to him.

'Niven!' she cried in a joyous tone. She gave him a hug and pulled him off to the side, whispering in his ear.

Another man exited the carriage, a younger man than

Lord Crawfurd, but not of an age with Niven either. He was not expected.

'Lady Dunburn,' Lady Crawfurd chirped. 'Let me present Mr Charles Hargreave. You remember the Hargreaves. The Earl of Barring's younger son.'

'Ah, Mr Hargreave.' Lady Dunburn laughed nervously. 'Yes. You are welcome, too.'

The young man bowed to Lady Dunburn. 'My lady, you are too kind when I know a surprise guest is always a difficulty.'

'Let me introduce you to my daughters.' Lady Dunburn called to Davina, 'Davina, what are you about? Come here.'

Hargreave's gaze turned to Miss Wallace and his eyes kindled with interest. Lucas frowned.

A maid was the last to exit the carriage and a manservant climbed from the top of the carriage. Lady Crawfurd's maid and Lord Crawfurd's valet.

'Come into the house,' Dunburn said.

Robert and Erwin saw to the luggage.

Lucas whispered to Mrs Cross, 'Have Betsy and Agnes prepare a room for Mr Hargreave.'

'Aye,' she responded. 'The blue room will be best.'

Lucas followed the family and guests into the hall and tended to their outer garments and hats.

'I'm afraid I did not bring my man,' Hargreave said in a haughty voice. 'He is to meet me at Lord Oxmont's. I will need someone to attend me.'

Lucas frowned. The man came uninvited and expected to have a valet attend to him?

'Yes. Yes,' Dunburn responded nervously. 'Lucas, our new butler, will see to it.' He turned to Lucas uncertainly. 'Is that not so, Lucas?'

'Indeed, it is, sir,' Lucas responded. 'I will attend you

myself.' There was no other choice. Neither Robert nor
Erwin would be up to the task.

'An English butler, Dunburn?' Hargreave said somewhat mockingly.

Niven piped up, 'Lucas is fairly new. Papa just hired him
not long ago.' Niven gave Lucas a wink.

At least Niven was quick to play along.

Lord and Lady Crawfurd wished to freshen up and rest
from their journey and Miss Wallace offered to show them
to their rooms. Lady Dunburn declared she would rest as
well. Niven and his friend ran off somewhere, Davina with
them.

'Come, have a whisky with me while your room is readied.' Dunburn took Hargreave into the library with him.

Mrs Cross helped Lucas hang the coats in the cloakroom.

'We have crossed the first hurdle, Mrs Cross,' he said,
although the rest of the day would be even more of a challenge.

'Imagine that young man arriving without warning or
invitation.' Mrs Cross shook her head. 'The Quality can
be so thoughtless sometimes.'

Lucas agreed.

As soon as Lord and Lady Crawfurd and their servants
were settled and their luggage brought to them, Mairi hurried down to the servants' floor to see if there was anything
she ought to be doing.

She met Lucas in the hallway. 'We did not expect that
other guest,' she said breathlessly. 'I can help get the room
ready.'

His expression seemed to soften when regarding her.
'Miss Wallace, you need to play the part of the baron's daughter, not the maid-of-all-work. Betsy and Agnes are tending
to the room.'

She liked that he dropped his butler persona for this moment with her. 'It is not so easy for me to do that.' She gave him a worried look. 'Do you object to acting as Mr Hargreave's valet as well as everything else?' Did he even know how to be a valet?

He met her gaze. 'I am well able to play the hand I'm being dealt, Miss Wallace. Go back above stairs. Use this time to enjoy yourself.'

She sighed. 'Enjoy myself? I fear I shall be on edge the whole time they are here.' Nothing about having these guests would be enjoyable.

'Please.' His voice turned low. 'Do not worry over any of this. Truly, you may be at ease.'

His tone touched something deep inside her, something long neglected—the need for someone to care about her feelings. It upset her to be so moved. It made her vulnerable and she never wished to be vulnerable again.

'I will do my part,' she said much too sharply.

He blinked and leaned away before again speaking, though his voice was no longer low. 'You should not visit the servants' floor. If Lord and Lady Crawfurd's servants see Baron Dunburn's daughter here, they might think it something to gossip about.'

She had not thought of that.

'Send for me if you need to,' he said. 'I promise to take care of your concerns.'

She hated the tension between them, especially because she'd created it. 'Thank you, Lucas,' she said softly. 'I will leave it to you, then.'

He bowed and his demeanour changed back into that of a butler. 'Very good, miss.'

The formality in his voice depressed her, until a corner of his mouth turned up and amusement filled his eyes.

She broke into a smile and her body suddenly felt light

as a feather. Perhaps it was because he had taken some of the burden off her shoulders.

Charles Hargreave glanced calmly around the dining room, with its portraits of ancestors and still lifes of dead game and fish. It was a pleasant room. More modern than he had expected.

He'd been a guest at the Crawfurds' when he'd learned they would be stopping by Baron and Lady Dunburn's for a day or two en route to the house party at Oxmont Castle.

How lucky!

Sometimes good fortune simply fell into his lap. Hargreave had been making enquiries about certain Scottish Barons and, from what he'd learned, the Baron of Dunburn would suit his needs perfectly.

Hargreave had a secret. He desired a title. And an estate. But he was the younger son. His brother would some day become Earl. His sister had married a title. What could he do?

He could purchase a title. He could purchase a Scottish barony.

Oh, a Scottish barony was not an elevated title, but it was a title all the same, the only option available to him unless his brother died without issue.

He could not count on being that lucky, however.

At least from an uncle's inheritance, he had a sizeable fortune. His plan, then, was to find a baron in such financial straits that he would be forced to sell his title and lands. Hargreave was willing to help that situation along, if necessary. The Baron of Dunburn, it was rumoured, owed a deal of money to a great many creditors and money lenders. That was mere gossip, but Hargreave was determined on this visit to discover if it was true.

The only other problem would be how to maintain the

respect of his peers if he pursued his goal. The purchaser of the last barony had been shunned for ruining the family, although the way Hargreave saw it, it was the man's own fault for losing his title. Hargreave was taking no chances.

He slid a sideways glance at Miss Wallace, seated on his right. She was much prettier than he'd expected, which pleased him, although her reserve made her tiresome company. It was unfortunate that the younger daughter was not a few years older. He much preferred a lively redhead.

But he was impatient. Mairi Wallace was marriageable now. The plan was to marry the daughter of the ruined Baron. The way he figured it, if he married her, he'd be seen as the hero of the situation, the rescuer of the family, who could remain in their house and stay on their land. He rather fancied that.

Because it would be his house and his land and he would become the Baron of Dunburn.

Chapter Nine

After the Wallaces and their guests retired for the night, Hargreave rang for Lucas to ready him for bed.

Lucas had almost enjoyed orchestrating the dinner. It had taken planning, organisation and vigilance, and he was proud of his performance and that of the other servants. They'd pulled it off without a hitch.

But the idea of attending Hargreave put a bad taste in Lucas's mouth.

What sort of gentleman arrives uninvited to spend the night? Moreover, Lucas did not like the way the man had fawned over Miss Wallace.

He took a fortifying breath before rapping on Hargreave's door and hearing the man say, 'Enter.'

Hargreave lounged in a chair, a glass of whisky in his hand. Without saying a word to Lucas, he extended his leg and waited until Lucas pulled off his boot. And, to Lucas's distaste, his sock.

'My nightclothes are in the trunk over there.' Hargreave gestured with his hand. 'Do not disturb the packing. We should be here only a day or so and my man packed it very well. I do not tolerate wrinkled clothing.'

That immediately made Lucas wish to crumple up the clothes.

Instead he sifted carefully through Hargreave's things to find the nightshirt. He laid it out on the bed. Hargreave stood—Lucas's signal, he presumed, to help the man off with his coat and waistcoat.

'Tell me of the family,' Hargreave said while Lucas unbuttoned the waistcoat. 'There are rumours about them.'

'Rumours?' Lucas responded as blandly as he could. Did this man really think the butler would engage in gossip about the Wallaces?

Hargreave lifted his chin so Lucas could untie his neckcloth and then his arms to pull off his shirt. 'The rumour is that Dunburn is nearly a bareman.'

'A bareman?' Lucas repeated. *What the devil was a bareman?*

Hargreave gave a dry laugh. 'You don't speak Scots, do you, Sassenach? A bareman is a man with grave debts.' He walked over to the basin, washed his face and waited for Lucas to hand him the towel.

Lucas let him drip for a moment. 'I have no reason to believe the Baron has grave debts.' He handed him the towel. 'The Baron hired me, after all.'

Hargreave smirked at Lucas before rubbing his face with the cloth. 'What do you know of the daughter?' he asked.

Lucas bristled. Why the devil did Hargreave ask that? He hedged. 'There are two daughters.'

'I mean Mairi Wallace, of course.' Hargreave laughed. 'Oh, the younger one is lively enough. She'll lead some man on a merry chase some day, but one must wait a few years for her. Her older sister is of age.'

Of age for what? Courting?

Hargreave was not good enough for her—although, given her situation, the younger son of an earl would be a good match.

Lucas baulked at the thought. 'Miss Wallace is a fine

young lady, from what I have observed.' He handed Hargreave his sleeping garment.

Hargreave took it and grinned. 'And she is not too difficult to look at.'

Lucas's hands curled into fists. How he'd like to throttle the fellow, bantering about Miss Wallace.

Hargreave donned his sleeping garment by himself, for which Lucas was grateful. He sat again in the chair and poured himself another glass of whisky. Lucas's nostrils filled with the scent of it and he felt like he could almost taste it. He gathered the man's discarded clothes and picked up his boots.

'Will there be anything else, sir?' He managed to speak in his butler's voice.

Hargreave lifted the whisky bottle and checked the volume of the contents. 'No, I think this is enough. You may leave.'

Lucas executed his most servile bow. 'Very good, sir.' He refused to wish the man goodnight.

Lucas left Hargreave's room, filled with disgust. He disliked everything about Hargreave—the way he assumed Lucas would help with his dress, how he spoke only when trying to get information.

Lucas knew many men just like him, convinced of their own superiority, oblivious to those whose job it was to serve them. Some such men had been his friends, fellow officers, other younger sons sent to the army to be cannon fodder. It mattered not one whit if those younger sons got killed in battle. It would not have mattered one whit if Lucas had been killed instead of his brother.

He should have been.

Why had Bradleigh been so mad for the glory of war? He'd be alive today if—

Do not think of Bradleigh!

He tried to shake the thoughts out of his head.

But the vision of his brother's shocked face as the
cuirassier's sword thrust through him flashed through
his mind anyway.

He yanked open the door to the servants' stairs.

'Whoop!' Niven jumped back, clasping his heart. 'You
startled me!'

Lucas frowned. 'What the devil are you doing here,
Niven?'

'I'm waiting for you, of course,' Niven responded amiably.

'What for?' Lucas started down the stairs.

Niven followed him. 'I have been dying of curiosity!
Imagine my surprise to find you are our butler. Davina told
me to pretend you really are our butler and to keep mum to
William and his parents about it. I have not had one moment
alone with her or Mairi to ask. How did this come about?'

'I volunteered,' Lucas said.

'Why?' Niven paused for a second. 'By the way, it is
capital to see you all recovered.'

'Thank you.' Lucas reached the lower level of the house.
He wished he could go to his room with a bottle of whisky
like Hargreave had.

He had the keys to the wine cellar...

No.

He wouldn't steal from Dunburn.

He turned to Niven. 'If you must, come with me to the
butler's room and I will explain what I can, but take care
not to show yourself down here to Lord and Lady Craw-
ford's servants.'

Lucas opened the door and peeked into the hallway. It
was empty. He signalled Niven to follow him. He went directly to the butler's room and dropped Hargreave's clothes
on the floor. He'd deal with them later.

'You cannot be a butler,' Niven said as soon as they were inside the room with the door closed. 'It's demeaning for a soldier like yourself!'

'I am not a butler,' Lucas clarified. 'I am merely pretending to be one and you must not give any hint that there is anything remarkable about this. You must stay away from me.'

Niven's expression turned sulky. 'I was hoping William and I could talk to you about the war. What battles you fought. What it was like. Papa already told everyone you were at Waterloo.'

That was unfortunate. Dunburn should not have called attention to him like that.

'Very well. Tomorrow seek me out. If I can, I will talk to you.' Two boys wanting to talk about the war would probably not be remarked upon and he did owe Niven his worthless life. He dreaded it, though.

He'd relive it again.

Niven sat down in one of the chairs. 'But tell me now why you volunteered to be our butler.'

Lucas stood over him. 'It was your doing, Niven. You invited the Crawfurds without consulting your parents. That was not well done of you.'

Niven looked shocked at the rebuke, then turned defensive. 'But everyone we know would have extended such an invitation in my place! How churlish would it be if they brought me here and we sent them on to stay in the village inn?'

'You might have returned the day you said you would, instead of staying longer,' Lucas countered. Niven opened his mouth to protest, but Lucas held up his hand. 'You knew your family was short of servants and could use your help.'

The youngster looked chagrined. 'I confess I did not think of it. I don't notice much about not having servants.'

Did the boy not notice how hard his elder sister had been working? 'Your parents feared your guests would notice the dearth of servants, especially the lack of a butler.'

'Would they not merely assume Papa has not hired a new one?' Niven asked.

Lucas gave the boy a direct look. 'Niven. The Crawfurds would guess that your family was having financial difficulties. If word of that got around, it might make matters very hard for your father and mother.'

Niven lowered his gaze. 'I did not think of it that way.'

'Your parents were greatly distressed and so I volunteered to pretend to be your butler. To repay you all for possibly saving my life. I might have died had it not been for you and Davina finding me.'

The reminder of Niven's better choices seemed to raise his spirits. 'But how is it you know how to be a butler?'

'I have been a member of a household. I have seen what a butler does,' he prevaricated and quickly changed the subject. 'Did you tell your friend William that you rescued someone?'

'Yes, of course,' Niven replied. 'It was the most exciting thing to have happened here in a long time.'

'Does he know it was me?' If so, all their efforts would be for naught.

'No. Davina told me not to say it was you.' Niven lifted his chin. 'I told William that the man we rescued left already.'

'Well done,' Lucas told him. 'No one must know there is anything strange about me being your butler.'

Niven straightened. 'I give you my word I will say nothing and I always honour my word.'

Lucas softened towards the youth. 'I do not doubt you.'

Niven rose. 'I'd best be off to bed, then.' He walked with as much dignity as a boy his age could muster after receiving a deserved dressing-down. He stopped at the door. 'Goodnight, Lucas.'

Lucas smiled at the boy. 'Goodnight, Niven.'

After Niven was likely out of the hall, Lucas picked up Hargreave's clothing and took it to the footmen's room. With luck, one of the maids would launder the shirt, neck-cloth and stockings. He began brushing off the coat, waist-coat and trousers.

Even touching the clothing was distasteful. To perform such intimate care for a man like Hargreave was abhorrent. One thing was for certain—Lucas would never again take the services of a personal servant for granted.

The next morning, Mairi rose early as she had needed to do every other morning to keep the household afloat, and, as usual, Nellie came to her room first to help her dress. The poor woman was so fatigued after staying up late to attend her mother that Mairi said she would help Davina get dressed. She sent Nellie back to her bed to rest until her mother awoke.

It was still a little too early to wake Davina, so Mairi went downstairs to see if Mrs Cross needed any help.

She found Mrs Cross in the drawing room, helping the maids tidy the place.

'Good morning,' Mairi said, more cheerfully than she felt.

The maids and Mrs Cross stopped working. They all curtsied to her.

'How are you faring?' Mairi asked.

Mrs Cross smiled, an unusual expression for her these days. 'We are doing fair, Miss Mairi. Better than you would expect.'

'That is so?' She was used to Mrs Cross looking tense and harried. 'I am glad to hear it.'

Mrs Cross leaned forward a little and spoke confidentially. 'To own the truth, Mr Lucas has stepped in like a champion.'

Betsy piped up, 'Aye, he has, miss.'

Agnes nodded.

Nellie had told her much the same thing. 'Indeed? What has he done?'

Mrs Cross shrugged. 'It is hard to say. He just seems to know who should do what and when.'

Agnes giggled. 'I wouldnae say no tae him.'

Mrs Cross frowned and clapped her hands. 'Now, now, we'll have none of that.'

Agnes and Betsy, still stifling smiles, went back to wiping the tables with their cloths.

'Well, I am glad matters are more to your liking,' she managed to say.

Agnes mumbled, 'The butler is more to my liking.'

Betsy snickered.

'Girls!' Mrs Cross admonished.

Agnes and Betsy's good humour irritated Mairi, although she had no idea why. She ought to have been glad they were happy.

'Do you need any help, Mrs Cross?' she asked.

'No, miss. Not today,' the housekeeper said. 'We have it all in hand.'

Mairi's brows rose in astonishment. 'Well. That is very good.'

She bid them all good day and walked out of the room. She might as well see if Davina was awake.

She passed through the hall where Erwin was on duty. He nodded to her.

'Is all well, Erwin?' she asked.

'It is, miss,' he said, sounding amazed. 'I don't think we have to worry.'

Because of Lucas, no doubt.

She climbed the stairs to the first floor, where all the bedchambers were. As she neared the landing, Mr Hargreave was on his way down. He stood in her way so she had to stop.

'Good morning, Miss Wallace.' He gave a little bow and smiled.

'Good morning.' She wanted to be on her way, but he blocked her path.

'I hope you are well this morning.'

'I am, sir.' She ought to say something polite. 'Did you sleep well?'

'Quite well. And you? How did you sleep, Miss Wallace?' His smile widened and his gaze swept over her in an intense manner.

It sent a shiver down her spine and her heart raced like it always did around unfamiliar men. Or at least around ones who looked at her in that intense way. The memory of her assault pressed against her brain, trying to break through.

She must not let the memories come. With them came the panic.

She took a breath and forced her voice to be calm and polite. 'Quite well,' she responded, mimicking his words. 'Breakfast is in the morning room. Erwin, who is attending the hall, will direct you.'

She took a step forward, but he hesitated a moment before stepping aside.

He'd engaged her in conversation the night before, but all she could remember about it was wanting to get away from him. She couldn't, really. He was their guest.

Before she reached Davina's bedchamber, she glanced down the hallway containing the guest rooms and saw Lucas emerge from Mr Hargreave's room.

'Lucas,' she called.

He turned and waited for her to reach him. 'Miss Wallace. May I serve you in some way?' he asked in that bland tone that servants so often used.

'Lucas, you do not have to talk like a butler with me.' Why did she not feel discomfort with him? He was more of a stranger than Mr Hargreave, whose family knew her family.

Lucas kept his bland expression. 'One never knows who might hear,' he said quietly.

She looked over her shoulder and glimpsed Mr Hargreave on the top step watching them. That uncomfortable feeling returned.

She tried to ignore it.

'Is everything going well?' she asked Lucas instead, making certain she still spoke quietly. 'Is there anything I might do?'

At least his eyes lost that distant expression. They softened as he gazed at her. 'Enjoy yourself. You may be at ease.'

She blew out an anxious breath. 'I feel so useless!'

'Overworked, more likely,' he said, adding softly, 'We will pull this off, I promise. So, truly, be at ease.' He glanced back at the stairs. 'But I should leave you, unless there is a service I might perform.'

'Is he gone?' she whispered.

He nodded.

'You were coming from his room.' She could not picture Lucas acting as valet to this man. 'How is it to serve him?'

His brows knitted. 'He asked several questions—about the family.'

'He did?' Why would he do that?

'I did not answer them,' he assured her.

'I should hope not!' She knew that without asking, though.

His voice turned soft. 'I will not betray you.'

Their gazes caught. Warmth spread through her like warm honey. Such a different reaction from how she'd felt towards Hargreave a moment ago. Mairi rarely felt safe around a man, but she felt safe with Lucas.

Maybe he had cast a spell on all of them. Her whole family and all the servants had put their faith in him.

He stepped back and smiled. 'Tend to your guests, Miss Wallace. That is all you need do.' He bowed and turned away to walk towards the servants' stairs.

She watched him until he disappeared, a jumble of feelings inside her.

She hurried on to Davina's room.

To her surprise, Davina had already risen and, like Mairi, had dressed herself as far as she was able.

'Oh, Mairi.' Her younger sister looked distressed. 'I thought Nellie would have been here by now.'

'I told her I would help you,' Mairi said. 'She is resting.'

'Resting?' Davina looked at her reflection in her mirror. 'How can she be resting? I need her to fix my hair. She is so good at it.'

'Mama kept her up late and, because of us, she had to rise early,' Mairi explained. 'It is difficult for her at her age. I told her to rest a wee bit before Mama needs her.'

Davina wailed. 'Not today, Mairi. I want to look my best.'

'Whatever for?' Mairi lost her patience. Davina was rarely thoughtless of others, especially of their beloved servants. 'It is only the Crawfurds. We've known them for ever.'

'There is also Mr Hargreave!' Davina responded, her tone somewhat dreamy.

'Mr Hargreave?' Mairi's guard flew up.

'Yes.' Davina crossed her hands over her chest. 'I like him.'

Mairi's heart beat too fast. 'He is too old for you!' Or more accurately, Davina was too young. Much too young.

Davina rolled her eyes. 'Oh, Mairi. He cannot even be thirty years yet and you know daughters like us often marry men who are as old as Papa.'

Mairi could not bear to think of that very real possibility. 'But not when they are fourteen!'

'Some girls marry at sixteen, though,' Davina protested.

But not Davina, Mairi vowed. It was much too young to handle what could happen between a man and woman. Mairi knew too well. 'Mama and Papa would not want you to marry at sixteen. Besides, you are only fourteen. You must not flirt with Mr Hargreave. You must behave like a lady.'

Davina plopped down in the chair at her dressing table. 'Oh, I will. I value my reputation, you know, but I do wish I were older.'

'You will be older in no time at all.' Mairi began brushing out Davina's auburn hair. Her sister was already a beauty and sometimes looked older than her years. 'And do not fear. I will arrange your hair attractively. It is not that difficult. Your hair is so lovely.'

Too lovely perhaps, paired with Davina's bright green eyes.

Just in case, she would watch over Davina in Mr Hargreave's presence.

Mr Hargreave remained at the breakfast table when Mairi and Davina entered the room. Niven and William Crawfurd were also present. When Mr Hargreave stood, Niven and William scrambled to stand as well.

'Good morning, ladies,' Mr Hargreave said smoothly.

Before Robert, who was serving the breakfast, could do so, Hargreave pulled out a chair for Mairi. William, following his example, did the same for Davina. When Davina turned to thank him, colour rose in his face. Mairi did not miss it, even though Niven seemed oblivious. William was smitten with their younger sister.

Hargreave slid a knowing glance at Mairi. 'The boy has good taste,' he whispered to her.

That this man acknowledged her sister's beauty, even in this indirect way, only raised her hackles even more.

Robert appeared at her side, offering a piece of ham. She nodded and he put it on her plate. He offered some to Davina next. Both Niven and William asked for more. Robert served cooked eggs and toasted bread as well.

'Shall I pour you some tea, Miss Wallace?' Mr Hargreave asked.

She wanted nothing to do with him, but was obligated to be nice out of politeness. 'Thank you.'

He poured and she pulled the cup closer to her plate.

'What plans do you ladies have for this fine day?' Hargreave asked amiably.

Davina looked up, but did not speak.

'We are at the disposal of our guests,' Mairi said quickly.

William cleared his throat. 'Niven and I are going riding after breakfast.' He turned to Davina. 'Miss Davina, perhaps you would like to join us?'

Davina glanced at Niven, who said happily enough, 'Yes, Davina. Capital idea. Come with us.'

Davina beamed with pleasure. 'I'd be delighted!'

'Well, let us eat quickly,' Niven said.

They busily talked about what horses each should ride and where they should go.

'I should like to see the standing stones,' William said. 'The ones where you found the sick soldier.'

'The sick soldier?' Mr Hargreave's brows rose.

Davina and Niven looked distressed. As did Robert.

'Yes,' Mairi quickly said. 'Davina and Niven found a soldier there who was travelling north. He was quite ill, but recovered quickly, thank goodness.' She added, 'He has gone on his way.'

'What luck to have two soldiers in your house,' William said. 'Your butler and the wanderer.'

'Your butler was a soldier?' Hargreave asked.

'Oh, yes,' Mairi said. Better not to make up too many stories.

'He—he was at Waterloo,' Niven added. 'He—he told William and me all about the battle. We were up early and spoke to him.'

'Did you now?' Mr Hargreave said unenthusiastically.

William turned to Davina. 'Is it true the stones have magic?'

Bless him for changing the subject.

'There are countless stories of strange things happening at the stones,' Davina happily answered. 'Apparently witches used to worship there.'

They talked then of magic stones and mysterious legends around them, and the conversation totally veered away from their butler.

When the young people finished their meal and hurried out, Mairi's mother and Lady Crawfurd entered the room. Hargreave again pulled out chairs and assisted the older ladies, much to their pleasure.

'Where is your father?' her mother asked Mairi after being served.

Hargreave answered. 'He and Lord Crawfurd ate earlier. I believe they are taking a tour around the estate.'

Mairi hoped Lord Crawfurd would not notice how run-down the property had become, or anything else that would give away the true state of things at Dunburn.

'I see we shall have to entertain ourselves, Jane,' Lady Crawfurd said to her mother.

'That we shall,' her mother replied. 'Mr Hargreave, I hope my husband did not neglect you.'

'Not at all, ma'am,' he said smoothly. 'I was invited to accompany them, but I declined. So if you have need of me, I am at your beck and call.'

The ladies tittered.

He turned to Mairi. 'Unless, of course, Miss Wallace might wish to show me the gardens and partake of this fine weather.'

There was nothing she'd rather do less.

Her mother replied, 'I am certain Mairi could do that, could you not, Mairi?'

'Yes, of course.' Her hands trembled. She had no wish to be alone with him.

'Excellent!' He rose. 'Suppose I meet you in the hall in an hour?' He glanced at the clock on the mantel.

'The hall in an hour,' she repeated.

He bowed to the ladies and took his leave.

Mairi's hands shook. She hid them in her lap.

Her mother leaned towards her. 'Mairi, isn't it grand! He may want to court you!'

Lady Crawfurd added, 'He is the younger son of an earl and has a nice income. It would be a good match for you.'

She looked from one eager face to the other. 'He merely asked me to show him the gardens, not to marry him.'

'But it might lead to that!' Her mother clapped her hands. 'He is handsome, too, is he not?'

Lucas's face flashed through her mind. Mr Hargreave was not nearly as handsome as Lucas. 'I suppose.'

'His family are great friends of ours,' Lady Crawfurd continued. 'Charles is like a son to us. He had a particular interest in meeting you, you know.'

Mairi immediately turned wary. 'Why was that? I have no great fortune to tempt him.' She likely had none at all.

'Well, you are not poor, are you? And I suppose we spoke highly of you,' Lady Crawfurd admitted.

Mairi wished she had not. 'How very kind of you, ma'am.'

Please do not act the matchmaker on my behalf. I do not wish to marry. I need to stay at Dunburn House and keep my father from losing it.

This was her place of safety and refuge. She could not bear it if her father had to sell. What would happen to Niven and Davina?

She concentrated on sipping her tea and, to her relief, the conversation moved on to talk of other people. Her mother appeared to be enjoying herself tremendously. That made Mairi happy. Of all of them, her mother could least cope with poverty. The strain would probably kill her.

Mairi vowed not to let that happen.

The clock ticked away the minutes until she must meet Mr Hargreave. She stood up from her chair. 'With your permission, Mama, I will take my leave.'

'Oh, yes, dear, go now,' her mother said. 'Take a little time to freshen up.'

'You look lovely just as you are,' Lady Crawfurd added with a smile.

Did she look lovely? Mairi did not know. All she knew was that she was damaged and that made the idea of court-ship and marriage abhorrent to her. To Hargreave or to any other man.

Chapter Ten

Robert came in to the kitchen with dishes from the breakfast table.

'How did you fare serving the meal?' Lucas asked.

Robert worried about serving all the guests alone when Lucas had given him the assignment.

'It was nae as hard as I thought,' Robert told him as he took the dishes to the scullery. 'But I thought they would never stop eating. First one came and then the others.'

'Are they all finished with the meal?' Lucas asked. 'I'll help you clear the table.'

They carried the dishes down on trays so Evie could wash them. When she was finished, Lucas would count the silver and make certain all the pieces were there, just like his family's butler did.

As they left the scullery, Robert remarked, 'Did ye know that Mr Hargreave may be courting Miss Mairi?'

Lucas frowned. 'Indeed?' So that was the man's intent.

'Anyways, that's what Lady Dunburn and the other lady think. And that Mr Hargreave, he was making eyes at Miss Mairi. Course, he did enough lookin' at Miss Davina, too.'

Hargreave had better not lay a hand on either Mairi or Davina.

'What did you think of that fellow?' he asked Robert.

'Mr Hargreave?' Robert paused as if choosing his words carefully. 'I dinna know why, but I cannae like the man.'

Lucas nodded. He agreed completely. 'Did he ask you questions about the family?'

'He didnae talk to me at all, except to bring him food.' Robert shook his head. 'But I wasnae in the room alone with him.'

'If he does ask questions, do not answer them,' Lucas warned.

Robert looked affronted. 'I never would!'

Lucas thought he'd better warn the other servants not to answer any questions about the family either. Hargreave was up to no good. Lucas was protecting the whole family, he told himself, not just Mairi.

Lucas returned to the breakfast room and removed the linens from the table. He took the cloth out the back door and shook off the crumbs. From the corner of his eye he spied Hargreave and Miss Wallace walking in the garden, Hargreave talking in an animated manner. Merely seeing the man with her made Lucas want to boot him off the property.

But it was really none of his concern, was it? Of course, his father's butler took protecting the family very seriously. Lucas must, too, while he played the role.

He walked back inside the house and made his way to the hall.

'How are you faring, Erwin?' he asked.

Erwin looked unsettled.

'Only the family and guests have been coming and going.' The footman frowned and knitted his brows. 'But I should tell you that John—' He looked at Lucas. 'You know John? The stable lad?'

Lucas nodded.

Erwin continued. 'John brought the mail from the vi
lage. When the Baron looked through it, something unse
tled him. He was really upset. I did not know what to do

Erwin, of all the servants, was the least likely to becom
distressed about anything.

'When did this happen?' Lucas asked.

Erwin rubbed his chin. 'About a half-hour ago, I'd guess

Was this something Lucas must care about? He coul
not help himself. 'Where is the Baron now?'

Erwin signalled with his head. 'He closed himself o
in the library.'

'With Lord Crawfurd?'

'No, he said he wanted no one to disturb him,' Erwi
replied. 'Lord Crawfurd went to his room before the Baro
looked at the mail.'

How bad could this be? He'd heard of men shootin
themselves in the head because of debts.

Ignoring Dunburn's wish not to be disturbed, Luca
knocked at the library door.

Dunburn did not respond to Lucas's knock and Lucas
anxiety rose. He tried again. 'Baron? It is Lucas.'

He still did not respond.

Lucas opened the door.

Dunburn sat at his desk, papers strewn everywhere, h
head in his hands. He rocked back and forth, moaning.

Lucas hurried over to him. 'Baron?' He touched him o
the shoulder. 'It is Lucas.'

'Lucas?' The older man looked up briefly, but the
dropped his head into his hands again. 'What am I to do?
What am I to do?'

Lucas picked up the papers that had landed on the floor.
'What appears to be the problem, sir?' Many of the papers
were demands for payment of bills.

Dunburn lifted one sheet from the desk and, without looking, extended it towards Lucas.

It was a demand for payment of a loan. A rather sizeable loan. Five thousand pounds. Apparently Dunburn had missed several payments and now the moneylender he'd gone to was threatening to seize his property unless he paid up.

'I cannot possibly pay this!' Dunburn wailed. 'This is the end of me!'

Lucas read further. 'You have two months, it says. Much can be done in two months.'

Dunburn picked up the papers on his desk and threw them in the air. 'But there are all these others! I fear I will have creditors knocking down my doors and taking everything I own.'

The situation looked much more dire than Lucas had imagined. 'Calm yourself, sir. Let us look through everything and make a tally. I am certain something may be done.'

He hoped so, anyway. With the exception of Miss Wallace, this family was ill-equipped to adapt to straitened circumstances.

By the time an hour had passed, Lucas had organised all the demands for payment and made a list showing which ones had to be prioritised. Next, they looked through the books and Lucas pointed out where Dunburn might economise in the future, but that would not help the current situation.

'You must raise funds now,' Lucas said. 'The only way to do so is to find what can be sold.'

Lucas started with the stable. Selling off some of Dunburn's horses would both raise money and save on expenditures.

They were deep in the discussion of how many horses he owned and how many were needed when a voice came from the doorway. 'What are you doing?' Lucas looked up to see Miss Wallace in the doorway. 'What are you talking about?'

Dunburn adopted a patient tone. 'Now, Mairi, dear, we are discussing finances. Not a subject for a lady to think about.'

'You were talking about selling some of the horses, were you not?' she challenged.

Lucas knew she would prefer the truth. 'That is precisely what we were discussing, miss.'

'Lucas is kindly advising me,' her father said.

She glared at him. 'Papa, I told you ages ago you should sell some of our livestock. You would not listen to me.'

The man's face turned red. 'I won't have you taking that tone with me, Daughter! I insist on being respected.'

She did not heed him. 'What has happened? Some new bill? Why are you discussing this with Lucas?'

Her father straightened. 'He is our butler.'

'Not really, Papa!' she cried. 'He is only pretending to be our butler. We do not know him and we have not actually hired him.'

Dunburn pointed to the door. 'You are excused, Mairi! This is none of your concern. Go now or I'll have Lucas throw you out!'

That Lucas would never do, no matter who instructed him.

She looked as if she might explode and the air in the room seemed to crackle with her anger, but she spun on her heel and walked out of the room.

'My daughter,' muttered Dunburn, 'thinks she can do a man's job. Can you fancy that?'

'Perhaps you should listen to her, sir,' he said.

Dunburn waved his hand. 'What could she know about a man's business?'

Lucas suspected she knew a great deal. Miss Wallace had a head on her shoulders and was not afraid to use it. He admired that.

But it would not help the matter at hand to argue this point with Dunburn.

Lucas stacked some of the ledgers and the papers. 'With your permission, sir, I will examine these some more and see what I can discover. If you sell what we discussed, though, you will be making a good start.'

Dunburn stood and extended his hand for Lucas to shake. 'I cannot thank you enough, Lucas. I was ready to put a period to my existence.'

Exactly what Lucas had feared. He'd done the right thing by interrupting the Baron's privacy. 'Never do that, sir. Your family needs you.' He picked up the ledgers. 'Return to your guests and give no indication that anything is amiss. You do not want to hint at trouble or the creditors will rain upon you.'

Dunburn clasped Lucas's shoulder. 'I believe I can do so now, thanks to your assistance.'

Lucas bowed. 'It is my pleasure to be of service, sir.'

Mairi paced the hallway of the servants' floor, angrier than she could remember being for a long time. It was one thing for Lucas to organise the servants and order them about; it was quite another for him to be directing her father in the paying of his bills. He was taking over everything and what did they really know of him? Nothing. Nothing at all.

She did not know how long she was there before she saw him enter the hallway carrying ledgers under his arm. Ledgers! Her father had never offered to show her the ledgers. Why would he trust them to Lucas?

He reached his door and opened it.

Mairi quickened her step. 'Lucas! I would speak with you!' She reached his doorway and strode past him into his room. She closed the door. 'Why are you interfering in my father's financial affairs?'

He faced her directly. 'Your father's finances are at a crisis point, Miss Wallace.' His voice was even and reasonable. 'I came upon him when he was quite in despair. There was nothing to do but offer my help.'

'What do you mean a crisis point?' she pressed.

'He took out a rather sizeable loan from a moneylender and did not meet the payments. The moneylender will call in the loan in two months' time.'

She paled. 'Or seize the house and property?'

'Yes,' he admitted.

Her hand went to her mouth. 'It cannot be! The house, the property, the title, all are Niven's birthright. Our family has held the title and lands for generations!'

'There are other creditors as well.' He was adding more salt to her wounds.

She started to pace again. 'I told Papa and Mama to economise! To stop buying horses and new dresses! I told them they should sell what we don't need! Did they listen? Not at all. Now, with one word from you—'

'They should have listened to you,' he said. 'But at this point it is more important to raise as much money as possible than to rail about what they should have done.'

She looked at him aghast. 'You are telling *me* this? When I have been begging them to do that for months? You are instructing *me* with what must be done?'

'What is it, Mairi?' He'd even slipped into using her given name. Who had given him permission to do that? 'You would rather blast me than seize on this opportunity to solve your family's problems? I do not know why your father confided in me. Perhaps I appeared at a crucial moment. It is no reason not to take action now.'

'Did I say I would not take action?' Her frustration spewed from her like a dam bursting. 'What part am I able to play? My father will not allow me to do anything about it.'

'*I* will need you,' he said.

Her gaze flew to his face at those words.

'I can advise him about livestock, but not about your family's personal items. And your parents seem incapable of such decisions.' He paused. 'You must choose.'

She could not see beyond her anger. 'You are telling me what I must do?' She averted her gaze. 'You are taking over everything.'

He clasped her arms and it almost sent her into a panic. 'I have no wish to take over anything. And I am not telling you what to do. Can you not see this as an opportunity? You tell me what can be sold. Work through me.'

He released her, leaving her with a tumult of emotions. She tried to calm down.

He spoke quietly. 'When the guests are gone, you can select what must be sold. I'll go along as if the ideas are mine.'

It wounded her that her father would trust this stranger— this *Englishman*—over the judgement of his daughter, but this was a chance to do what she'd wanted all along, a chance to save her family. And if she was honest, she had trusted him, too—with the planting, with the silver, with her family's reputation. What other choice was there?

It was only later she realised that while her father and mother clearly did not have faith in her, Lucas did.

Mairi left Lucas, still whirling with emotion. She'd been so angry at him—she still was. Angry and resentful. But not afraid, at least not until he had grasped her arms. Even then the edge of panic she'd experienced seemed to have nothing to do with him.

And everything to do with the memories she fought to keep at bay.

She hurried down the hallway and climbed the stairs, stopping and resting her cheek against the stone wall. Lucas seemed so solid, like someone who could be trusted, but, truly, they knew nothing about him. Still, she felt more at ease with Lucas than she did with Mr Hargreave, a man from a family known to hers, friends of their good friends, the Crawfurds, a man vouched for by Lady Crawfurd as a good match for her.

That was laughable. This new turn of events made it even more ludicrous that Mr Hargreave would wish to court her. He'd drop his suit soon enough if he knew the true extent of their finances.

But she had to pretend all was well, did she not? That meant at least being hospitable to Mr Hargreave.

The walk he'd insisted upon had been torturous. Any time the shrubbery hid them from the house, Mairi was reminded of the man dragging her into the bushes where no one could see. She found Mr Hargreave's charm unsettling. So often he seemed to put some secret meaning behind his words, a significance she did not understand, but which made her uneasy. Not only that, but she also noticed every detail of the gardens that had not been tended. Poor old Kinley could not do everything himself. Had Mr Hargreave noticed? He'd not let on.

Mairi did not like that Mr Hargreave had asked Lucas questions about the family. What was it he wished to learn and why? She did not want him to know anything about her or her family.

All she wanted right this minute was to walk through the house and make a list of items that might help raise some money, as Lucas had suggested.

She pushed away from the wall and made her way back to the library, intending to speak with her father, but, upon entering the room, it was not her father who looked up from his desk, but Mr Hargreave.

He stood and bowed. 'Miss Wallace. What a pleasure.'

She was shocked. 'What are you doing at my father's desk?'

He smiled sheepishly. 'Looking for pen, ink and paper. I thought to write a letter.'

It was a smooth answer and one she did not readily believe. She walked over to a small leather-topped rosewood writing table and opened the drawer. 'You will find writing materials in here.'

'Ah.' He moved away from her father's desk towards what was obviously a writing table. He lifted a piece of paper, but placed it back down again. 'I confess I intended merely to fill the time writing a letter. Your father and Lord Crawfurd are, I believe, playing billiards, and your mother and Lady Crawfurd are in your mother's sitting room. If you are at liberty, I would welcome your company.'

No, she wanted to cry.

'I am at a loss to entertain you. There is not much to interest anyone in this house.'

His smile did not waver. 'I would enjoy a tour. I noticed several curious family portraits. You could tell me about your family history. I do love history.'

This seemed an odd request. And she certainly did not want to spend more time alone with him. 'If you wish.' She felt trapped, but could think of no way out of the situation. 'Shall I start in this room?'

'At your pleasure,' he said, bowing again.

She pointed to the Wallace crest, prominent over the fireplace. 'My father is a descendent of William Wallace, which is a source of great pride for him and for our family. The relationship is a distant one, but Papa likes to say that William Wallace's blood flows through our veins, none the less.' She gave this speech without enthusiasm.

It struck her that her father's pride in being a descendent of the hero of the first war of Scottish independence was so important to him that the shame of a financial downfall would probably destroy him.

She talked about the other paintings in the room, paintings that had hung on those walls her whole life—and during many other lives before her. What would happen to it all? Would selling some of it save her family?

Mr Hargreave was an attentive audience and did not show any indication of being aware that her dispassionate discourse masked the pain she felt inside.

Hargreave contrived to spend every spare minute with Mairi Wallace, engaging her in conversation during dinner, sitting with her at tea afterwards, turning the pages of her music sheets while she played the pianoforte. He was certain he had the support of her mother and Lady Crawfurd, but Miss Wallace herself remained distantly polite.

It made her a challenge. He greatly liked challenges.

He insisted on escorting her to her room when it was time to retire for the night. When she turned the latch of the door, he put his hand on hers.

'I have so enjoyed your company, Miss Wallace,' he murmured in an earnest tone.

At his touch, her whole body stiffened and she whipped around to stare him in the face. 'Have you?' She pulled her hand away.

He smiled as if she'd made a jest. 'I have, very much.

And I look forward to spending more time with you at Lord and Lady Oxmont's house party.'

She looked less than eager at this prospect.

It made him move even closer. Her eyes flashed with alarm. He moved back again. Obviously he'd not played that moment well. Too bad. There was no one else in the hallway. It would have been a perfect time to steal a kiss.

Instead she lifted the latch. 'Goodnight, Mr Hargreave.'

It was a firm dismissal.

He chuckled inside. He'd win her eventually. One way or another.

He took a step forward. She gaped at him in alarm. He withdrew slowly and gave her his most engaging smile. 'Sleep well, Miss Wallace.'

The next morning after breakfast had been served, the guests' trunks and valises were carried down to be placed on the carriage. Lucas stood outside with the other servants while the family bid the guests goodbye. He waited, ready to receive from Lord Crawfurd and Hargreave the vails servants could expect from guests. These servants could certainly use payment from someone and they deserved to be compensated for the extra work they'd done.

Lord Crawfurd passed him by with not even a glance.

Hargreave walked up to him. 'Sassenach, I understand your kind expect vails to be paid to servants by guests. We Scots gave up that practice years ago. I am inclined to be generous, though, since you undoubtedly expect it.' He dropped some coins into Lucas's hand.

This was a show of power, of superiority, although why this man needed to lord it over Lucas was beyond him.

Lucas had no wish to let his contempt of Hargreave show. He removed any expression from his face and spoke in his emotionless voice. 'Thank you, sir.'

Although he would have gladly thrown the coins into the man's face.

He'd divide the money among the others. They'd earned it. Lucas was surprised that he felt as proud of the servants as he'd been of his soldiers. They'd done the work; he'd merely given the orders.

Lucas watched Hargreave approach Miss Wallace, always with that charming smile and leering eyes.

Hargreave took her hand in his. 'Miss Wallace, I will count the days until we meet again at the house party.' He lifted her hand as if preparing to kiss it, but released her instead.

What affectation. Was Hargreave trifling with her?

'Goodbye, sir,' Miss Wallace replied in her crisp voice.

Lucas smiled inwardly. Hargreave had not fooled her.

Lady Dunburn and Lady Crawfurd said tearful goodbyes as if they were not to see each other again for years instead of merely a fortnight. The Baron and Lord Crawfurd shook hands. Niven and the Crawfurd boy stood with Davina. William Crawfurd was smitten with Davina, that was evident. Lucas hoped Niven was looking out for her.

Lucas glanced away. Good God, he was becoming attached to this family and their servants. Not so long ago he'd cared for nothing and no one.

Finally, Lady Crawfurd was assisted into the waiting carriage and her husband after her. Hargreave tossed one more look towards Miss Wallace before climbing inside. Last was Mrs Crawfurd's maid. Lord Crawfurd's valet and William climbed on top and the carriage was off. The family and the servants all remained where they were, watching until the carriage disappeared from sight. Then Niven uttered a loud whoop and tossed his hat in the air. They all gave a cheer and hugged each other.

'We did it!' Niven cried and the maids joined in. 'We did it!'

Lucas could not help but smile. His gaze caught Miss Wallace's and he thought he saw gratitude in her eyes. She and he were the most subdued of the group, though they ought, perhaps, to have been the most joyous, having done the most to disguise the true state of affairs on the estate. She, who'd worked all along at maintaining the house and its grounds; he, who'd merely played the role of butler.

Niven pulled on Davina's arm. 'Come on, Davina. Let's ride.' They were both dressed for it.

As they hurried away, Dunburn walked over to Lucas. 'Thank you, Lucas. We owe you a great deal.'

'My pleasure, sir.' It had been a pleasure helping them. He caught Miss Wallace watching him. He turned to her father again. 'We have more work to do, sir.'

'Oh, yes. Yes,' the older man sputtered. 'Finding items to sell. Wouldn't do well at that. Not at all. Mairi will have to help you.'

Chapter Eleven

'Mairi!' Her father gestured for her to come over to him. She walked over to him. 'Yes, Papa?'

'You and Lucas here go through the house and find some things we might sell.' He waved his hand in the direction of the house. 'Listen to Lucas. He has a good head on his shoulders.'

She flared at her father's words. No one knew the value of their furniture and paintings better than she did.

'You will speak to Mama about her jewellery, will you not?' Mairi countered.

Her father blinked and looked everywhere but at her. 'Yes. Yes. I will. Straight away—soon.'

'Now, please, Papa,' she said. 'Mama's jewellery will bring the most money.'

'You know how your mother loves her jewels,' her father protested.

Yes, Mairi knew. And her father had been happy to indulge his wife with any pretty bauble she fancied—even when their servants were going unpaid.

'It must be done,' Mairi insisted.

Her father glanced at Lucas. Seeking Lucas's opinion? Mairi saw red.

'Must we sell jewellery?' he asked Lucas.

'Yes, you must,' Lucas responded. He gave Mairi a knowing look. 'Shall we start now, Miss Wallace?'

'As you wish,' she replied, hating that her father turned to Lucas for approval before agreeing to do as Mairi asked.

Before following her, Lucas raised his voice to the others. 'You should return to work now. There is still much to be done.'

The maids and footmen almost stood at attention, as if they were soldiers under his command. Even Mrs Cross and Mrs MacNeal sobered at the sound of his voice.

He met Mairi at the door and opened it for her.

'It seems everyone listens to you, Mr Lucas,' she said hotly as she passed him to enter the house.

He entered behind her. 'Your father should have listened to you, Miss Wallace.'

She crossed the hall and started up the stairs. She stopped to face him again when they reached the first floor. 'We will start in my bedchamber.'

Lucas understood better than she could know how it was to have a parent prefer another over oneself. At Foxgrove Hall, the sun had always risen and set on his brother, Bradleigh, while Lucas had merely been a troublesome afterthought. When his parents had found out Bradleigh had secretly purchased a commission in the First Royals, a person would have thought it was the end of the world. His father had commanded Lucas to serve with Bradleigh and keep him alive.

When Lucas came home alone, broken in spirit and consumed with guilt, his mother had screamed that she wished it had been he who died. Not Bradleigh.

So had Lucas.

He still was not certain that Mairi Wallace had done him any favours by nursing him back to health, but perhaps he could save her life, so to speak, when he couldn't save his brother's. At least the style of her life.

He desired her happiness. He'd never met anyone more deserving of it, yet he sensed a deep sadness inside her. A bit like his own.

There was no question, though, that at this moment her unhappiness stemmed from her parents' treatment of her. He hoped that helping her through this task would make matters better for her.

She led him to her room and opened the door. 'I've already decided what we should sell.'

'You must do the choosing, Miss Wallace,' he told her. 'No matter what your father said, you are the best judge.'

She glanced at him and again he sensed her pain. He stepped inside.

The room was so much like her. Without frills, but elegant in its simplicity. The walls of her room were a pale green with white plasterwork in the style of Robert Adam above the white mantel. The paintings on the walls were watercolours of various flowers and one a whimsical painting of a little girl with her cat. The bedcovers were a restful peach. The amount of furniture in the room would be considered almost spartan. A dressing table. A chest of drawers. A side table next to the bed.

The bed.

His gaze caught on the bed, so neat and tidy, but Lucas could imagine her in it, a tangle of linens and her bare skin matching the colour of the bedcovers.

He glanced away and caught her staring at him, her expression taut, her eyes wary. He kept his back to the bed.

'What have you selected?' Better to get down to the business at hand.

She walked over to the mantel and took down the only

objects that were the least bit frivolous: a matched set of porcelain figurines. 'Here. Sell these.'

Lucas knew almost nothing about porcelain figurines. One of these was a young woman holding a lamb in her lap, the other, a young man gazing adoringly at her, a lamb at his side. Both were romantically rendered, colourfully dressed country figures. They were seated on fanciful chairs made of tiny delicate porcelain flowers.

He wanted to ask why she would give up such pretty things. 'Are these English?' he asked instead.

'No,' she responded, her voice still sad. 'My father would never buy me something made in England. They came from Frankfurt.'

'They were a gift from your father?' Surely they meant something to her?

She set her chin. 'Yes, I love them, but such trifles are not as important to me as this house and this estate and the family title.' She shoved the figurines into his hands. 'I have more.' She walked over to a small chest on the dresser and opened it. Inside were necklaces of garnets, strings of pearls, gold chains, matching earrings.

'These are your jewels?' Was she to give up all her treasures?

'I've kept enough to get by.' She gestured to a corner of the room. 'I want to sell the mirror, too.'

It was a lovely cheval mirror in a mahogany frame, the sort a young lady would use to see her full-length reflection. 'Do you not need a mirror?'

She set her chin. 'There is one in Davina's room I can use.'

These were too many sacrifices for one young woman. Undoubtedly she would not ask her mother or sister to give up their mirrors or their treasured gifts or most of their jewellery.

'No,' he said firmly, though she would not agree to his reasons. 'No. It would be too difficult to transport without breaking.' That sounded plausible.

She glanced back at her mirror, looking disappointed. 'That is all I can think of in this room. The paintings are my own work. They have no value.'

He examined the paintings again with renewed interest. They showed a talent and an appreciation of simple beauty that she otherwise seemed to keep hidden. He gave himself an inward shake. He did not need to be more admiring of this woman.

'Where to next?' he asked.

'Let us bring the items to the nursery,' she responded. 'It will be a good room to gather what we select and also to pack it up.'

It was obvious she'd given this project a great deal of thought already. 'Excellent idea,' he agreed.

The nursery was set up as a schoolroom—its most recent use, no doubt—but the school materials were stowed on bookshelves along one wall. There was a long wooden table where Miss Wallace and her brother and sister must have sat during their lessons, now empty and perfect for gathering what they selected to be sold.

Lucas placed the figurines on the table. She set down the jewellery chest.

'Should we secure your jewels?' Keep them locked in a safe?

She shook her head. 'Our servants understand what we are doing. They are honest.'

'Very well,' he said. 'Where next?'

'Let us start in the attic,' she responded. 'And work our way down.'

They took a lamp from the nursery and lit it from the dying fire in Mr Hargreave's recently vacated guest room.

Lucas followed her up the stairs to the attic floor and past the maids' quarters to a door at the end. Miss Wallace opened it to reveal a shadowy jumble of wooden boxes, chests and dustsheet-covered furniture. One small window at the end gave the only light besides the lamp.

Miss Wallace had pulled off the cloths from the furniture and, under the lamplight, the air sparkled with dust particles. 'We have several pieces of furniture made by William Brodie.'

'Brodie,' Lucas repeated. 'I do not know the name.'

She walked through the maze of furniture. 'He was an infamous cabinetmaker from Edinburgh, crafting furniture by day and robbing houses by night to support his mistresses and pay his gambling debts. My grandfather purchased the items before Mr Brodie's criminal escapades came to light. The pieces were replaced, because my mother detested them. She could not forget that the maker of her furniture was hanged on the very gallows he'd built before his crimes were discovered.'

Lucas gave a wry grin. 'That is quite a story.' He ran his fingers over a small side table.

She went on. 'Perhaps some people would value the pieces for the very reason my mother detests them. No matter what, they are of no use covered with dustsheets up here.'

They went through boxes and chests and found a few other items. Lucas moved their furniture close to the doorway for Robert or Erwin to carry down later. They took the other items to the nursery, as well as some boxes and chests in which to pack the items to sell. Room by room, they covered the entire second floor, except for Davina's and Niven's rooms.

'I'll speak to them later,' Miss Wallace said. 'But I do not expect them to give up very much.'

Of course she did not.

As they walked through the hallway again, she pointed to the many landscape paintings hung there. 'My grandfather collected paintings of Scottish landscapes,' she replied. 'We come from a long line of Scottish patriots, you know.'

'I know.' He smiled. 'Your father is fond of mentioning his relation to William Wallace.'

She grimaced. 'It is rather a distant connection, but, yes, he is intensely proud of it.'

Any man descended from greatness had no wish to become the family's prime failure.

'I have heard of Wallace.' Lucas recalled a mention in a history book.

'Yes,' she said. 'William Wallace was the hero of the Battle of Stirling Bridge and one of our greatest Scotsmen.'

Lucas seemed to remember that the man had been hanged, drawn and quartered as a traitor. According to English history, that was.

He turned back to the painting. 'Who are the artists of these landscapes?'

'This one is by Nasmyth.' She gestured to the others down the hall. 'We have others by Stewart and More.' Her lips turned down into a frown. 'I think they should be sold,' she said softly.

He felt the ache inside her. Her grandfather was not the only family member who loved these paintings. Even though romantically idealised, they did show Scotland's wild beauty.

But he vowed he would help them raise the funds. 'If you find them valuable, others might as well, but it is for you to decide.'

She glanced away, a pained look on her face, but she steeled herself before his eyes. 'We should sell them.'

He admired her strength of resolve.

'But perhaps not all of them,' he added. 'Save the ones that mean the most to your family.' To her, he meant.

She nodded.

They worked their way down to the next two floors, choosing more paintings and decorative items. They found her parents in the library.

Her father rose as they entered the room. 'Well? How are you faring?'

Miss Wallace clamped her lips shut and stepped behind Lucas.

He spoke for them. 'We've found many things to sell, my lord. We've collected most of them in the nursery, but I strongly suggest neither of you look at them. It will be easier for you that way.'

'I cannot see why we must sell our things!' Lady Dunburn cried.

Her husband's face creased in anguish. 'I have explained to you, my dear.'

Miss Wallace spoke up. 'Mama, if we do not we will lose everything!'

Her mother glared at her. 'You are always saying so, Mairi!'

Possibly because she was right.

Dunburn sat on a sofa next to his wife. A rosewood box inlaid with ivory sat on the table, along with several smaller velvet boxes. 'We have brought your mother's jewels,' Dunburn said quietly.

Lady Dunburn swivelled away, holding a handkerchief to her nose. Lucas waited for Miss Wallace to take the chair near them. He stood behind her.

Dunburn opened the rosewood box. 'You must tell us which to sell, Lucas,' he said.

Lucas knew nothing about jewellery.

Dunburn lifted out several brooches, pendants and rings,

with glittering emeralds, diamonds, topaz, amethysts and rubies in settings of gold and silver. Next he opened the velvet boxes, which contained matching sets of necklaces, earrings and bracelets. The number of jewels was staggering, even in Lucas's experience. His mother, a countess, did not have nearly as many. Lucas would wager that these valuables were worth what Dunburn owed.

Her mother let out a sob.

Dunburn spread his hands in a helpless gesture. 'Tell us what to do, Lucas.'

Lucas did not know what to say.

Miss Wallace straightened in her chair. 'We save the old family pieces, first of all,' She quickly put several pieces in one pile off to the side, then turned to her mother. 'Mama, do you have some favourites?'

'They are all my favourites!' her mother wailed.

'You must choose some, Mama,' her daughter said, her voice low but firm.

Lucas could see how difficult this was for Miss Wallace, forcing her mother's unhappiness.

They managed to sort through every piece of jewellery, saving more than Lucas thought prudent, but far fewer than Lady Dunburn begged to keep. Most of the pieces had been gifts from Dunburn, a habit the man must learn to break if he wanted to keep his estate.

When the final selections were made, all at Miss Wallace's direction, her father turned to Lucas. 'What say you, Lucas? Should we sell so many?'

He looked the older gentleman in the eye. 'I would say your daughter was far kinder than I would have been. I would have selected only the family pieces to save.'

'No!' cried Lady Dunburn. 'That is too cruel.'

Lucas spoke to her in a low, kind voice. 'Your daughter has not been cruel. Her choices are sensible and considered.'

Lady Dunburn turned her face away, refusing even to look at her daughter.

Lucas turned to Dunburn. 'We will see to the packing of the items. Your daughter has agreed to record an inventory of every item.'

Such mundane matters did not interest Dunburn, though. He stood and clapped Lucas on the back. 'Well. Well. The hardest part of the task is done. How can I thank you, Lucas? You must dine with us. That is what you must do. Dine with us.'

Lucas glanced at Miss Wallace, but his finely tuned sensing of her feelings failed him. He could only guess she would not approve.

He hedged. 'Sir, is it appropriate for me to dine with you?'

'Why not?' Dunburn said. 'It is not like you are really our butler.'

He glanced at Lady Dunburn. 'My lady, you may not wish me to dine with you.'

Lady Dunburn's frown cleared when she looked up at Lucas. 'Of course you must dine with us, Lucas.'

Jewellery boxes in hand, Lucas and Mairi left the library. He asked her, 'Do you object to my dining with your family?'

She avoided looking at him. 'If it pleases my parents, how can I object?'

They climbed the stairs and brought the jewellery to the nursery, where Miss Wallace made a detailed inventory.

When they were finished, Lucas stepped back and frowned. 'I do not think we should leave the jewellery here. It should be locked up. It is too important.'

She shrugged. 'If you wish.'

He found a portmanteau they'd brought down from the attic and he packed all the jewellery in there. It was an item that could easily be kept about one's person and just as easily locked up.

He lifted the bag. 'Your mother's jewellery alone should bring enough to pay off your father's loan.'

They wrapped the paintings in cloths and packed the other items in boxes.

Miss Wallace lifted one of the figurines from her bed-chamber. She hesitated before wrapping it in a cloth.

Lucas touched her arm, stopping her. 'These figurines will not fetch much of a price. I suggest we do not sell them.'

'Every bit counts.' She resolutely placed the figurine in a box.

He took it back out again and unwrapped it. 'Not enough to risk them breaking while we transport them. Put them back on your mantel.' He handed it to her.

She glanced at him as his fingers touched hers. Her hands were soft and warm and he was reluctant to move away.

She placed both figurines away from the other items. 'I will put them back later.'

Lucas smiled inwardly. He was glad he'd made her keep her treasures and it was rare for him to feel glad about something he'd done.

After they finished the packing and the inventory, Mairi carried her figurines back to her room and placed them back on her mantel, brushing them with her fingertips after they were in place. They'd been a gift from her father, back when she'd been a little girl and innocent. Now they seemed like a gift from Lucas. Whenever she looked at them, she would think of him.

Had Lucas noticed that she hadn't asked Niven and Davina to donate any of their possessions? The truth was,

Mairi could not bring herself to ask them to give up anything. Their lives were already altered because of the financial mess her father and mother had made of things. Niven had lost his tutor and would never have a Grand Tour, nothing to help him grow from a boy into a man. Davina had no governess to instruct her in music or drawing, no money for a dancing master to teach her the latest steps, no finishing school to refine her social graces. Perhaps if their father and mother economised as instructed, there might be some sort of dowry for Davina when she came of age to marry.

Davina entered her room without knocking. 'Niven said you and Lucas are making us sell half of our belongings. I said it could not be true. It is not true, is it, Mairi?'

Mairi sighed. She'd tried to protect Niven and Davina from her worst fears about the state of their finances, but she could not protect Davina from everything. 'Help me dress and I'll explain.'

'It is not true, is it?' Davina repeated.

Mairi glanced at her mirror, the mirror that had once belonged to her grandmother. Another gift from Lucas now.

Davina stood directly in front of her, elbows akimbo. 'So? Is it true?'

Mairi turned her back so Davina could untie her laces. 'Well, it is not true that Lucas and I are making anyone do anything. And we did not choose half your belongings. We did not ask you to give up anything.' She slipped off her dress and laid it over a chair.

Davina pressed on. 'I peeked in the nursery. What were you doing with all those boxes, then?'

'We chose things our family does not need. They will be sold to pay off Papa's debts.' She walked over to her wardrobe and pulled out a dress.

'Not that old thing.' Davina took the dress from her hands and selected another one, a blue silk that complemented her eyes. 'Are Papa's debts so great that we have to sell our things?'

'Yes,' Mairi told her. 'Papa's debts are that great.' She stepped into the dress.

Davina buttoned up the back. 'But I thought we were rich.'

'We are not poor.' Yet. 'But Papa owes money to several creditors. And our unfortunate servants have not been paid in over a year. That is why your governess left. And Niven's tutor. And the butler and the other servants.'

Davina's expression turned sober. 'But I thought Niven no longer needed a tutor. Or I a governess.'

'You are both old enough to forgo a governess and tutor, that is true,' Mairi admitted. 'But Niven's tutor should have taken him on a Grand Tour, like William Crawfurd's will do. Papa cannot afford that. And you might have had a dance master or some other instruction in refinement.'

Davina's brows knitted and she pursed her lips.

'Sit down,' Davina finally said. 'I'll fix your hair. It looks terrible.'

Mairi's hand went to her hair. Had she looked a mess? She sat at her dressing table and Davina pulled the pins from her hair before she could tell if it had gone askew.

'Well...' Davina spoke more like her typically cheerful self '...did Mr Hargreave propose marriage to you? Lady Crawfurd was certain he would.'

'He did not.' Thank goodness. 'And I doubt he ever will.'

'Really?' Her sister brushed the knots from her hair. 'He certainly acted charming around you.'

'He was merely trifling with me, Davina,' she said. 'Some men do that.'

'Lady Crawfurd did not think he was trifling with you.' Davina pulled Mairi's hair high on her head, securing it with a blue ribbon and letting it fall into loose curls instead of putting it in a chignon.

Mairi shot back, 'Lady Crawfurd ought to have known that I do not possess a dowry sufficient to tempt a younger son.' Given her father's debts, she suspected there was no dowry at all.

Davina used pins to keep Mairi's hair in place. She surveyed her work. 'Hargreave should have seen you with your hair loose like this. He'd have been even more smitten with you.'

Oh, the romantic heart of a fourteen-year-old girl! Mairi hoped her younger sister would never learn that men were not always what they seemed. She glanced at her image in the mirror. Davina had made it look as if she fussed over her appearance for dinner. Would Lucas think so?

Mairi did not know if she hoped he would notice or wished he would not.

She stood. 'Come. It is almost time for dinner.'

Chapter Twelve

Lucas stood behind some chairs in the drawing room when the door opened and Niven walked in. On his heels were Davina and Mairi.

Niven broke into a smile. 'Lucas! I thought you were done playing butler.'

'He is not playing butler,' their mother said without cheer. 'He is our guest for dinner.'

'No!' Niven looked even more pleased. 'Capital idea.'

Davina skipped to Lucas's side. 'I am so glad!'

Mairi said nothing.

'Pour Lucas a drink,' Dunburn told Niven.

Niven gladly poured some claret into a wine glass and brought it over to Lucas. 'Maybe when the ladies leave us, you can tell us more about the battles you've fought.'

Lucas hoped not. Talking of the war meant remembering his brother's death. His failure. And the foolishness of those seeking glory on the battlefield. Lucas was uncomfortable enough about dining with the family. How would he answer questions about himself? He did not wish to be the person he was.

Dunburn placed a hand on Niven's shoulder. 'We have more important matters to discuss, my son.'

Would Dunburn actually talk about his debts?

Lucas glanced over at Mairi and saw her features tighten. He wished she could feel good about what she'd accomplished. It had been a difficult job to select items of value to sell, some of which meant a great deal to her and her family. She'd pushed her mother, who now seemed very glum and was perhaps blaming her daughter for it. Lady Dunburn would not even look at her.

And Miss Wallace looked exceptionally lovely this evening. The blue of her dress perfectly matched her eyes and it was difficult not to stare at them. Her hair was looser than she usually wore it. He fancied that if he pulled the end of the ribbon, her dark brown waves would cascade to her shoulders.

'Why did you help Mairi pick things to sell, Lucas?' Davina asked him.

'Your father asked me to,' he replied, which was really no answer at all.

'Some of the paintings are gone from the hallway,' she went on. 'Did you take those from the wall?'

'Yes,' he replied.

'To sell them?' she asked.

'Yes.'

Davina's expression turned petulant. 'I think it is extremely dreadful that we must sell our things.'

'It is better than a poorhouse,' he countered.

Davina's eyes grew wide. 'A poorhouse? Surely we won't have to go to a poorhouse!'

'Indeed not!' piped up Dunburn.

Niven joined them. 'See? I told you, Davina.'

'Mairi would be delighted to see us all in the poorhouse,' Lady Dunburn said.

Mairi flinched as if struck.

Lucas jumped in. 'I can assure you, my lady, your daughter took no enjoyment from today's task.'

Lady Dunburn lifted her chin and turned away.

At that moment Erwin appeared in the doorway. 'Dinner is served.'

Lady Dunburn took her husband's arm and Lucas was uncertain if he should escort Mairi. What was his place in this pretend life of his? In England his new status as his father's heir made him higher in precedence than even the Baron of Dunburn. He was glad he did not have to assume that role here. As it was, Niven and Davina walked behind their parents. Lucas offered Miss Wallace his arm and their gazes caught for a moment before she accepted him.

In the dining room, he sat between Mairi and her mother, who took her place at the end of the table opposite her husband. Niven and Davina sat on the other side. Even in the cavalry, Lucas had been served his meals, but it felt awkward here. In just these few days, he'd become accustomed to being a servant, not the served.

The mood at the table was sombre, he thought. The day had been difficult, after all. Only the two youngest members had been relatively free of the burden and stress.

Davina spoke first. 'Papa, why did you let Mairi and Lucas take so many of our paintings and things? Why are they being sold? Are you really in so much debt?'

How honest would Dunburn be? Lucas wondered. And why was it everyone put the blame for these difficult decisions on Mairi—Miss Wallace, he meant? How was he supposed to think of her? As a butler or as the son and heir of an earl?

'Now, now, my little one, you must not fret about this,' her father replied. 'Nothing is as bad as it might seem. You ladies must not worry yourselves about this.'

'Are you going to be taking the items to be sold?' Niven asked. 'Where?'

'Edinburgh would be best,' Mairi broke in. 'More people in that city would find our things desirable.'

Dunburn gave her a sharp look. 'I will make those decisions, Mairi. It is not your place to do so.'

Lucas felt her recoil from the unfair rebuke. Especially because she had better judgement than all the other family members.

'Will you go to Edinburgh, Papa?' Niven asked. 'I would so like to go with you.'

'If Niven goes, I want to go, too,' Davina said.

'I will not go,' their father said. 'Oh, dear me, no. I simply cannot go.'

'You must, Papa,' Mairi insisted. 'Who else can do it?'

'Why, Lucas, of course,' he said.

'Lucas?' Mairi exclaimed.

Her father turned towards Lucas. 'You will do this for me, will you not, Lucas?'

'Yes, Lucas,' her mother added. 'You must. You will get us the best price, I know you will.'

'Then you must go with him,' Mairi told her father.

He lowered his brows and glared at her. 'And you must mind your tongue, my girl. You have become most high-handed in this matter. Lucas does not need me. He can handle the affair very well.'

'You do not know that, Papa,' Mairi cried. 'We don't really know Lucas at all!'

Dunburn half-rose in his seat. 'I'll have you know I am an excellent judge of character, young lady, and I say that Lucas is the man for the job.'

Mairi was correct. They did not know him at all. He'd not wanted them to know him.

'Perhaps you should do this, my lord,' Lucas said.

Dunburn's face contorted in stress. 'Oh, no. It would not be proper for me to carry out such business. I will provide you with a letter under my seal authorising you to act on my behalf.'

Mairi spoke up again. 'If you will not go with Lucas, I will accompany him.'

'You will do no such thing!' her mother broke in. 'A young lady doing business like that? It simply is not done.'

What was simply not done was a single man escorting a marriageable young lady over a two days' drive without a chaperon.

'I insist, Papa,' Mairi said. 'You cannot merely hand over all our property to Lucas.'

Dunburn's face turned red. 'You have said quite enough, young lady. I will not be contradicted in this matter.'

'I will go with Lucas,' Niven offered eagerly.

'If Niven goes, I want to go, too,' Davina added.

'No!' her parents and sister said in unison.

Davina leaned back in her chair and folded her arms across her chest.

'This is madness, Papa,' Mairi said again.

Her father leaned forward in his seat, pointing a finger at her. 'Have you lost all sense of propriety and sensibility? You are excused from this table and may spend the rest of the evening in your room.'

She stood and Lucas could tell she was trembling with rage.

'Sir—' he said.

'This is a family matter, Lucas. Say no more.' Dunburn waved away the soup and signalled for the fish to be served.

Mairi did not heed her father's orders. Instead she grabbed her cloak and walked outside into the fresh air. She was so angry and upset she could not bear to be confined to her room like a naughty child. She needed fresh air and exercise and the freedom to move around as she wished.

The night was clear and the moon full enough to light

her path to the garden. She walked the paths, the same ones she'd been forced to show Mr Hargreave. Her mind raced.

How could her father be so imprudent? Lucas had been wonderful to her family in so many ways, but they really knew very little about him. One did not trust an unknown person with one's jewels and other treasures or with the money they might earn when sold. Could her father not see that? And how could her mother go along with such a scheme as if it was the most natural thing in the world?

Why did they trust him, a virtual stranger, but not their own daughter? Had she not proved she'd been right about everything? Why did they constantly brush aside anything she had to say, as if she were nothing but a nuisance?

Mairi paced the garden paths, trying to figure out a way to keep her father from behaving so foolishly. True, Lucas seemed trustworthy. He'd done nothing but help them—he had saved their reputation with the Crawfurds; he had planted the kitchen garden; he'd even polished boots and brushed out clothes—but that did not alter the fact that they did not *know* him. Men who seemed safe and harmless could still be disguising a dangerous nature.

Mairi had learned that lesson well.

She had no idea how long she remained outside, but long enough for her slippered feet to become tired and achy. She sat on the bench, wishing she would be allowed to observe the sale of the jewellery and other items. She'd make certain they were sold at a high enough price and that all the money came back to her father.

If she accompanied her father to Edinburgh, he would not listen to her. If she accompanied Lucas, though, perhaps he would allow her to manage the sales. Although a man—especially one as tall and strong as Lucas—could overpower her and she'd be helpless—

No. Lucas would not do such a thing. She knew he would

never hurt her. She did not know why she knew that, but she did.

On the other hand, he still could steal their money.

'Miss Wallace?'

She jumped at the voice and instinctively recoiled.

Lucas stepped into her view. 'How long have you been out here?'

'Since I was sent from the dinner table,' she replied sharply. She was not angry at him, though. He'd been the only one to attempt to support her.

'Your parents were wrong to chastise you,' he said. 'You were entirely correct. Your father should handle the sale of the items. He should have charge of the money.'

'You told him that?' She looked up.

He glanced away. 'Not in so many words.'

He hadn't supported her in the end.

He turned back and met her gaze. 'I think your father is much better at purchasing things than selling them.'

'So you agreed to do this for him?' Her spirits sank.

'Niven is to come with me.' He did not sound very excited about this prospect.

Neither was she. 'Niven?'

Of what use would Niven be? He'd not had enough experience of the world to know the value of things.

She stood. 'I am returning to the house.'

He walked next to her, but did not say another word until they reached the door. He opened it, and as she stepped over the threshold, he grasped her arm. 'Miss Wallace—'

Mairi jerked away in panic. She again felt a man's grip on her arm. She could smell whisky and sweat.

An instant later the sensation dissolved. Her heart still raced.

Lucas stepped back and gaped at her in confusion. 'Miss Wallace?'

'I—I— You startled me by seizing my arm.' She could barely make herself talk.

He looked concerned. 'I did not hurt you, did I?'

'No. Just startled me.' She shrank away. 'I must go to my room. They might look for me.'

She hurried to the servants' stairs, the better to make it to her bedchamber without anyone seeing. She stopped before reaching the floor. What had happened? For that brief moment she'd not known it was Lucas touching her. It had been that other Englishman, the one from whom she could not escape. She'd momentarily returned to that horrible afternoon.

At least Lucas did not press her as to why she had reacted so strangely. He'd accepted her excuse, which was good, because she would never, ever, tell him what had happened to her.

Very early the next morning Lucas, Erwin and Robert loaded a wagon with the furniture and boxes. They all reentered the house to eat breakfast.

Lucas had changed into his own clothes, but he'd packed his butler's garb as well. Best to look somewhat respectable if he was to sell items of value. He made certain he had Dunburn's letters, signed and sealed, authorising him to act on the Baron's behalf. He hoped merchants in Edinburgh would accept an Englishman as a Scottish baron's man of business.

First a labourer, then a butler, now a man of business. He'd played so many parts for these Wallaces, so caught up in their problems that he'd nearly forgotten his despair. He'd hardly thought at all of war, even without whisky to wash it all away.

Who was he fooling? It was not the family who preoccupied him; it was Mairi. He'd been in her company the greater part of yesterday and everything about her increased his admiration. Everything but that look on her face when he'd grasped her arm. What had that meant? It had seemed more like fear than anger, but he'd done nothing to frighten her. He had certainly angered her, though.

Niven stepped into the servants' hall. 'I've finished breakfast.' He'd eaten in the kitchen. 'I am ready now, Lucas. Shall we be off?'

It felt wrong to leave without Dunburn to see them off, but he had insisted it would be too difficult and he would rather sleep late. It felt even worse to be sneaking off without even telling Mairi they were leaving. He'd intended to tell her the night before that he and Niven would be leaving early, but, after she reacted so strongly to his touch, she'd run from him.

'Yes,' Lucas said. 'Let us leave now.'

'Not before taking a basket with you.' Mrs MacNeal appeared with a large wicker basket, fragrant with freshly baked bread.

'Thank you, Mrs MacNeal.' Lucas passed the basket on to Niven. 'I need to take the portmanteau.'

Lucas fetched the portmanteau containing the jewellery from the butler's room and he and Niven left via the servants' entrance to the waiting wagon. Niven climbed up first. Lucas handed the portmanteau to him and started to climb up next.

'Wait!'

He turned to see Mairi running towards him. She was dressed in her nightclothes and a dressing gown. Her hair was loose and flowing as she rushed towards them. She looked like an angel in flight.

'You are leaving?' she cried. 'Without a word?'

He had to hold his hands out to stop her from running into him. 'I tried to tell you.'

'I saw the wagon from my window, but it is so early. You are sneaking away.' She was breathing hard. 'Does my father know?'

He held her shoulders. 'He knows, Mairi. This is as he wanted it.' He'd slipped into using her given name.

'You were all hiding it from me?' she cried.

'No.' She must not think that. 'I came to tell you last night—'

She blinked rapidly. '*You* came. But Mama and Papa made no effort to tell me.'

Her pain affected him more than he wanted to admit. 'I am sorry, Mairi.'

Her eyes filled with angry tears. 'You had better do as Papa wished, Lucas!'

'Don't be bottle-headed, Mairi,' Niven called down. 'Of course we will do as Papa wished. What else would we do?'

Lucas knew better than Niven what pained her. Her parents had not even done her the courtesy of telling her.

He leaned closer to her, speaking low. 'You can trust me, Mairi. I will return with the funds. I promise.'

'You say that.' She looked into his eyes. Hers glistened with tears.

'Zooks, Mairi,' Niven said. 'Lucas is a fine fellow, but I will make certain he does as he should.'

Niven could not stop Lucas if he wanted to steal the money and he knew that Mairi knew it. Lucas could tell her he had no need of her family's money. He had plenty of his own. His brother's fortune and his father's some day.

'I will return with the money,' he said softly.

'You had better!' she rasped.

Lucas wished he could hold her and comfort her fears, assure her that everything would work out as she hoped, but he certainly had not earned that right. He took her hand in his and clasped it firmly, wishing his were not gloved so he would be able to feel the warmth and smoothness of her skin against his.

'You have my word, Mairi.' He released her reluctantly and climbed up next to Niven, who handed him the reins of the horses. 'We will be back.'

Lucas drove away, feeling her gaze upon his back. Without looking, he knew she stood watching them and would do so until they disappeared from view.

Lucas and Niven had travelled about an hour before a rustle sounded from behind them in the wagon. Lucas halted the horses and both he and Niven turned around in alarm. The oilcloth they'd used to cover the boxes and furniture was lifted up.

Davina sat up, grinning. Lucas swore to himself.

'Davina!' Niven cried. 'What the devil?'

'You didn't think I would let you have this adventure without me, did you?' She climbed over the boxes and took a seat beside Niven.

'Miss Davina! This is not well done of you. Not well done at all.' Lucas could not keep his extreme irritation out of his voice. 'We will have to turn around now.'

'No!' she and Niven both cried at once.

'Do not turn around,' she pleaded. 'I want to go with you. I have never been to Edinburgh. But do not concern yourselves. I will be no trouble at all and nothing could be objectionable about me accompanying my brother and our servant. I left a letter for Mama and Papa so they won't worry.'

'If we turn around, we might be delayed by a day at least,' Niven complained. 'And that might make us late for the house party and that will inconvenience our hosts. Lady Oxmont will be counting on us to arrive when we said we would.'

Lucas did not credit either of these excuses, but he knew time was of the essence or it would not matter how much money they raised.

It looked like he was saddled with both of them.

Mairi watched Lucas drive away, then spun on her heel and re-entered the house. There was nothing she could do. She was powerless and she hated that feeling. Her heart accelerated and a wave of anxiety accosted her.

This was intolerable. Intolerable.

Had Davina known of these plans to sneak away shortly after dawn? Was Mairi the only one who hadn't known? She had no doubt that her parents had wished to hide this from her. They knew she'd make a fuss.

Not that any of it did any good.

Her dressing gown came open as she climbed the stairs. She stopped and retied its sash. She did not even care that she'd run out of the house barefoot and in her nightclothes. She'd seen the wagon from her window and known instantly what was afoot.

She knew better than to wake her parents and confront them, but Davina might be persuaded to tell her the details of this plan, not that it would reassure her much.

At least she'd not flinched from Lucas's touch as she had the night before. Perhaps her anger had protected her from reliving that…event again. When Lucas took her hand in his she'd almost felt comforted. Reassured.

When he was looking into her eyes and speaking softly and earnestly, she'd believed him. But as soon he'd disappeared from sight, she'd begun to worry ag Would he truly return with the money?

She tapped on Davina's door and, hearing no opened it quietly. Her sister might still be asleep. She into the room to see.

The bed was empty and looked as if it had just been made up. Mairi stepped into the room. 'Davina?'

There was no answer.

Davina was not in the room. Had she risen early?

Mairi was about to leave when she noticed a piece of folded paper on the bed.

She picked it up and opened it.

Dear Mama and Papa,
Do not worry about me. I have gone with Niven and
Lucas to Edinburgh. It was not fair that Niven could
go and not me.
Yours, etc.
Davina

'Davina!' Mairi cried aloud. 'You silly fool!'

She hurried into her room and pulled her riding habit out of the wardrobe. If she rode one of the very fast horses, she might catch up to them. She struggled with her laces, but could not reach them. No matter. She'd ride dressed as she was. She grabbed her cloak and gloves and ran out of the room and halfway to the stables.

She stopped. She had no idea what roads to take to Edinburgh. What if there was more than one way to go? How would she know which route they'd taken? She had very little money of her own to take with her, perhaps not enough to stay in an inn.

And she would be alone on strange roads where nobody knew her. She would be at more risk alone than Davina could ever be with Lucas and Niven to look after her. As long as Davina stayed with them. That was the worry, though, was it not?

Would Davina stay with them?

Chapter Thirteen

It took them two days to reach Edinburgh. The first night on the road they stayed at an inn in Linlithgow and Niven and Davina insisted upon visiting the ruins of the palace where Mary, Queen of Scots, had been born and where Bonnie Prince Charlie had briefly visited a few months before the Duke of Cumberland had burned most of the building. There were several delays like that one, the two young people treating the trip more as a lark than as a means to save their family from losing everything.

He was lucky enough to sell the jewellery and many of the decorative items to John Howden and Son, a watchmaker and jeweller. With recommendations from Mr Howden for other places that might take the furniture, he managed to sell everything over the following three days.

Rather than watch over Lucas's efforts, Niven and Davina explored the sights of the city, managing to visit both Holyrood Palace and Edinburgh Castle. Lucas gave them orders as stern as he'd done with his soldiers that they were not to engage in any mischief. They'd listened to him when he'd explained about the family's debts, as well, and promised to be more responsible in helping their sister. Niven immediately rose to the occasion to watch over Davina.

With their promises to behave properly, they happily went off on their own and Lucas was able to conduct the serious business as he desired.

He managed to raise enough blunt for the payment of Dunburn's loan, plus extra for the other debts and, as Lucas would insist, the long overdue salaries of the servants. With bank notes safely kept always on his person, the trip back was almost enjoyable.

Davina and Niven sang as they neared the home this trip would save for them.

The wagon passed through the wrought-iron gate with their name, Wallace, arching over them.

'I wonder if anyone will see us coming,' Niven said.

Lucas suspected someone would take notice. Was he being foolish to hope it would be Mairi?

He pulled up to the front entrance and Erwin stepped out of the house. 'You are back.' He eyed the near-empty wagon. 'You had some success?'

'We did well,' Lucas admitted.

Niven jumped down and turned to help Davina down. 'It was a great adventure, Erwin!'

'And matters here?' Lucas asked.

Erwin shrugged and reached for the small bags they'd each carried with them. 'Much the same as always.'

If he were driving up to his father's country house he would have handed the reins to the footman and left him to deal with the horses and wagon, but instead he told Erwin, 'I will take the wagon to the carriage house.'

As he pulled up to the carriage house, John, the stable boy, opened the doors. He drove the wagon inside and helped John unhitch the horses.

'How did ye make out?' John asked.

'I was able to sell everything,' Lucas replied.

MacKay, the head groom, heard this as he walked in. 'Aye, good news, that is. And I was able to sell those two new horses the Baron purchased. Made a wee profit.'

'That is excellent news,' Lucas responded.

'Now, if the man can only keep his money and not throw it away,' MacKay said. 'Get what ye can, and keep what ye hae, that's the way to get rich.'

'Aye,' responded Lucas.

John and MacKay laughed. 'Turning into a regular Scotsman, he is,' MacKay said.

They heard footsteps hurrying towards the building and all three men turned to see who was rushing towards them.

Lucas's breath caught. It was Mairi Wallace. She stood in the doorway for a moment, probably waiting for her eyes to become accustomed to the dark interior of the carriage house. She strode towards them and the lantern that hung near them illuminated her. She wore a wide-brimmed hat, apron and heavy gloves, as if she was coming directly from digging in the garden again.

Erwin's words came back to Lucas. Yes. Things were much the same as always. He was surprised he had missed the place.

Had missed her.

'Well, Lucas?' Her breath was coming fast and her eyes, vivid blue even in the dim light, were anxious.

'All sold and we made enough.' Best to go directly to the point with her.

Her shoulders relaxed. 'Thank goodness.'

He stifled a smile. 'See? I kept my word.'

'Yes. Well.' She turned away. 'It is a good thing.'

MacKay waved his hand. 'You go on back to the house. I'll bet Cook will make you something to eat.'

Lucas was hungry. They'd had little to eat on the journey, wanting to return home as quickly as possible. 'Thank you both.'

Mairi walked back to the house with him. 'I have not seen Niven and Davina yet. How did they fare?'

'They behaved themselves,' he responded. 'Showed an independence I had not seen in them before. They did not impede the errand on which I was sent, which helped.'

Before they reached the door, she stopped. 'Do you truly have the money to pay Papa's debts?' she asked in a low voice.

He placed his hands on her arms and looked directly into her eyes. 'Yes, Mairi,' he murmured. 'You may rest easy on that score.'

Her blue eyes seemed to touch his. 'Then I thank you.'

Before they entered the house, she pulled off her gloves and put them in the pockets of her apron. When they walked in, the Baron and Lady Dunburn were in the hall still making a fuss over Niven and Davina.

'And your sister was all at sixes and sevens when she found your note,' their mother said cheerfully. 'But I told her Niven would take care of you and so he has. Look at you both.' She extended her arms.

'Ah, here is Lucas.' Dunburn strode over to him and clapped him on the shoulder. 'Niven says you did it, Lucas. You raised enough.'

'Indeed, sir.' Lucas patted his coat. 'It is all safely on my person.'

'Come. Come,' Dunburn said. 'We should put it in the safe.'

'Yes, do.' Lady Dunburn laughed. 'Then come into the drawing room.' She turned to the footman. 'Erwin, ask Cook to make some tea and biscuits.' She took the arms of her two youngest children. 'You must tell me of all you saw and did.'

Niven, Davina and their mother, all talking at once, headed to the drawing room. Dunburn urged Lucas to follow him to the library. Mairi was left standing alone.

Lucas stopped. 'I want Miss Wallace to see the money into your safe.'

'Mairi?' Her father waved the idea away. 'She involves herself too much in men's matters. It is not seemly.'

Mairi stood apart, her hat in her hand, apparently unnoticed by the others.

Lucas disliked seeing her that way. 'She has been the most worried of all of you about your finances and worked the hardest at finding what to sell,' he told her father. 'She should see for herself how much profit was made.'

Mairi followed her father and Lucas into the library.

If Lucas had not called attention to her presence, her father would probably not have noticed she'd been there. Her parents had barely spoken to her since that night before Lucas left for Edinburgh.

He'd come back, as he'd said he would. He'd saved their home and property. How would she ever thank him?

Once in the library, Lucas pulled a coin purse from one pocket and a thick leather envelope from another. Out of the leather envelope he took bank notes and several other pieces of paper and placed them on the desk. He separated the bank notes from the other papers.

He looked up at Mairi. 'Miss Wallace, is there pen and ink or a pencil you might write with?'

She walked over to the small writing table, the same one from which she had brought out pen and ink for Mr Hargreave. At least Lucas did not rummage through her father's desk drawers.

She brought over pen and ink.

'Would you sit at the desk?' Lucas asked her. 'You might be more comfortable writing there.'

'What the devil must she write?' her father asked.

Lucas turned to him. 'I want you to have a clear record of what sold and for how much, so you might see that it matches the money.' He placed a paper in front of Mairi. 'This is the list we made of everything to be sold.'

She perused it and nodded. It was the list in her handwriting, but monetary amounts were written next to each item.

'I have the receipts from the shopkeepers. I will read them to you and you can put a mark beside each one if it is correct.'

'This is a great deal of trouble—' her father broke in.

Lucas quickly answered, 'I want you both to see that the list, the receipts and the amount of money all match.'

Lucas wanted her to see that he'd been honest in his dealings with their possessions and money, she realised. Her father lowered himself into one of the upholstered chairs near the fireplace and folded his arms across his chest. By the time Mairi and Lucas had finished the task, her father was snoring softly.

Mairi raised her voice. 'Papa!'

He started, then blinked rapidly. 'Yes. Yes. No need to shout, girl. I was merely resting my eyes.'

'We are finished,' she said. 'The money goes into the safe now.'

He rose and fished through his pockets for the key.

'I have one more request, sir,' Lucas said.

Her father glanced up.

'I want you to pay the servants and the other workers.'

Mairi had not expected that. How good of him to think of the servants.

Lucas went on. 'There is enough money for it.'

Her father sighed. 'Will you see to it tomorrow?'

'With pleasure,' Lucas responded.

Her father walked over to one of the bookcases and removed the false-book spines that hid the safe. He opened it with his key and Lucas brought the money over and placed it inside. Her father closed the door to the safe, locked it and put the false-book spines back.

Mairi relaxed. The money was safe, the disaster averted.

Her father clapped his hands and glanced at Lucas. 'Let us join Lady Dunburn for tea.' He grinned. 'Or perhaps something stronger.'

Her father sauntered out of the library, but Lucas waited, letting her walk through the doorway ahead of him. She went over to the hall table and picked up her hat.

He had not followed her father as she had expected him to. 'You are not taking tea?' he asked.

She shook her head. Her family had so clearly indicated that her presence was not desired.

She hung the hat over her arm by its ribbons and pulled the gloves from her pockets. 'I have too much work to do.'

Mairi had finished in the kitchen garden and moved over to the formal gardens, where she'd found Kinley pruning bushes. He'd directed her to weed and rake the flower beds. She'd started on the furthest beds, mostly to avoid being seen by her mother, who would certainly have much to say to her about digging in the dirt.

Perhaps her father could soon hire more servants, more gardeners to help poor Kinley. When that time came she would probably miss this work. It kept her from thinking too much.

Lately she'd been thinking entirely too much of Lucas.

She'd missed him when he'd been away. The house had become depressed and stuffy without him in it. And so very lonely. Only when he'd gone had she realised how much life he'd restored to the house. Because of his presence.

He'd agreed to stay only while they had needed a butler, but he'd wound up staying longer to help her father out of the fix he'd got himself into. He was now under no obligation to stay. Perhaps he had come to say goodbye.

She stood, afraid to breathe, afraid that this would be the last moment she would see him.

When he came close enough, her breath caught in her throat. His handsome looks had become so familiar to her, so dear. And now she must say goodbye to him.

He wore the clothes he'd had on when Davina and Niven had found him, but now, of course, he looked hale and hearty.

He came close enough to speak. 'What work needs doing today?'

'Work?' He must be making idle conversation. 'I am merely cleaning up the flower beds.'

He stood over her. 'I meant what work might I do?'

She looked up in surprise. 'You want to work? I thought you were coming to say goodbye to me.'

His gaze was soft upon her. 'Not today.' He glanced away and back. 'I might as well be useful.'

She put her spade in the dirt to loosen the roots of a weed. 'Believe me, Mr Lucas, after what you have done for our family, you owe us nothing. It is we who owe you.'

He cocked his head. 'I would prefer to work.'

She could only stare at him. Offering to help. How very kind of him. 'Ask Kinley what needs doing.'

He glanced around until catching sight of Kinley pruning the bushes. 'I'll do that.'

Mairi watched him walk over to Kinley, her heart unreasonably glad. She would not have to say goodbye to him today after all.

* * *

A little while later she spied him with the wheelbarrow filled with gravel, a shovel and a rake. He poured gravel over the paths and raked them smooth. It was work that would have been difficult for her or the ageing Kinley to do.

Another kindness.

When the sun dropped low enough in the sky, Mairi stopped working. She looked around, but did not see Lucas. Perhaps he had finished ahead of her. She returned the tools to Kinley and went back into the house to dress herself for dinner.

In her room she stripped down to her shift and corset and washed herself as thoroughly as she could.

She was drying herself when her door opened and Davina burst in. 'Where have you been all afternoon? I wanted to tell you about Edinburgh, but you didn't come to tea after helping Papa with the money.'

She'd not felt welcome.

'You can tell me about Edinburgh now,' Mairi said. 'But please do not ever do something like that again, Davina. Going off like that. I was worried to a frazzle about you.'

'That's what Mama said,' Davina responded, laughing. 'I was perfectly safe, you know.'

'This time you were.' Mairi stepped into her dress and presented her back to her sister.

At that moment Nellie knocked on the door. 'Do you need me, miss?' she asked.

'Thank you, no, Nellie,' Mairi responded. 'Davina is helping me.'

The lady's maid looked relieved. She curtsied and left.

'What did you see in Edinburgh?' Mairi asked as Davina tied her laces.

'What did we not see!' Davina exclaimed.

Mairi sat at her dressing table and took down her hair
She combed it while Davina chattered on about seeing the
castles, the shops and other sites of Edinburgh, the city o
so much exciting learning and thought. She was glad her
sister had had such an enjoyable time; there was little fur
to be had at home these days, even if things had been more
exciting since Lucas's arrival.

'How did you have time to see all those things and sti
sell every item?' Mairi asked.

'Oh, Lucas did all that,' Davina said. 'He didn't come
with us to see all the sights.'

Davina and Niven had not helped Lucas at all? He'd left
them on their own?

She plaited her hair and twisted the plait into a chignor
at the nape of her neck. It was tidy at least.

'What did you do while we were away?' Davina asked
as they left the room to go to the drawing room.

Did she mean besides being alternately ignored or chided
by their parents? 'I helped the maids and worked in the
garden.'

'Poor Mairi!' Davina said. 'Maybe now that Papa car
pay his debts he can hire more servants and you won't have
to do all that drudgery.'

'I like feeling useful,' Mairi said.

Those were nearly the same words Lucas had used.

When they walked through the door to the drawin
room, Mairi immediately saw Lucas standing there. He
changed into his butler clothes and looked quite like
gentleman. Her parents had not yet come down.

Davina skipped over to him. 'Lucas! I was just tellin
Mairi about Edinburgh.'

Niven appeared from behind a chair. 'We saw every
thing, Mairi. You should have been there.'

'It sounds wonderful,' she responded.

'Did you tell her about New Town? How fashionable it was?' Niven asked.

'Of course I did,' Davina retorted. 'I told her everything.'

Brother and sister began to bicker about what was most important to have told Mairi.

Mairi stepped closer to Lucas. 'I heard they left you to tell everything.'

He tilted his head. 'It was easier that way, if you can believe that.'

She frowned. 'You left them alone.'

'They had very strict instructions to behave,' he said. 'They were up for the challenge. They are not children, you know, Mairi.'

True, Mairi had to admit. She also had to admit she might be too protective.

Her parents entered the room and Mairi withdrew. They soon all went to dinner, where the conversation continued about Edinburgh. Mairi quietly ate her food.

When the subject of Edinburgh was exhausted, her mother turned to her. 'I do hope the dresses you had made over will do for the house party. We should have ordered new gowns as I originally wanted. If our clothes are commented upon, I will lay the entire blame on you.'

'Yes, Mama,' Mairi said.

Her father broke in. 'I confess, I am in a quandary about this house party.'

'Why, Papa?' Davina asked.

'Wilfred is saying he cannot make the trip,' her father answered. 'And I say he must. I need a valet.'

'Papa, of course Wilfred must not go,' Mairi said. 'Such a trip is far too strenuous for him. Even if he rode in the coach—'

'Oh, no.' Her mother scowled at her. 'No manservant could ride in the coach, at least not on the inside.'

Her father continued talking. 'Erwin and Robert cannot do it. They do not have the faintest idea how to be a valet.'

'Indeed not!' her mother agreed.

Her father turned to Lucas. 'Will you do it, Lucas? No one will comment if my butler acts as my valet, especially because you did so for Mr Hargreave.'

Mairi broke in. 'Papa, Mr Lucas has his own affairs to attend to. He's already delayed his journey for us. Don't you think he's done enough?'

Her father simply ignored her. 'Will you do it, Lucas? It promises to be a fine party.'

'And we must make as good an impression as possible, even though we are among friends,' her mother added. 'We do not want anything to deter Mr Hargreave from courting Mairi.' She glared at Mairi. 'Do we, Mairi?'

Mairi felt Lucas's eyes upon her. She lowered her gaze. The house party was not going to be fine for her.

'Lucas?' her father prompted.

Lucas took a drink of wine before he answered, 'I will do it.'

Chapter Fourteen

Once again Lucas had agreed to stay on. Mairi had said he had done enough for this family and he agreed. He'd more than paid his debt to them after the Edinburgh trip. But here he was, riding Dunburn's horse alongside the coach transporting the Baron and Lady Dunburn, her lady's maid and Mairi. Davina and Niven rode along with him, both wanting their horses for use at the Oxmonts' house party.

At least the weather was fine. Lucas wondered what the two younger Wallaces would do if it poured rain. The trip took two days with a night's stay in Perth. On the second day Lucas watched the landscape change from rolling hills to mountains that seemed to rise straight to the sky. Every once in a while he could see lines of stag on the green and gold peaks, looking as if they wondered quite who these intruders were.

Lucas had seen great houses throughout England and castles in Spain, France and Belgium, but he was still impressed at the first glance of Oxmont Castle. The road brought them to the crest of a hill and the house appeared below them encircled with trees that had started to change to their autumn colours. The mountains soared behind the house. Painted white, it appeared more like a country house than a castle and one haphazardly built at that. No homage to symmetry in this house. If one looked closely, though, a castle tower could be seen, one of several wings of the house that seemed put together like a child would build with blocks.

When they finally reached the gate, they rode down a long avenue shaded by flaming red-leafed linden trees on both sides, as majestic an entrance as Lucas had ever seen. When they reached the house, the family was properly greeted and it was a new experience for Lucas to be virtually ignored by the couple he presumed to be Lord and Lady Oxmont. One of their footmen showed him to Dunburn's room and gave him directions to get to the servants' hall, where he would be free to spend leisure time and where his meals would be served.

How odd to be unpacking for the Baron. Lucas was not looking forward to providing such personal care to Dunburn. Why had he agreed to this role again?

Because the problem of Dunburn's valet had become another point of conflict between Mairi and her parents and he'd wanted to prevent it. And he was not at all certain he liked the prospect of Hargreave courting Mairi. What he might do to interfere with that he did not know. He only knew he was determined that Mairi should be happy.

Hargreave would not make her happy.

The room Dunburn was given was not grand, probably befitting his lower title. There was a small closet with a cot. This would be where Lucas would sleep. Not as rough as some places he'd had to sleep during the war, but by far the saddest accommodations he'd ever had in a country house.

Lucas quickly changed into what he thought of as his butler clothes. By the time he'd dressed, Dunburn came in to change out of his travel clothes.

The man was in high spirits. 'Well, well, Lucas. What do you think of this place, eh? Have you ever seen its like?'

He adopted the persona of a manservant. 'Never, sir.' Perhaps if he remained very detached, he'd get through this.

He helped Dunburn off with his coat, his boots, his trousers, and on with clean ones.

'I'm off,' the Baron said cheerfully.

After he left, Lucas located the clothes brush, but should he brush the Baron's clothes and his own here? They were filled with the dirt of the road.

There was a knock on the door and he bid whoever it was to come in.

To his surprise it was Mairi. 'Forgive me for intruding, Lucas,' she said. 'But Nellie cannot get my mother's trunk open. Can you help?'

He put down his clothes brush. 'Certainly.'

Lady Dunburn's was the next room. And after fiddling with the key he was able to open the trunk for Nellie. Mairi helped her unpack her mother's things and Lucas stayed to move the empty trunk to the closet for them. Mairi left the room at the same time as Lucas.

'Was your ride comfortable?' he asked her.

'As well as one can expect,' she replied.

'What happens now? Some entertainment planned for you?' At house parties he'd attended in the past there was always something planned.

'Davina is off to find Lord and Lady Oxmont's daughter. She is the reason Davina was invited. To keep the daughter company. Niven went to find William Crawfurd. I suppose I shall have to join some of the ladies in one of the sitting rooms. I dare say that is where Mama is.'

'You do not sound eager to do so.'

'I am not. There is nothing to do but sit, and I am so unused to being idle.' She lifted a shoulder. 'At least it will delay encountering Mr Hargreave.'

'You wish to avoid him?' Lucas couldn't help feeling cheered by this.

Her eyes flashed. 'Yes!' She seemed to compose herself. 'I cannot like him.'

They were in agreement on that score.

She lifted her arms in a helpless gesture. 'My mother and Lady Crawfurd are determined, though.'

'That he should court you?'

She nodded.

Lucas was reluctant to leave her. They stood together in the hallway, not speaking.

'I am sorry you had to come, Lucas,' she whispered finally. 'I am certain this house party will be even worse for you.'

'I will manage.' He gazed down at her. 'But you must let me know if I might be of assistance to you. You are not alone here, Mairi.' He slipped again, using her given name.

She lowered her lashes and blinked rapidly.

Voices sounded at the stairway and they stepped apart.

'I'd best be on my way,' she said.

He bowed slightly and returned to Dunburn's room to gather the travel clothes. In this vast castle there must be a valet's room where the clothing might be well brushed. He walked to the servants' stairs and descended as far down as they went. A servant in the corridor directed him to the room where two others were tending to clothes.

What was the etiquette for being a guest's valet at a house party? He'd had a quick lesson from old Wilfred about what duties he'd need to perform for Dunburn, but he had not thought to ask how one interacted with the other servants.

He nodded to the men present. 'Good afternoon. I am Lucas. With the Baron of Dunburn.'

One fellow glanced up for only a moment; the other's brows rose. 'English, are ye?'

'That I am.' Being English was not all that welcome in Scotland.

'Been in Scotland long?' the man asked.

'I was recently hired as butler at Dunburn House.' That much was true.

'English butler,' the man said mockingly. 'Quite fancy.'

'I am glad to have the work,' he said. 'Many soldiers home from the war are not so lucky.' Hargreave and the Crawfurds knew he'd been in the army, so he might as well mention it and hope no one asked him about Waterloo.

'A soldier, were ye?' That at least earned him a modicum of respect from the fellow. 'I'm Anderson, first footman. I tend to William, the eldest son. Among many other duties, as you well know.' He gestured to the other man. 'He is Mr Hargreave's valet.'

'One of the guests?' Lucas asked, but he knew very well who Hargreave was.

'Aye,' Anderson said. 'Son of the Earl of Barring.'

'I am not well versed in the Scottish peerage,' Lucas admitted. Perhaps they would not expect so much of him as a result.

'Most of the important ones are here.' Anderson eyed the clothes in Lucas's arms. 'And some of the not-so-important ones.'

Lucas ignored that affront and hung Dunburn's coat on one of the forms in the room and got to work brushing it. Anderson talked on about who the guests were and about how important Lord and Lady Oxmont were. The other valet, who never provided his name, did not speak.

'Before you return your gentleman's clothes, I'll show you

to the servants' hall. You are welcome to spend any leisure time you have there.' Anderson gestured for Lucas to follow.

In the servants' hall were some maids and footmen having refreshment. Some were talking, some reading, others possibly napping. A couple of men there were not dressed as house servants. More like stablemen.

Anderson raised his voice. 'Everyone, this is Lucas, the Baron of Dunburn's valet.'

One of the stablemen whose back was to him turned and his mouth dropped open. 'Lucas?' he said in a puzzled voice.

Lucas blanched. It was Findlay, his batman, the man who'd served him throughout his many campaigns in the First Royals, the man who'd held him together after Bradleigh was killed.

Findlay strode over to him. Lucas sent a fierce warning with his eyes; Findlay knew him as Captain Johns-Ives and he obviously did not want that name to be known.

'Lucas?' he said again as Lucas extended his hand for Findlay to shake.

'Good to see you again, Findlay.' He meant that. Findlay had served him well.

'You know each other?' Anderson asked. A few of the others looked up out of curiosity.

'From the army,' Lucas was quick to explain.

Anderson told him when meals were served and excused himself. 'Must be off.'

Lucas was left with Findlay, but the room was filled with curious ears. 'I should be off, as well,' Lucas said. 'Good day to you, Findlay.'

The batman took hold of his arm and left the room with him. He led Lucas to a door at the back of the house where deliveries were made and, he presumed, the door the servants used.

Once outside Findlay walked them to a corner of the

house where they were alone. 'Now, sir, tell me why?' He did not even have to finish his sentence.

Lucas nodded. 'I will tell you the longer story when we can find more time.' How to explain. 'I—I— Things were difficult with my parents. I wanted to get lost for a while and I wound up in Scotland.' He felt a rush of pain. 'I became ill and this family—' Mairi, primarily '—helped me. I am helping them in return. They have no idea who I am. They know I was in the war, but they do not know I was an officer. I transposed my name. John Lucas instead of Lucas Johns-Ives.'

Findlay frowned. 'Why do I ken there is more to this than ye are saying?' He shook his head. 'But a servant, sir?' Instead of an earl's heir, he meant.

'Do not give me away.' He used the voice he used when commanding soldiers. 'This is a family in dire straits and I will see them settled before I leave.'

'To return to England?' Findlay said, still sounding puzzled.

Lucas looked away. 'I do not know.'

Returning to his father's estate, to his role as heir and to his parents' disappointment seemed every bit as unbearable as before.

'I'll keep your secrets, sir,' Findlay said. 'You can rely on me, sir.'

Lucas touched his arm. 'I know that, Findlay. I have relied on you more than anyone else these last few years.'

Findlay straightened as if standing to attention. 'My duty, sir.'

Lucas turned to go and both men walked back to the door.

'One more thing,' Lucas said as his batman reached for the latch to open the door for him.

'What is that, sir?' he asked.

'Do not call me sir.'

* * *

Davina sprawled over the bed in the chamber she shared with Mairi. 'I do wish Elspeth and I were invited to the dinner.'

'Believe me, it is not so exciting,' Mairi told her. 'You are better off dining with Niven and William.'

'It is like being banished to the nursery!' Davina wailed.

'It is not,' Mairi countered. 'I am sure you will be in a perfectly lovely sitting room.'

Davina rolled over on to her back. 'I do like that we will eat with William.'

Mairi fixed her garnet-and-gold earrings on her ears, one of two pairs of earrings she'd not sold. She wore a necklace to match, a simple garnet pendant on a gold chain. The jewellery matched the pale pink dinner dress the dressmaker had made over.

She stood and surveyed herself in the mirror.

'You look lovely, Mairi,' Davina said. 'I am certain the divine Mr Hargreave will agree.'

Mairi wished he could see her in the dress she wore to work in the garden instead. What would he think of her then?

There was a knock on the door and Mairi opened it.

Lucas stood there. His gaze flicked over her only for an instant, but she felt the colour rise in her cheeks in response. Had he approved of her appearance? His eyes met hers and she fancied that he had approved.

'Hello, Lucas!' Davina called from the bed.

He tossed a glance to her and back to Mairi. 'Your father wishes you to accompany him and your mother to the drawing room,' he said in the servant's voice that annoyed her so much.

'I will await them,' she said.

'Doesn't Mairi look pretty, Lucas?' Davina said.

His eyes perused her again. 'Indeed,' he said softly. He bowed and left.

Mairi swivelled around to her sister. 'That was not well done, Davina. You should not have spoken to Lucas like that.'

Davina sat up. 'Why not? It is not like he's really a servant.'

'He is here, though,' Mairi countered. 'You must be on your very best behaviour. How you comport yourself reflects on Mama and Papa.'

Davina slipped off the bed. 'Mama and Papa are not half so stuffy as you've become, Mairi. I do wish you would simply enjoy yourself instead of being grim all the time.'

Her sister's words stung, but only because Mairi heard the truth in them.

'I will try,' she said.

Hargreave looked over as the butler announced the Baron of Dunburn and Lady Dunburn and Miss Wallace. Miss Wallace wore that placid look that made him itch to rile her into some heightened emotion.

He enjoyed a challenge.

She smiled graciously to Lord and Lady Oxmont, no doubt thanking them for the invitation. Perhaps by next year, Lord and Lady Oxmont would be greeting a new Baron of Dunburn. And a new Lady Dunburn.

The old Dunburns saw some people they obviously knew and left their daughter's side. She walked through the room alone, nodding to people with whom she'd been acquainted her whole life, as he had been.

Hargreave crossed the room to her. 'Miss Wallace. How delightful to see you and looking so lovely, as well,' he said smoothly. 'You arrived today?'

'Yes. Today.' She did not quite smile.

'I am glad of it,' he said. 'I look forward to your company. And that of your parents, of course.'

She wore a pale pink dress, one not quite up to the latest fashion, but that suited her complexion. He had no desire to see the family looking prosperous. When he'd visited Dunburn House, he'd discovered a drawer full of unpaid bills and a letter demanding payment of a sizeable loan. But Miss Wallace had discovered him there before he could assure himself that Dunburn was indeed deep in dun territory.

He smiled his most charming smile. 'Shall I get you some wine?'

'Thank you, yes.' She was already looking away from him.

He noticed she walked over to another young woman standing alone. Hargreave knew the chit. Eldest daughter of Viscount Annanfell, Miss Johnstone. Well dowered, which was to her credit, but Hargreave had his heart set on ruining Dunburn, taking his title and land, and playing the hero by marrying his daughter.

Miss Johnstone and Miss Wallace exchanged pleasantries.

Hargreave took two glasses of wine from the attending footman and brought them to Miss Wallace and her companion.

Miss Wallace took the wine glass from his hand. 'Mr Hargreave, allow me to present Miss Johnstone to you.'

Miss Johnstone smiled and curtsied. 'We have met before. How do you do, Mr Hargreave?'

He returned her smile. 'I am delighted to see you again, Miss Johnstone.' He handed her the second wine glass. 'Please. Take this.'

'But it is yours!' she protested.

'I am certain I was meant to give it to you,' he said smoothly.

Miss Johnstone took a sip and asked, 'When did you arrive at the house party, Mr Hargreave?'

'A week ago,' he responded.

'How nice,' she said.

'Please excuse me,' Miss Wallace broke in. 'There is someone I must speak to.' She walked off and he was stuck with a young woman in whom he had no interest.

When dinner was announced, though, Hargreave managed to extricate himself and find Miss Wallace again.

He offered his arm. 'Allow me to escort you in to dinner.'

In the dining room he was seated next to her—Lady Crawfurd had arranged it for him. Hopefully every dinner would have the same seating arrangement.

During dinner he tried to engage her in conversation about the food, the wine, the room's decor. She responded unenthusiastically.

He tried another topic. 'Was that your sister and brother I saw this afternoon? I had forgotten they were included in the invitation.'

'As companions to Lord and Lady Oxmont's daughter,' she responded. 'I believe that is why William was included as well.'

'He and your brother will take part in some of the hunting, as I understand.'

'Niven will love that,' she said.

That worked a bit better.

He turned to an older woman seated on his other side and conversed with her while the gentleman on Mairi's other side spoke to her.

When Hargreave turned back to Mairi, he remarked, 'Will your brother have a Grand Tour this year?'

'Not this year,' she replied.

He nodded. If her brother was planning a Grand Tour,

Hargreave would be less certain of the family's financial problems.

'I believe William Crawfurd is getting ready to go abroad. I thought the two of them might have travelled together.'

See what she says about that.

'That would have been nice for them.' She took a bite of her food.

She was not very forthcoming, but he would not be deterred. He had the entire duration of the house party to make her warm to him.

He took a sip of his wine.

Chapter Fifteen

When the hosts and guests were at dinner, the kitchen also served a meal to the guests' servants. Lucas sat at the table with the other valets and lady's maids. There were about thirty of them, more valets than lady's maids. More men than women guests, he surmised. Several of them knew each other already, perhaps from other years, other house parties. No one knew Lucas, of course.

He tried not to call attention to himself, but the valet who'd virtually ignored him earlier while they'd been brushing out coats suddenly found a voice. He pointed to Lucas. 'He's a Sassenach, ye ken.'

'English?' one of the maids said. 'What in heaven's name brought you to Scotland?'

'I needed employment,' he said.

Another maid laughed. 'That's why we all are here.'

'Ye dinna wear livery,' one of the men said.

The once-silent valet spoke before Lucas could respond. 'He's the butler. Filling in for the Baron's valet.'

'The Baron who?' someone asked.

'The Baron of Dunburn,' he responded.

The once-silent valet spoke again. 'Dunburn is a right dobber.'

'Dobber?' Lucas asked.

The maids tittered.

'An…idiot,' one fellow said.

'And your employer is Mr Hargreave, I understand.' Lucas directed his gaze at the once-silent valet.

'Aye. Mr Hargreave,' the man said. 'He is the son of the Earl of Barring, in case you did not know it.'

'Son of an earl,' Lucas responded. 'Quite impressive.' For the first time since his arrival in Scotland he wished he could own to his true identity.

'Mr Hargreave visited Dunburn House recently,' the man said.

'Yes,' Lucas replied. 'I remember him.' He was disinclined to say much at all to this fellow.

Another one of the men said, 'You were in the army, I heard. With that coachman.' He meant Findlay. That information had spread swiftly.

'I was.' This change of subject was no better received by Lucas, though.

Lucas was compelled to tell them where he had served. In Portugal. At Waterloo. But the conversation quickly veered to those in the room who had relatives who'd fought in the war or whose lives had been lost.

Lucas excused himself as soon as he could do so without offence, but instead of returning to the confines of Dunburn's room, he walked outside. The air was chilly with a fine mist of rain. He quickened his pace to the stables, quite a distance from the house. The sun had set and, with the rain, the sky was starless. Not the best time to go looking for Findlay. He spied the lights of the stables and, turning up the collar of his coat, headed towards them.

Once he got close he could hear voices. Chances were their hall was above the stables where their rooms also

ikely were. He entered a door that opened to a stairway
and, even though it was closed off from the stable, the familiar scent of horses filled his nostrils. He climbed the
stairs and found the hall.

Several men turned when he reached the doorway.

'I am looking for Findlay,' he said loudly enough to be
heard over the din.

'Guests' coachmen are in the next building,' a fellow
growled.

Lucas walked to the next building and found another
hall filled with men talking, drinking, gambling.

'Is Findlay here?' he called.

'Yes! I am here!' Findlay stood and walked towards him.
When he reached Lucas he said, 'Now you will tell me the
whole?'

'If you like.'

Findlay gestured for him to follow. 'Come with me. I
want to check on our horses.'

There was another stairway leading directly into the
stables.

'Wait until you see these horses, sir,' Findlay said as
they passed the stalls of several horses, all matched teams.
He stopped in front of stalls holding matched bays. 'Magnificent, eh?'

The horses were large and muscular with silky hair on
their lower limbs. 'They look grand,' Lucas said, stroking
one on its neck.

Findlay sat on a nearby stool. 'So tell me now. And tell
me why you'd come looking for me tonight.'

Lucas did not need to say much about the effect of his
brother's death. Findlay had been there, had seen him
through it. He told Findlay how he could not bear taking his
brother's place, how he'd numbed himself with whisky, how

he and his parents had argued. He'd impulsively packed a satchel, written his parents a letter and left.

'But why come all this way? To Scotland?' Findlay asked.

Could he explain? It seemed impossible. 'It was far away. Whisky was easy to obtain. I had no destination. Just travelled from inn to inn.'

Findlay grinned. 'And you wound up a butler?'

'Precisely.' Lucas told him all about being ill, being rescued and feeling at first obligated to help the family, later feeling they needed him. He did not tell him about Mairi, how she needed someone to help her. He did not tell him that caring about her, helping her, pulled him out of his dismal mood. Every time he helped her and her family, he felt a little more healed.

'So, what now?' Findlay asked. 'Are you remaining a butler for ever?'

Lucas shook his head. 'I must leave them after this farce is over. And then, I am not certain.' He pushed away from the door to the horse's stall. 'I must decide soon, though.'

'Seems to me you should go back to your home. Make up with your parents,' Findlay said.

Lucas did not want to hear that.

He leaned against the wall. 'There is another matter. A Mr Hargreave, son of a Scottish earl and one of the guests here, may be planning to court the eldest Wallace daughter. He was a visitor at Dunburn House and something about him concerns me. I cannot like this fellow. I need to know more, if I am to warn her about him.'

'Warn her?' Findlay gave him a sceptical look. 'You really have involved yourself with this family, haven't you?'

'I owe them my life. Miss Wallace especially.' In a way

he owed Findlay his life, too. The batman had kept him from destruction that horrid day.

Findlay rubbed his neck. 'Well, I'll keep my ears open. This lot has a great deal to say about their employers. It takes nothing to get them talking.'

'Hargreave came with Lord and Lady Crawfurd. Their people might know something.' Lucas pushed away from the wall. 'I had better get back to the house.' He gave a wry grin. 'I have my duties, you know.'

The two men bid each other goodnight and Lucas left the stable. The misty rain had stopped, but the air still felt damp and cold. He quickened his step and headed back to the house, where the lights of many candles and lamps shone through almost every window.

He entered the house through the servants' entrance and walked through the corridor towards the servants' stairs that would take him up to the hallway where Dunburn's room was. When he passed the hall, Hargreave's valet stepped in front of him.

'Where were you?' the man asked in his hostile tone.

Lucas straightened and glared at the man like he might at a recalcitrant soldier. 'Explain yourself, man.'

The valet blinked in surprise. 'What?'

'Why do you need to know my whereabouts?'

The man baulked at responding.

'Well?' demanded Lucas.

He still did not speak.

'Why this hostility?' pressed Lucas. He'd nip this in the bud now.

The valet seemed to gain some courage. 'I do not like Englishmen.'

'That is your sole objection?' Lucas lifted a brow.

'Yes.' He tried to look Lucas in the eye, but could not quite meet his steely glare.

Lucas had seen his like before, needing to display a bravado precisely because they felt cowardly inside. Or felt smaller. Lucas knew he was no better than this man who had to make his way in the world by serving the intimate needs of a man such as Hargreave. He actually felt some compassion for the valet.

Lucas spoke in a milder tone. 'I understand that you Scots have reasons to dislike Englishmen. I will try to stay out of your way.'

Lucas might just as easily have intimidated the man with his officer's demeanour. He could have reminded the man he was larger, stronger and accustomed to battle, but this Scottish valet was neither his enemy nor a soldier under his charge. He was just a man trying to get through life the best he could. Like Lucas himself.

Lucas nodded cordially, and the valet, looking surprised and confused, stepped to the side to let Lucas pass. He climbed the stairs and entered the hallway on which was Dunburn's room.

Coming in the other direction, towards her own room, was Mairi, her pale pink dress swirling around her legs as she walked. Should she not be with the other guests after dinner?

'Miss Wallace?'

She lifted her chin as if he had challenged her. 'I developed the headache.'

He could not help but smile. 'Was it that dreadful?' He'd attended many a country house dinner. He knew how wearying it could be, merely sitting and making conversation, especially with people in whose company you did not wish to be.

She rolled her eyes. 'Mr Hargreave seemed unable to leave my side.'

He wished—

But he had no right to wish. Not now he was so tangled in the family's affairs and his own half-truths.

She directed her gaze at him again. 'At least you have tasks to perform. I must be idle.'

He could list her a dozen tasks she would be grateful not to have. Emptying chamber pots, for one. 'Surely something is planned to entertain you. Is there nothing tonight?'

'The ladies are playing the piano and singing, but I did not wish to participate. Not with Hargreave insisting upon turning the pages for me.'

'What do you make of his persistent attention?' Lucas asked.

She blew out a breath. 'Mama thinks he will make me an offer, but I believe that is absurd.'

'Why?' To think of her married to Hargreave was intolerable.

'I cannot imagine that there is a penny left for my dowry and Mr Hargreave is not a man to marry without furthering his own interests.'

'Some men, if wealthy enough in their own right, do not care about such things.' Lucas could not imagine marrying for money—although he'd never had to entertain the prospect.

'Mama and Lady Crawfurd seem to believe he is wealthy enough, but I do not want to marry.'

She didn't want to marry?

He was about to ask her why, but she threw up her hands. 'I've done nothing to encourage the man. I do not understand why he seeks my company.'

His eyes swept over her. 'Do you not? You are quite lovely, you know.'

Her gaze flew to his face. 'Lucas?'

He took a step back. 'Forgive me. I should not have said that.'

'Why did you say it?' she challenged.

He could not help himself. He leaned closer to her again. 'Because it is true. Because I do not believe you know your worth.'

'My worth?' Mairi rasped.

She alone knew that she no longer had worth. The man she'd happened upon on that walk to the village five years ago had stolen whatever was of value about herself, leaving her with nothing.

Lucas looked puzzled. 'Do you not believe me? That you are courageous, intelligent, beautiful, loyal to your family, no matter how they treat you—'

'Stop.' She pushed one hand against his chest and just as quickly realised she was touching him. Their gazes locked and she could not move.

He took her hand in his and held it against his heart.

'You must not speak to me so.' She did not deserve it.

His gaze was soft. 'It is the truth.'

She drank in his words and his admiration as if she were dying of thirst. She was so in need of comfort. She wished he would put his arms around her and simply hold her.

So she would not feel so utterly alone.

Instead he released her hand and stepped back.

And she steeled herself. 'No need to flatter me, Lucas, kind as it was for you to do so.' His flattery at least sounded genuine; Hargreave's always seemed calculated.

There was a clatter of feet on the stairwell and voices approached.

'It is not fair!' It was Davina.

Niven's voice came next. 'Fishing is a man's sport. William and I will see you later in the day.'

Her brother and sister came into view.

When Davina saw Lucas she brightened. 'Lucas! You will take my side, I am certain of it.' She did not give him a chance to refute that statement. 'William and Niven are going fishing tomorrow and they will not take me along with them.'

'There are other activities for the ladies,' Niven said. 'Davina is supposed to do them with Lord Oxmont's daughter. That's the whole reason she was invited to the house party.'

'And why were you invited?' she countered, with hands on her hips.

He leaned right into her face. 'Because William was invited.'

'Well, Elspeth has no need of me tomorrow.' She huffed. 'So there is no reason I should not go fishing with you.'

'It will be cold and it is rugged. Not at all a place for a girl,' he protested.

'Stuff!' she cried. 'You and I have gone fishing dozens of times at home. This is no different.'

'Maybe we don't want girls there,' Niven said, perhaps finally getting to the truth of the matter. 'Maybe we want a man's activity of our own. The other men will be hunting stag and William and I were not invited. You don't see us complaining, though. Not like you.'

'I'm not complaining,' Davina insisted. 'I do not want to sit all day and do sewing or something. I want to be outside. I want to go fishing with you.' She turned to Lucas. 'Tell him, Lucas. Tell him he must take me along.'

Davina excelled at putting people on the spot to make them say or do things they did not want to do.

But apparently Lucas was made of sterner stuff. 'Miss Davina.' He kept his voice low and calm. 'I am not in charge of you here. Not like in Edinburgh. You must discuss this with your mother and father.'

'Mama will say I can go!' Davina marched into her bed-chamber and slammed the door.

William peeked around the corner. 'Is she done yet?'

Niven strode over to him. 'She is impossible! Such a child. Let us see if we can get food in the kitchen. I'm famished.'

When the two boys had left, Mairi looked up at Lucas. They both burst out laughing. And when they stopped, they still stared into each other's eyes.

'Who won that skirmish?' he asked softly.

'Davina,' said Mairi. 'But it concerns me. She must not always think she is entitled to her own way.'

'She is wilful,' he agreed.

Mairi lifted her gaze and met his. Her body felt as if every nerve and muscle had come alive. She wished—

She wished Lucas were a guest instead of a servant, so she might spend her time with him. But even if Lucas were a gentleman or she was an ordinary young woman, would he not despise her for what happened to her?

The thought depressed her. 'I should go to my room to see if I can reason with Davina.'

He reached up and touched her arm. 'Yes. Goodnight, Mairi.'

His touch surprised her, but did not frighten her, which surprised her even more. It was so gentle, yet made her skin tingle and her pulse quicken. He leaned closer, so close his breath brushed her face and the heat of his body warmed her.

Before her assault she used to dream of being kissed by a man. Afterwards, she had not even wanted to be touched, but now, suddenly, Lucas's touch thrilled her. And it seemed as if her lips yearned to taste his. He moved even closer and she rose on tiptoe.

Abruptly he stepped away, leaving her baffled and filled with desire and disappointment. His face was stony. Unreadable. He must feel a kiss between them to be very wrong, yet she yearned to tell him she did not care if their stations in life were unequal. She simply wanted to be held by him.

'That was not well done of me,' he said. 'I must leave you.'

He turned and strode away.

'Goodnight, Lucas,' she whispered and retreated to the room she shared with Davina.

Lucas strode back to the servants' stairway, but merely waited there until he was certain Mairi had entered her room.

What the devil? He'd just about kissed her. He still wanted to kiss her.

There was no reason not to kiss her, though, was there? He was a gentleman, son of an English earl, heir to that earldom. All he need do was tell her. Admit who he was.

Then what? Return to his parents? Accept his fate? Accept their disappointment? His own guilt?

No. He did not want to be Lucas Johns-Ives, the man who would some day gain all that should have been his brother's, the man who had run away and tried to kill himself with drink. The man who had let his brother die.

But could he remain John Lucas?

The money in his purse would eventually run out. What would he do then? Become some Scottish lord's valet or footman? Live a life of changing chamber pots and cleaning someone else's clothes? Serving food or answering doors? Or working in a garden or farm field?

It was good, honest work, all of it, and he had a new respect for those who performed it. Such good, honest work had saved him from himself—that and Mairi's voice pulling him back from the doorway of death—but maybe he only relished the work because he knew he could leave it any time and return to a life of ease. Could Erwin or Robert or even Hargreave's valet do that? They could only look forward to a lifetime of serving people who happened to have been born into the gentry.

As John Lucas he could not kiss Mairi. Or court her. Or ask her to marry him. As Lucas Johns-Ives he'd be a good match for her, but would she want him after she found out he had deceived her and her family about who he was?

He yanked open the stairway door and walked back to Dunburn's room to await the gentleman, undress him and help ready him for bed.

Chapter Sixteen

That night, Mairi lay awake for what seemed like hours, replaying in her mind the almost-kiss from Lucas. Had she tempted him unwittingly? Or did he feel, too, that strange affinity she felt towards him?

She finally slept, but fitfully, and woke the next morning to find herself alone in the bedchamber. She sat up and looked out of the window. It was barely past dawn.

Davina never rose so early, nor was it like her to be so quiet that she wouldn't wake Mairi. Mairi climbed out of bed and hurried to wash herself. She pulled on a dressing gown and went out into the hallway to her mother's room. Without knocking, she opened the door. The curtains were drawn and the room was dark. She could just make out her mother asleep in her bed.

Nellie rose from a chair and tiptoed over to the door. 'Miss Mairi! What may I do for you?' she whispered.

Mairi motioned for the maid to come into the hallway. 'Have you seen Davina?'

'Yes, miss, she woke me a little while ago to help her dress.' Nellie frowned in disapproval. 'She was half-dressed already, needing only for me to do her laces. I told her she should not have walked in the hallway that way. Someone might have seen her, or worse, it might have woken your mother.'

Mairi's insides twisted. 'How was she dressed?'

'In her travelling dress,' Nellie responded. 'But she carried her half-boots and her cloak like she was going outside.'

Davina's travelling dress was the plainest and oldest of the clothes she'd packed for this visit, the sort of dress she'd put on if she planned to go fishing.

Mairi turned to the maid. 'Will you help me dress? Maybe I can catch her.'

They returned to Mairi's room and Mairi slipped out of her dressing gown and nightdress as quickly as she could. She, too, chose one of her plainest and oldest dresses. As Nellie was tying her laces, Mairi glanced out of the window and spied Davina crossing the yard below.

'Where is she going all alone?' Mairi's heart pounded.

'She is alone?' Nellie sounded as alarmed as Mairi. 'She cannot know the land here.'

Mairi quickly put her hair into a plait. 'I need help going after her. Do you know where Mr Lucas would be?'

Nellie answered, 'He sleeps in your father's room.'

'My father should be at breakfast by now. He is to go on the stag hunt today.' She hoped Lucas would not be required to accompany him.

'Would you like me to ask for Mr Lucas below stairs?'

'Would you, Nellie?' She gave her a grateful look. 'And see if Niven and Lord Crawfurd's son have gone out yet, if you can. I will wait in the hall.'

'Right away, miss.' Nellie rushed out.

Mairi pulled on her stockings and her half-boots. She wrapped a woollen scarf around her neck, gathered her cloak and her gloves, and made her way to the hall.

The footman attending the hall enquired if she needed assistance.

'Do you know if Lord Crawfurd's son and the Baron of Dunburn's son went out this morning?' she asked him.

'I believe so,' he responded. 'Two youths, miss?'

'Yes.' It must have been Niven and William. 'With fishing poles?'

'Aye, miss. The very ones.'

At least she knew that much. 'And did Miss Davina Wallace enquire of them as well?'

'The young miss?' He obviously noticed her worry. 'Aye, miss. She asked questions about fishing. I did think it odd.'

'Did she learn where the boys might have gone?'

He frowned. 'Aye. I fear I told her as much.'

She felt sorry for the servant. 'It is difficult not to tell her something she wishes to know. You did nothing wrong.'

She was about to ask him about Lucas, when Lucas appeared in the hall, Nellie following.

'Miss Wallace?' he said formally. 'You wished to speak to me?'

She felt her face flush at the sight of him, but she answered in a similar tone, 'Yes, Lucas. This way, please.' She searched for a room where they might not be overheard and found a small drawing room that looked as if it was meant for waiting callers with no particular status.

'Davina went off alone?' he said as soon as they were private.

'She intends to find Niven and William, I am sure, but she cannot know the land. She should not be out there alone!'

He nodded. 'I will go after her. Let me speak to someone who would know where they went fishing.'

Nellie stood a short distance away, looking worn to a frazzle.

Mairi went over to her and placed her hands on the maid's arms as if to steady her. 'Nellie, thank you so much for finding Lucas. Please get your rest while you are able and do not worry. Lucas will find her.'

'Very well, miss,' the elderly maid said uncertainly. 'If you are certain there is nothing else to be done.'

'You have helped so very much. Just—just do not tell Mama. Say Davina and I took a walk to explore the gardens and we will see her later. She will believe that.'

Nellie nodded, curtsied and walked away with a slight limp, from her arthritic hip, no doubt.

Mairi turned to Lucas. 'I am going with you.'

She expected him to protest. Surely he would not wish to spend time with her after what had happened between them the night before, but he merely nodded. 'Wait here. I must change. I will be quick.'

After he left she sat in one of the chairs and tried to calm herself. But Davina was off by herself on a strange estate and she was too trusting to have any notion of danger. Mairi rose again and paced. If nothing else, she could become lost in the wood or injure herself in a fall. She could wander towards where the gentlemen were hunting stag.

She could come across a man who would see her as prey.

Mairi's anxiety grew. She could barely breathe.

Lucas was not gone more than ten minutes, but it seemed ages until he returned. He'd changed into the clothes he'd worn when they first found him.

'Let's be off,' he said.

She put on her cloak and followed him through a labyrinth of rooms until reaching a door that led to the outside.

'I have directions to the head ghillie's office. We should ask there.'

The head ghillie was with the hunters, but they found a man who could direct them to the best places to fish. They chose one in the direction Davina had been seen walking.

'She left so long ago,' Mairi said. Would they be able to find her?

'There is every chance that she's followed the same directions we are following and will find Niven easily.'

She darted a glance to him. 'Are you trying to patronise me, Lucas? If you are, I do not appreciate it.'

He turned to her and spoke kindly. 'Do not spin in your mind all sorts of calamitous ends to our search. It is most likely she will be safe and unharmed.'

But she could not help her anxiety. 'If you believe that, I wonder why you agreed to come.'

He stopped and faced her directly. 'Because you asked me.' Before she could draw a surprised breath, he started walking again. 'And because she is alone and might need protection.'

So he was not free of worry either. That reassured her more than his consolation.

They must have walked for an hour—and talked little—over fields and through woods before they heard the sounds of water.

'This may be near where Niven is fishing,' he said.

If they'd followed the directions correctly, this was the River Tilt of which the ghillie had spoken. The river was like a blue ribbon threading through the landscape. On one side the mountain, brushed with shades of brown and gold, rose almost straight up, like a wall. Dotted here and there on the mountainside were the red deer, the stags majestic with their crowns of antlers. These were the animals the gentlemen were hunting today and their dignified beauty made Mairi hope they all escaped the hunter's shot.

They walked towards a bend in the river where trees had turned yellow. The views almost made Mairi forget why they were here. To search for her sister. To keep her safe.

Finally, in the distance, they heard voices above the music of the water and the figure of a fisherman could be seen at the river's bank.

'Look!' She pointed and quickened her step.

As they came closer, Lucas said, 'It is Niven.'

Her heart pounded in fear. If Davina was not with them—?

Niven spied them and reacted with surprise. 'Mairi! Lucas! Is everyone to come fishing?'

Sitting together on the bank were William and Davina. William rose.

Mairi ran to her sister. 'Davina! I have been so worried about you!'

Davina met her with a defensive expression. 'Whatever for? Did I not tell you that I wanted to go fishing with Niven and William?'

'But you went off alone!' She wanted to hug her sister. And throttle her.

'I take walks alone at home,' she protested, a fact that also worried Mairi.

Mairi sank down next to her. 'At least you are safe.'

'Of course I am safe!' Davina said.

Niven left the bank of the river and came over to his sisters. 'Mairi! Look at the fish we have caught already!' He showed her the basket with four large fish. 'These are only the keepers—there were lots of small ones we threw back. The fishing here is grand!' He carried the basket over to Lucas. 'Look at these fish, Lucas.'

Lucas might not have shown it, but he, too, breathed a sigh of relief to see Davina safe with her brother. Some how his vow to care for no one and nothing had dissolved into a need to protect all of the Wallaces. He'd certainly felt it in Edinburgh, acutely aware then that the safety of the brother and sister lay solely in his hands.

As it had been with Bradleigh.

But he must not think of him. He turned his attention to the basket of fish Niven proudly showed him. 'Those are fine! The Oxmonts' cook will be quite pleased.'

Davina called over to him, 'Hello, Lucas! Mairi should not have made you come with her. I was perfectly safe.' She laughed. 'Even if I became lost for a little while.'

He did not like to hear that. 'You should not have gone off alone. You might still be lost.'

She smiled enigmatically. 'No harm done.'

'Lucas! Come here. You can practically see the fish swimming!' Niven had returned to the riverbank and picked up his fishing pole.

William had wandered to the riverbank as well.

Lucas joined them and gazed out at the water. Right beneath the surface could be seen dark shapes swimming with the current.

As he watched the water, William came up to him. 'Mr Lucas? May I tell you something?' The youth's expression was serious.

'Of course,' Lucas replied.

William hesitated before speaking. 'Miss Davina did not find us. We found her. We were walking the bank, looking for another spot to fish, and we came upon her.'

'Yes?' Lucas frowned.

'She was not alone,' the boy said. 'She was with Mr Hargreave.'

Lucas really did not like hearing that. 'And?'

William's words came sputtering out. 'And he was standing a wee bit too close to her. Her back was to a tree and he had one arm leaning against it. It—it did not look at all right.'

Lucas felt his insides burn.

William went on. 'As soon as he saw us he moved away from her and she did not seem upset or anything. He acted as if he'd been helping her find us, but I thought it looked strange.' He glanced at his friend. 'I was going to ask Niven if he noticed, but I'm not certain he even saw what I saw.' He made a gruff laugh. 'I am not certain I saw what I saw.'

Lucas suddenly liked this young lad. 'You were right to tell me.' Hargreave knew Davina was only fourteen.

'It did not seem right,' William repeated.

'I agree,' Lucas said. 'I will take care of it. Do not fear.'

He and Mairi stayed a while with her brother and sister, but Lucas knew he could not be gone all day. He'd have to return before Dunburn came back from the hunt. Davina could not be persuaded to come back and she clearly did not want her sister to stay.

'Do you promise not to go off on your own?' Mairi asked her.

'Of course I promise,' Davina responded. 'I want to be with William and Niven. That is why I came.'

'I will make certain no harm comes to her,' William assured Mairi.

Davina regarded him with doe eyes. 'You can depend on William.'

Lucas believed that was true. Niven might not think of his sister as another man's prey, but William sensed it, even if he could not articulate it.

'Stay together, all of you,' Lucas ordered in his sternest officer's voice.

Davina rolled her eyes. 'We will.'

He and Mairi left them, but Mairi turned back for another look, as if they'd disobey as soon as she was gone.

'I think we can trust William to keep Davina in line,' he told her.

She turned back. 'Yes. William. Niven is just as likely to wander off himself and not give his sister a thought.'

They walked along the riverbank, retracing their steps.

'I suppose you are going to say you told me so,' Mairi said after a time.

'Told you so?' he asked.

'You said she'd be safe.'

Her foot slipped and he caught her arm to steady her. 'I hoped she'd be safe,' he clarified, releasing her.

'She doesn't know what could happen when she does these things. First sneaking on the wagon to Edinburgh. Now this.'

'I made certain she was safe in Edinburgh.'

She gave him a sceptical look. 'You left them on their own.'

'They had their orders,' he reminded her. Besides, a little trust sometimes went a long way. 'One slip and they knew they'd be in trouble.'

'One slip might be a fatal one.' Her voice cracked.

He stole a glance at her. Was she talking about Davina or herself?

She stopped and gazed across the river. 'The mountains look so beautiful. It is hard to say what time of year is the most beautiful in Scotland, but right now I'd say October.'

He agreed. It had its own unique beauty. Like her.

The faint sounds of gunfire wafted in the wind.

'The hunt is still on,' she said sadly.

Lucas had heard the gunfire on and off throughout their walk. He pushed away memories the gunfire provoked. 'Maybe that is why we see so many deer on this side of the mountain. They are hiding.'

'Hide well, deer,' she murmured.

They continued walking, crossing a patch of grass. The ground was uneven and again Lucas held her arm to steady her. When he released her, she threaded her arm through his and held on to him as they continued walking.

After a while she asked, 'Will you talk to me about last night, Lucas?'

He knew instantly what she meant. He searched for the right words to say.

'To beg your forgiveness? I should not have touched you.' *Or almost kissed you*, he added silently.

'Why?' she said softly. 'It is not as though you are really a servant, are you, Lucas? You were a soldier.'

This was his chance to tell her who he really was, but the gunfire sounded again.

'I was a soldier, but I grew up in a great house.' Let her believe he was John Lucas. 'In any event, I should not have behaved as I did towards you. It was wrong of me.'

She let go of him and walked a little faster, putting herself a step or two ahead of him. He caught up to her.

'I know you are right,' she said, but her tone was sharp.

Had she wanted the kiss? He'd thought so. He'd been too familiar with her. In his father's house he would not dream of becoming so involved with—say—one of the maids. But she was not a maid and he was not really a butler. How had this become so complicated? In any case, he should have kept his distance from her.

She regarded him with a sad expression, but she did not question him any more. Instead she asked him, 'Tell me about selling our things in Edinburgh. Was it difficult?'

He responded, 'Not too difficult.'

'How did you know where to sell them?' she asked.

She was simply making conversation, he realised. She'd seen some of his pain and had changed the subject to free him of it. He willingly let her steer the talk to Edinburgh and described all he'd done there to get the best prices he could for her family's possessions.

Oxmont Castle came into sight and Lucas regretted he'd soon lose her company. To reach the castle they had to walk through a small wood with tall trees whose autumn leaves made a canopy of orange and red. Ahead of them, a figure emerged from another path. When they came closer they saw it was Hargreave.

He greeted Mairi with a smile. 'Why, Miss Wallace, what a pleasure to encounter you in these lovely woods. Whatever are you doing here?' He glanced at Lucas, but did not ask the obvious question of why she was strolling the grounds with the family butler.

'We were searching for my sister, Davina,' she responded, her voice tightening.

'Your sister?' Hargreave's expression turned to one of concern. 'Is your sister lost?'

Lucas broke in. 'Did you see her, sir?'

Hargreave hesitated a moment before turning to Mairi to answer. 'Why, I did earlier. I did not go hunting, you see, preferring to take a long walk. I assure you, she was not lost. She was with your brother and Lord Crawfurd's son. Did something happen of which I am not aware?'

'No,' Mairi said. 'All is well.'

'Are you heading back to the house?' Hargreave asked.

She hesitated as if reluctant to reply. 'We are.'

He extended his arm. 'Then allow me to escort you. It would be my pleasure.'

She darted a glance at Lucas, one that seemed to say she did not find any pleasure in his escort. There was nothing Lucas could do but drop back and follow them.

When they reached the house, Hargreave continued to escort Mairi up the stairs. Lucas used the servants' stairs and emerged in the hallway as Hargreave was leaving Mairi's door. The two men were alone in the hallway.

'Well, Lucas,' Hargreave said with false cheer. 'What a surprise to see you here at Oxmont Castle.'

Lucas ignored the man's remark. 'I am glad to have this moment alone with you.' He fell in step with Hargreave as they strolled towards another wing of the house.

'Well?' Hargreave asked as they turned the corner and entered another corridor. He looked amused.

Lucas blocked his path. 'You were seen with Davina today. Her brother found her with you, not the other way around. Do not dally with that child, do you hear me, Hargreave? Stay away from her.'

Hargreave laughed. '*You* are saying this to *me*?'

Lucas raised his voice. 'I am and you will listen to me, sir. She is fourteen. *Fourteen.* Stay away from her.'

Behind Hargreave's back Lucas noticed Hargreave's valet turn the corner and step into the hallway, but the man retreated immediately.

Hargreave's expression blackened. 'Who are you to order me around?'

Lucas leaned in closer. 'I serve that family and I will not see them hurt in any way. Not by you or anyone.'

'You are that attached to them?' Hargreave smirked. 'To the daughters, I would guess, ludicrous as that is.' He patted Lucas's arm condescendingly. 'Do not worry about Miss Davina, Sassenach. It is not the younger one who interests me, pretty though she is.'

Lucas pushed him against the wall, pinning him there. 'Do not cross me in this, Hargreave. I've seen your kind before.' He released him. 'And dealt with them.'

Hargreave straightened his clothing. 'I could have you arrested for assaulting your betters!'

'Try it, Hargreave.' Hargreave was not his better. 'I will

explain what provoked it. Your attempt at seducing the innocent child of a baron.'

Hargreave laughed again. 'She was a shameless flirt.'

Lucas leaned forward again. 'Say another word like that and I will flatten you.'

Hargreave dusted himself off. 'We shall see who gets the better of whom.'

Chapter Seventeen

In the drawing room before dinner there were even more guests who'd arrived that day, but Hargreave waited only for Miss Wallace. When he saw her walk in, he was ready with a glass of wine for her.

He crossed the room to her and handed her the wine. 'I assume your sister is accounted for still?' He smiled.

'Yes.' She took the glass. 'She is with the young people in another room for the evening.'

'Your sister is a charming girl.' Very charming. And nubile. One of the new guests greeted him and he acknowledged the man with a nod. He turned back to Miss Wallace. 'Your butler helped you search for your sister?'

'Yes.' She seemed puzzled he would ask.

Hargreave had taken a dislike to the man even before he had acted the ruffian with him. There was something in the butler's demeanour, even back at Dunburn House.

Arrogance? No, not quite.

'He seems an encroaching sort, do you not think?' he said to Miss Wallace. 'Not quite knowing his place.'

The butler certainly had acted out of place that morning. Using brute force on a man far above his station.

Miss Wallace's eyes narrowed. 'His place? His place was to help me when I asked. Which he did.'

Hargreave's smile faltered. He had not expected her to defend the fellow. 'Would it not have made more sense if you had asked one of Oxmont's footmen? They would have known the land.'

One brow lifted. 'Do you mean I should have pulled one of Lord Oxmont's footmen from his duties? Gone off alone with a man I did not know,' she retorted, 'and left open the possibility that my sister would become the subject of gossip?' She gave him what seemed like a patronising smile. 'I am certain, sir, that *you* will not tell tales of why she went off by herself to join her brother fishing, but I would not depend on someone else's discretion.'

'You are right, of course.' She was being troublesome. He intended to be in charge of her, not to make her a sparring partner. 'I meant only to warn you about servants who attempt to become too friendly.'

'I am certain your advice was kindly meant,' she added, 'but Lucas is the finest…butler our family could hope to employ.' He did not know what was behind her words, but he intended to regain control of the conversation.

Dinner was announced and, as on the night before, Hargreave offered her his arm. In the dining room the table had been made longer than before to accommodate the newly arrived guests. Precedence dictated that he and Miss Wallace would sit near each other, but he just as easily might have been seated across the table from her instead of next to her, which would prevent any further conversation. Thanks to Lady Crawfurd, he had engineered the possibility of always sitting next to her.

As dinner progressed, the lady and gentleman on the other side of him began a discussion about titles.

'This is Scotland,' the gentleman said. 'We are all Scots whether we have a title or nae. It is who you are that matters, not what title you inherit.' He was an untitled younger son, but a member of the House of Commons and, thus, a man who fought for all Scots.

'But a title is a measure of prestige,' the lady said.

Hargreave joined their conversation. 'A title automatically conveys respect, as it ought. We may all be Scots, sir, but we are not all equal. Superiority over the common man is proven in the possession of a title.' He turned to Miss Wallace. 'Would you not agree, Miss Wallace?'

She seemed to weigh her answer carefully. 'I believe we are all more alike than we are different, no matter what our status. That said, I am intensely proud of my family's heritage.' She shrugged. 'So, sir, I am all contradictions.'

He laughed, but it was the thought that the title would soon be his which kept the smile on his face. 'Indeed you are, but charmingly so.'

Mairi was relieved when the dinner was over and the ladies retired to the drawing room for tea. Her mother and Lady Crawfurd gestured for her to sit with them.

'It looks as if it is going splendidly,' her mother gushed. 'He favoured you both nights! I am certain he intends to make an offer.'

'He has money, you know,' Lady Crawfurd added. 'And he is the son of an earl. I could not be happier for you!'

Mairi attempted to diffuse their enthusiasm. 'Do not put the cart before the horse, Mama, Lady Crawfurd.'

Lady Crawfurd patted her hand. 'I have a feeling about this, my dear.'

And just as Mairi feared, when the men joined the ladies, Hargreave managed to sit next to her. After some inane conversation, he gave her that smile that had begun to make her cringe.

'I feel a need to stretch my legs,' he said. 'Would you

care to take a turn in the gallery? A nice walk up and down should do the trick.'

Her mother and Lady Crawfurd beamed.

She did not wish to spend any time alone with him, but she could not bear to sit idle in the drawing room either.

'Very well,' she said. At the very least it would afford her the opportunity to put a stop to his attentions once and for all.

Findlay sought out Lucas and the two men stood outside while Findlay smoked a pipe.

'I have nothing useful on Hargreave,' Findlay told Lucas. 'Lord Crawfurd's coachmen know only that the two families are friends.'

That much Lucas already knew. He told Findlay about his search for Davina that day and about William seeing Hargreave with her. 'He saw only enough to give him concern,' Lucas explained. 'I confronted Hargreave about it—'

'You confronted him?' Findlay shook his head. 'You are supposed to be a valet or a butler. You don't confront them, sir. It's akin to me confronting an officer.'

Lucas shrugged. 'Well, I did confront him—rather forcefully, too. But he was taunting me. Speaking of the girl in a manner which was not to be borne.'

'Do you think he seduced her?' Findlay asked, drawing on his pipe.

'Not yet.' Lucas's anger rose again at the thought. 'I warned him off fairly sternly.'

Findlay exhaled. 'Then I think it matters not what ye learn of him. You already ken he is a bad one.' He peered at Lucas through his cloud of smoke. 'But what of you? Are you in fair shape? Outside of skelping your betters.'

'Skelping?' Another foreign Scots word.

'Striking.'

'I did not strike him,' Lucas clarified.

'Are you in fair shape, then?' Findlay persisted.

'I'm no longer fevered, if that is what you mean,' he answered. 'I mean to see the Wallaces set in fair shape. After that I do not know.' Truth was, he did not want to think beyond returning to Dunburn House after the party.

A maid came to the doorway and called out, 'If ye want dinner, ye ought to come now.'

Findlay nodded to Lucas. 'I'll bid ye goodnight, then.'

'I'm grateful to you, Findlay,' Lucas said. 'Goodnight.'

Findlay returned to the stables where their dinner would be served and Lucas re-entered the house. He made his way to the servants' hall and took his place at the table along with the lady's maids and valets and other senior servants of the guests. Lucas was definitely an outsider, even more so for being English, so, the conversation went past him. He did, however, notice Hargreave's valet staring at him. Was he going to have a conflict with the valet as well?

When dinner was over, Lucas had no wish to linger and even less of a wish to confine himself to Dunburn's room. He put on his topcoat again and went outside. It wasn't long until he heard a man's voice behind him call out, 'Mr Lucas!'

He turned. In the dim light of evening he could not make out the person until he came close. It was Hargreave's valet.

Lucas sighed and braced himself for yet another confrontation.

But the man stopped some distance away. 'May I speak with you?'

Lucas nodded assent.

'I overheard you and Mr Hargreave in the hallway today,' the man said.

'I saw you.' The valet could be Hargreave's witness to

Lucas's…rough treatment. That could mean trouble—for him and for the Wallaces.

'You accused Hargreave of improper behaviour?' the man challenged.

'Not precisely,' Lucas responded. 'I warned him against improper behaviour.'

'I—I wanted you to know—' The valet hesitated as if unsure what to say. 'I wanted you to know that such behaviour is common in him. Hargreave is not…gentlemanly.'

Lucas's brows rose in surprise. He spoke plainly. 'You think Hargreave capable of seducing a young girl?'

The valet's voice grew stronger. 'I know he is.'

Now Lucas was puzzled. 'Why tell me this?' Surely this was disloyalty.

'I am fortunate to have this job,' he responded. 'But Hargreave is not a good man. I've seen it. With one of the young maids.' He rubbed his face. 'I have a sister in service. I wouldna want any man to take advantage of her in the same manner.'

If Hargreave ever discovered his valet confiding in him, no doubt the man would lose his job. Lucas stepped towards him and extended his hand. 'I am grateful you told me. This confirms my suspicions.'

The valet accepted the handshake.

'If you learn anything else that concerns you, I hope you will let me know,' Lucas added.

The valet nodded and went to leave. He turned back. 'The daughter. I've seen her. She is what he likes.' He disappeared into the darkness.

Lucas walked behind the house, intending to sit on a bench in the garden until he must return to the bedchamber and wait for Dunburn. He heard a squeal and he could make out figures in the garden. It looked much like a game of tag, but he could not be certain. Two ladies. Two men. He moved closer. One of them dashed by, laughing. Not ladies and gentlemen. Girls and boys. It was Davina and, he guessed, the other young people.

'Miss Davina!' he called.

She stopped and looked around and laughed when she saw him. 'Lucas! We are playing a new game. Would you like to play?' She wore a shawl, but nothing suitable for protection from the chilly evening.

'Should you be outside at this hour?' he asked.

She giggled. 'Elspeth says no, but who is to make us come in?'

'Me, I think.' He turned towards where he thought the others might be. 'Niven! William!'

They all came to him.

'You should go in before you alarm your hosts with your absence,' he told them.

'Yes,' William said. 'Lucas is right. We should go in.'

The other girl looked at him with worried eyes.

'Elspeth,' Davina said. 'This is our—our butler, Lucas. He is acting as Papa's valet, because Wilfred is much too old for the journey.'

'Lady Elspeth.' Lucas bowed like a proper servant.

They all headed to a garden entrance and walked through a labyrinth of corridors before entering a drawing room.

'Miss Davina, one moment,' Lucas said. He gestured for her to walk a distance away so he could speak in private.

'Tell me what happened between you and Hargreave today,' he commanded.

Her mouth opened in surprise. Then her cheeks coloured as if she were embarrassed. 'How did you know—? Oh, I suppose Niven said I was with Mr Hargreave.'

'Tell me,' Lucas demanded.

'He was taking a walk and I told him I was looking for Niven and he helped me find them. He was very charming.'

'Did he behave improperly in any way?'

'No!' she protested. Then she changed her tone. 'Oh, well, he was all flattery and nonsense like that, but I knew he was not serious, because he is going to marry Mairi. At least, I think he is.'

Lucas gave her a piercing look. 'You are telling me the whole?'

She nodded her head. 'Mairi would say I was acting like a flirt, but I was just practising. I think he was pretending, too, for a wee bit. Pretending like he was going to kiss me, but then we found Niven and William and it was all a game.'

It sounded more like a narrow escape.

Lucas held her gaze. 'You must not play such games with Mr Hargreave, Davina. You must not be alone with him. Your reputation depends on it.' He intensified his gaze. 'Promise me.'

She rolled her eyes. 'Oh, very well. I promise, but, I tell you, you do not have to worry, because he is sweet on Mairi, not me.'

He leaned back. 'Remember. You've given your word.'

'Yes…' She groaned. 'May I go now?'

He waved her away and hoped she had listened to him.

Mairi's anxiety rose as she and Hargreave approached the gallery. No one else was walking through what was a long, dimly lit room filled with portraits of Oxmont ancestors and paintings by Dutch masters.

'I am delighted you agreed to this little promenade,' he said smoothly. 'I have wanted to be private with you—'

Fear crawled up her back. 'I did not know we would be alone here and you must see that it is most improper. I would rather see the gallery another time.'

Before he could argue, she started back towards the drawing room.

'Miss Wallace, I had hoped—' he started to say, catching up to her.

'Mr Hargreave, we must return to the party.' She did not have to explain.

They reached the corridor that led to the drawing room.

He touched her arm. 'I wish you would wait a moment. It gives me such pleasure to be in your company.'

She brushed off his touch and faced him directly. 'It is clear to me that you have sought out my company, both here and at Dunburn House. Why is that, sir?'

He blinked, but appeared to compose his features into a smile. 'I thought my intentions were obvious, my dear. I wish to court you, to offer you marriage, but I did not wish to speak of it before the time was right.' He gave her an earnest look. 'Is the time right at this moment?'

She ignored that question. 'Why would you wish to make an offer for me? Marriage to me cannot bring you any advantage.'

He drew her closer, even though anyone could appear in the corridor at any moment. 'I would be prepared to overlook any...deficiencies in your dowry.'

She pushed him away. 'You assume my dowry is insufficient?' Her eyes flashed. 'Then there can be no advantage to you.'

His gaze flicked over her. 'You do not think you have other attractions?'

Lucas's words came back to her—*I do not believe you know your worth*—the same sentiment, but Lucas's words had not made her feel sick inside.

'I will not trifle with you. I do not wish to marry you.' There. She could not make it more definite.

'You refuse me?' His demeanour changed suddenly and he was no longer smiling.

Her fear started to creep back, but she pushed it away. You should look elsewhere. Not to me.'

He glared at her. 'I cannot believe you. My offer is more than you ought to expect in your situation.' His gaze narrowed. 'Who put you up to refusing me?'

'I beg your pardon?' She was taken aback.

'You cannot have come to this conclusion on your own,' he insisted. 'Someone must have put you up to it. Not your parents, I am certain. With their debts, I am certain they would be more than eager to see you married to me.'

How insulting. Believing she did not possess her own mind, let alone her own judgement.

'You purport to know many things—my family's finances, my parents' opinions, my ability to judge for myself—'

'I *do* know your family has serious debts,' he insisted. 'The rest is easily surmised.'

She straightened. 'You *think* you know.' Because those debts would soon be paid and he could not know about that.

In any event, she'd had enough of him. She moved to walk past him.

He blocked her way. 'Someone has poisoned you against me. It is the only explanation.'

She did not even credit that statement with a response.

'It was that butler!' he said, his voice like a growl. 'The butler. I will wager he told tales about me.'

She took a step back. 'Lucas?'

Hargreave sputtered, 'Whatever he told you about me and your sister is not true. He threatened to ruin me in your eyes. You cannot trust that man.'

She gripped his arm, forgetting everything else. 'What you and my sister?'

He looked unnerved for a moment, but quickly collected himself. 'Nothing. Nothing. That is the point. I happened to meet your sister on her walk and saw her safely to your brother, as I thought you would wish me to do. That Sassenach butler threatened to make more of it.'

But she heard only that he'd been alone with Davina. She released him and spoke in a low, trembling voice. 'Leave my sister alone, do you understand me? Stay away from her!'

He lifted his hands in a helpless gesture. 'Really, Miss Wallace. You misunderstand. She is a child, after all. I merely made certain she reached your brother safely. No matter what your butler says.'

Lucas had said nothing to her. She would speak to him of that. 'Leave me alone as well!'

She started to stride off, but he caught her arm. 'I am not giving up, Miss Wallace. I *will* renew my proposal and you *will* say yes.'

She pried his fingers off her. 'Do not touch me!'

Someone appeared at the far end of the corridor and she took the chance to escape Hargreave. The detestable man!

Never would she marry him! Never! She fled to the stairs and strode directly to the door of her father's bed-chamber.

She opened it and burst into the room. 'Lucas! Lucas! Are you here?'

The bedroom was empty, so she looked inside the dressing room where he probably slept. He was not there.

'Lucas, where are you?' she whispered, stepping back into the bedchamber.

At that moment the door opened and Lucas stood framed in the doorway. 'Mairi?'

'Where were you?' she demanded.

'Below stairs.' He entered the room and put his topcoat on a nearby chair. 'Why? What has happened?'

'You know what has happened.' Her anger poured out

on to him. 'What happened between Hargreave and Davina and why did you not tell me?'

His expression told her he knew something. 'I had no opportunity to tell you.' He spoke in a low calm voice and his gaze upon her was gentle. 'I do not think anything happened, but that is not to say nothing could have happened. I do not trust Hargreave. He lied to us when he said he saw Davina with Niven and William. He'd already been with her when she was looking for Niven.'

'There is more to tell,' she guessed.

He stood close to her, but being close to him felt nothing like being near Hargreave.

His voice remained composed. 'Davina said—'

'Davina said!' Her anger erupted again. 'You spoke with Davina?'

'Yes. Only a moment ago.'

How could he have spoken to Davina about this and not her? She waved that thought away. 'So what did she say?'

He took a breath. 'Hargreave apparently flattered and charmed her, but that is all. She thought it a game.'

That sounded like Davina. 'She has no idea. Everything is a game to her.' Mairi had tried to warn her. 'I must try to talk to her again.'

'I warned Hargreave,' Lucas said.

She glanced up. That explained why Mr Hargreave had mentioned Lucas.

'I warned him not to trifle with her,' Lucas said. 'I think he will listen, but I also told Davina to stay away.' He lifted a shoulder. 'I fear she does not put any credit in what I said. She thinks Hargreave is interested in you, not her.'

She leaned against the bedpost. 'He wants to marry me.'

His expression stiffened. 'Did you accept him?'

'Of course not,' she snapped. 'But he says I will marry him anyway.'

She remembered the anger in Hargreave's eyes, remembered his grip on her arm. So much like before. Her body began to tremble as it had after the soldier had left. She could not calm herself.

Lucas took a step closer and enveloped her in his arms. Instead of panic, his arms comforted her. His chest was warm against her ear and his steady heartbeat calmed her. She savoured the scent of him, the strength of him. Her trembling stopped, the fear dissipated, the memories vanished. She simply felt safe in his arms.

And he held her a long time, but eventually he gently eased her away. 'You cannot be found in here with me, Mairi,' he murmured. 'You need to leave.'

She looked up at him. 'What am I to do, Lucas? Mama and Papa will want me to marry him. He is wealthy.'

'When your father's debts are paid, his wealth will not matter.' He touched her arm, but gently. 'You will decide what is best for you.'

Lucas. Such a contrast to Hargreave.

Lucas's strong arms lent her strength. She moved into them and again he embraced her.

But he also released her. 'You must go, Mairi.'

She nodded and backed away. She peeked out of the doorway to make certain no one saw her leave.

What would their fellow house guests think if they caught her in the arms of the butler in her father's bedchamber? She'd already be condemned if they knew what had happened to her five years ago. Ironically, those same people would likely applaud a marriage with Hargreave.

But, as she fled down the hall, she realised that the only place she wished to be was back in Lucas's arms.

Chapter Eighteen

Lucas stared at the door after she left. Holding her had shaken him down to his boots. She helped ease the ache inside him that never seemed to go away. She'd roused his emotions—and his desire—and he worked hard to tamp them down again. He didn't want to feel anything. Life was less painful that way.

In the solitude of Dunburn's bedchamber, there was nothing to do but think, and his thoughts kept drifting back to her. How her face glowed when she'd gazed at the beauty and majesty of the Scottish landscape earlier in the day. How wistful she sounded when she'd whispered to the deer on the mountain. How fiercely she cared about her sister and brother. There was something more, though, a pain she held deep inside her. Her pain seemed to call to his own, like kindred spirits intertwining.

He opened the window and leaned out, gulping in the cold night air. This dead time was making his mind whirl and he guessed he had another two hours before Dunburn would retire for the night. He closed the window and headed below stairs again. Perhaps the servants had managed to pilfer some whisky, not unheard of at a house party such as this. He craved the oblivion of drink. He'd even be willing to pay for a bottle, but what butler did that?

In the servants' hall, Anderson, the footman who'd been mildly helpful the first day, was lounging in a chair. The footman lifted a bottle. 'Care for a wee bit?'

Lucas nearly wrenched it from the man's hand, but instead of the comfort he expected, the drink turned sour in his mouth.

He sank into the chair next to the footman and nodded thanks anyway.

Anderson took another swig from the bottle. 'Need a wee swallow to make it through the night.' He inclined his head. 'They are still at it above stairs.'

'At it?' Lucas repeated.

'Card playing, whisky drinking and gossiping,' he said. 'Tuneless playing and even worse singing.' He groaned. 'I dislike these house parties. The work never stops.'

'At the moment I have too much idle time,' Lucas said. Too much time to think.

'Some lads have all the luck.' Anderson rose from his chair and ambled towards the door. Before leaving, though, he turned back to Lucas. 'Are you bored enough to do some actual work?'

Anything was better than the thoughts whirling through his head. 'What do you propose?'

'Well, it would not do for you to be seen serving the guests, but I am supposed to set up the breakfast room, among about a dozen other tasks. No one would see you setting the tables.'

Lucas rose to his feet. 'Show me what needs to be done.'

He helped Anderson carry up stacks of plates and napkins to set the tables. Had he ever realised all the work that was done behind the scenes? From the breakfast room he could hear the sounds of the entertainment, people talking and laughing, someone playing the pianoforte.

Had Mairi returned to the entertainments? he wondered. He was thinking about her entirely too much.

At least those thoughts were of the present and future, instead of the past, but it all mixed together and the only clear path he could see to the future led him places he did not wish to go.

He placed the plates and napkins the proper distance apart, using the measuring rod Anderson provided him. It was exacting but mindless work.

Someone stopped in the doorway and Lucas looked up. It was a man in a Scots Greys uniform, an officer Lucas had met once or twice in Brussels before the battle.

'Captain?' the man said in a disbelieving tone. 'Johns-Ives? What the devil are you doing?'

Good God. Who would have ever thought he'd meet someone else he knew in Scotland? First Findlay. Now this fellow.

No use pretending he wasn't who the man thought he was. 'I am found out,' Lucas admitted.

The man entered the room, getting an even closer look. 'You are a footman? But you are an earl's son!'

'A reversal of fortune,' Lucas said. 'I'd be obliged if you would not speak of me to anyone.'

'But a footman?' the man said incredulously. 'How can it be? Surely any reversal of fortune could not sink you so low.'

Lucas felt the insult. Footmen did honest work, after all.

But he was not going to debate it. 'May I count on your discretion?' he asked instead.

'Why, yes,' the man said. 'I do see why you would desire it.'

Lucas nodded, but glanced away. 'I should not be seen conversing with guests.' He picked up the empty tray. 'If you will excuse me, I must return to the kitchen.'

'Of course.' The man stepped away.

Lucas left as quickly as he could. The Wallaces would stay at the castle for a full two weeks. He feared the Scots Grey would not be able to keep a confidence that long.

Lucas returned the tray to the pantry and went back to Dunburn's bedchamber. Now he had something new to occupy his mind.

He did not really care if the house guests discovered he was an earl's son. He need not see any of these people again, but think how his subterfuge would embarrass the Wallaces. They did not deserve to be made fools of on his account.

He could just see the hurt and censure in Mairi's eyes if he were exposed in front of their friends.

When Dunburn finally came in, he was staggering with drink.

'A bonny time!' Dunburn cried out, too loudly. 'A bonny time. Played cards mostly.'

'Cards? For stakes?' That did not sound good.

'Keep your head. I win at cards.' He swayed as Lucas helped him off with his coat.

'Then, Baron, I beg you, walk away while you are ahead.' Gambling, even friendly games at house parties, always led to losses.

'Dinnae fear. I've been playing with Mr Hargreave.' Lucas unbuttoned his waistcoat. 'Grand fellow! You may know he wants to marry Mairi—*marry Mairi*—' He broke into a fit of laughter. 'Ah, me! Whew!' He caught his breath. 'As I was saying—' He lifted a finger, making it hard for Lucas to slip off the man's waistcoat. 'He wants to marry my daughter, so he's trying to butter me up. So I am winning!' He collapsed into a chair.

Lucas pulled off the man's boots. 'Sir, do not play cards. You cannot afford more debt.'

'Playing for pennies, Lucas, my boy. For the enjoyment of it.'

Lucas managed to get Dunburn into his nightclothes and quickly helped him climb into bed. In moments the man was snoring loudly. How Lucas wished he could find a decent bed to sleep in, one with more privacy…and quiet. But, then, he'd endured far worse on campaign in the Peninsula.

At least it was not Hargreave he was serving. Lucas felt sorry for Hargreave's valet, having to dress, undress and otherwise clean a man he despised and having no other prospect for work. At least for Lucas this was temporary.

Perhaps when Dunburn hired more servants there would be a position for Hargreave's valet. Lucas could try to arrange something.

He retreated to the dressing room and the cot that was too small for his six-foot frame.

For the next three days, Lucas saw only glimpses of Mairi, never enough to speak with her. He had no way of telling whether Hargreave still pursued her. He had as much difficulty keeping watch over Davina, but she seemed mostly in the company of the Oxmonts' daughter and the daughter seemed well supervised.

His valet duties were not at all demanding and he had quite a bit of free time. He walked the estate and observed the running of it, from the kitchen to the stables to the farm workers and shepherds. As a boy he'd spent a considerable amount of time around the servants and workers on his father's estate, but he'd not really thought about how an estate ought to be run. His idle time gave him plenty of opportunity to do so here. He even befriended the head ghillie, who was quite willing to answer questions. Proud of how well he performed his duties, the ghillie never asked why a butler had such an interest in estate management.

Lucas's interest was on Dunburn's behalf. He learned ways Dunburn could make his estate more efficient. The Baron had no interest in discussing estate management while Lucas tended to him here, but when they returned to Dunburn House, Lucas could shed the role of butler and push for his ideas to be discussed.

Perhaps he would stay long enough to see that Dunburn successfully implemented some cost-saving plans. After all, he had no other place he wished to go. He knew he could not stay for ever, but perhaps a few more weeks…

This day was clear and sunny and crisp like only an autumn day could be. A good day for hunting grouse, which was what the gentlemen were doing. Niven and William were included this time, Niven had excitedly told Lucas.

Lucas had gone to the stables to spend time with Findlay, but his former batman was helping with the hunt. Lucas could not abide the idea of going back inside the house, though. The servants of the other guests lingered in the servants' hall, playing cards or passing the time with each other. Although more of them spoke to him, he was still the Sassenach outsider. Perhaps they sensed somehow he was a true outsider, not a servant at all.

He took a chance there would be no objections to him walking around one of the ponds in the vast walled garden. As he made his way there, he almost turned around. There were others walking there—a man and Davina and the Oxmont daughter.

Lucas stepped on to the path in front of them as they got close.

'Lucas!' Davina greeted him with a mixture of pleasure and dismay.

'Good morning, Miss Davina.' He bowed to her friend. 'Lady Elspeth.'

Davina gave a nervous giggle. 'You remember Lucas, Elspeth. You met him when we played outside the other day.'

'I remember,' Lady Elspeth said quietly. This girl did not look at all comfortable.

Lucas directed his steeliest gaze at Hargreave. 'I would speak with you, sir.'

'We'll go away,' Elspeth said.

'No,' Hargreave countered. 'I do not let servants dictate to me.'

'Do not be nonsensical, Mr Hargreave.' Davina giggled. 'Lucas is more than a servant.'

'Is he?' Hargreave raised one eyebrow.

Lucas shook his head at Davina and she clamped her mouth shut.

'In what way?' Hargreave asked.

'He's—he's our butler,' Davina replied.

Hargreave made a derisive sound. 'Well, I do not allow *butlers* to dictate to me. So I will take my leave and spare you ladies any unpleasantness.' He bowed to them and strode off and left the garden through the gate.

Davina put her hands on her hips. 'Now do not chastise me, Lucas. I did not tell him anything. And just so you know, we happened upon Hargreave by accident and he desired to ask me about Mairi. She is being so difficult. He does not know how to proceed. He asked my advice.'

Hargreave needed a fourteen-year-old's advice on having his proposal of marriage accepted? Lucas doubted that.

Elspeth spoke up. 'Well, I am glad he left. I cannot say that I liked him very much.'

'Sound judgement, my lady,' Lucas said. He turned to Davina. 'Do you really think he needed your advice?'

'Well, I do know Mairi better than anyone,' she responded.

Unbidden, the thought came to Lucas. *No, I might know her better, because you cannot see how hard she strives for you and your brother.* Still, there was so much of Mairi he did not know at all. So much he wanted to know.

And never would.

'If you want what is best for her, then perhaps you should honour her decision not to marry a man she cannot like.' He paused, then asked, 'How is your sister faring?'

Davina rolled her eyes. 'She finds the house party tedious—' She turned to Lady Elspeth. 'Forgive me for saying so, Elspeth. You know *I* do not think it is tedious.' She spoke to Lucas again. 'Every day there is an entertainment and tonight there is to be a ball. Elspeth and I will be allowed to come down and dance one set with William and Niven and we are over the moon about it. Mairi is not. But we have a surprise for her. A new dress for the ball. It's an old one of Elspeth's mother's and we have remade it into today's fashion.'

Lucas would like to see Mairi in a ball gown.

He averted his gaze. He thought about her entirely too much.

'I hope you will all have an enjoyable evening.' He bowed to them. 'Now I must also leave you.' He directed a severe look at Davina. 'Remember, you gave me your word about Mr Hargreave.'

She rolled her eyes. 'I remember.'

That evening after Davina and Elspeth had dressed for the ball in Elspeth's bedchamber with Elspeth's maid to help them, they burst into the room Mairi shared with Davina.

'You both look so beautiful!' Mairi said truthfully. 'And so grown up!'

The girls beamed with pleasure.

'Elspeth lent me one of her dresses. Is it not lovely?' Davina spun around.

'Very lovely.' In fact, Davina looked ravishing. Mairi feared she would turn the head of every man at the ball. She was both proud of her sister and fearful that her allure would prove a danger to her. 'Have you come to help me dress?' Mairi asked.

The girls giggled.

'We have a surprise for you!' Davina cried.

'Stay where you are,' Elspeth said as she opened the door.

A young maid with another gown draped in her arms stepped into the room.

'This is Innis, my maid,' Elspeth explained.

'And the gown is for you!' Davina took it from the maid's hands and placed it against herself to show Mairi what it was like.

It was a pale green silk with an overskirt of white net that made the cloth shimmer when it moved. The neckline, puffed sleeves and hem were trimmed in narrow white lace with green ribbon laced through it. It was the prettiest dress Mairi had ever seen.

'I cannot wear this!' she cried. 'It must belong to someone else.'

'It is my mother's ball gown from last year,' Elspeth said. 'And we asked her if we could make it over for you. She said yes.'

'We've been working on it for two days!' Davina cried. 'You must wear it.'

'It will go well with your colouring, miss.' The maid held the dress against her. 'It makes your eyes look bluer,' she added. 'And I have a matching green ribbon for your hair.'

All three of them looked at her expectantly.

'Very well.' Mairi did not have the heart to disappoint them. 'I will try it on.'

She removed her dressing gown and the maid helped her into the dress.

'Let us see! Let us see!' Davina cried excitedly.

She turned so the girls could see first.

Davina clapped her hands. 'It is perfect!'

Mairi turned towards the mirror. The maid was correct. The green gown somehow brought out the blue in her eyes. The bodice fit her figure perfectly.

'Yes. It even fits you very well,' the maid said. 'Now we will take the dress off and I will arrange your hair.'

The young woman used a papillote to create a frame of curls around Mairi's face.

'What else did you do today besides sewing this beautiful dress?' Mairi asked the girls while Innis worked. 'Weren't William and Niven at the hunt? You were on your own, then.'

'We took a walk in the garden,' Davina said, adding, 'Guess who we happened upon?'

Oh, dear! She'll say Hargreave. 'Please do not make me guess.'

'We saw Lucas!'

Lucas. Mairi's shoulders relaxed. How she missed Lucas. She'd hardly seen him since—since he'd put his arms around her and held her against his warm body.

Elspeth looked at her friend. 'We also saw Mr Hargreave, Davina.'

Exactly as Mairi had feared.

Davina waved her hand. 'That was a trifle. You do not want to hear about that.'

'I certainly do,' insisted Mairi. 'Especially as you know I do not want you spending time with him.'

'I cannot like him,' Elspeth admitted.

Davina rolled her eyes at her, but turned to Mairi. 'Really, Mairi. Just because you do not want him—'

'That is no reason for him to befriend you.' Mairi was tiring of having this conversation over and over with Davina. 'He has no business passing his time with girls as young as yourselves.'

'If you will *listen* to me, you will hear the reason he walked with us.' Davina huffed. 'He wanted to speak with me, because of *you*. He wants to marry you.'

'That is his misfortune,' Mairi said.

Hargreave had mostly stayed away from her, but not entirely. He'd been exceedingly polite and respectful, but Mairi sensed a simmering resentment beneath his civility.

'I wish you would not talk with him about me.' Mairi added, 'Do not talk to him at all.' She just wanted him to go away.

And she wished Lucas would stay. She feared he would leave once they returned from the house party. He'd stayed so much longer than the ten days the doctor had dictated.

That seemed so long ago.

Perhaps he would stay and become her father's man of business. He could help her father and mother manage their money. Then she could still see him.

They merely needed to get through this horrid house party.

'There!' Innis said. Mairi's head was a mass of twisted tissue paper. 'Next we will do your face.'

'My face?' Mairi looked at her in the mirror.

'Just a tint of rouge for your cheeks and lips. Then a little powder. No one will guess, I promise.'

Davina tittered. Mairi shot her and Elspeth a look. 'You've tinted your cheeks and lips?'

'You did not know, did you?' Davina moved her face closer.

'No,' admitted Mairi. 'But I would not tell Mama or Papa.'

'Of course not!' Both girls nodded vigorously.

Innis was true to her word. Even Mairi would not have guessed she'd tinted her cheeks and lips. She was helped into the gown again and sat at the dressing table for Innis to arrange her hair. Innis pulled off the papers, leaving a cascade of curls. When the maid finished dressing her hair, curls framed Mairi's face and tumbled from the ribbon high on her head.

'That looks very pretty,' Elspeth said.

Innis gathered her things. Mairi thanked the girl. 'You've done wonders!' She must give the girl some vails when they left.

Mairi put on her pearl pendant necklace and pearl earrings, the two other pieces of jewellery she'd kept besides her garnets.

Davina surveyed her. 'She will dazzle everyone, will she not, Elspeth?'

Mairi did not want men looking at her, but it was too late to change into her old ball gown and dress her hair plainly.

'I suppose we should go,' she said without enthusiasm.

The three stepped into the hallway.

Davina cried, 'There's Lucas.'

Lucas had just left their father's room.

Davina hurried over to him. 'Hello, Lucas!' She twirled around. 'What do you think? We are dressed for the ball.'

Lucas gave Davina a soft smile. 'You look very pretty, Miss Davina.' He glanced at Elspeth, but his gaze rested on Mairi. 'You all look very pretty.'

Mairi felt her senses flare. Not with anxiety or fear at his admiration, but with something akin to excitement. She remembered that he had once almost kissed her and she yearned to feel his arms around her again.

'Just think,' Davina exclaimed. 'We will be dancing at a ball tonight!'

Lucas's expression was kind. 'I hope you will enjoy the dancing, Miss Davina.'

Davina twirled around again. 'I know I will! My first ball!'

He looked over at Mairi and smiled. 'Can you help her calm down?'

She smiled back. 'I will try!'

Lucas gave Davina a stern look. 'You must compose yourself, Miss Davina. This is your chance to behave like a lady.'

'Oh, I will, Lucas!' She sighed. 'I am just so filled with excitement!'

One of the gentleman guests appeared at the end of the hallway, stared at them for a minute and turned back, as if lost in the maze of corridors.

Lucas stepped back. 'You should be off. Not standing here talking to me.'

Mairi would have preferred to stay with Lucas, but she needed to be at the ball, if for no other reason than to supervise her wayward little sister.

Chapter Nineteen

Mairi, Davina and Elspeth peeked in the ballroom while they waited to be announced. The large room, filled with grandly dressed ladies and gentlemen, was like stepping into the past. Its wood floor gleamed with polish and mirrored the timbered ceiling. The walls were wainscoted and above the wainscoting were set after set of antlers, covering every space of wall up to the ceiling. Chairs were lined along the walls and huge vases in each corner held fragrant flowers. On one side of the room was a balcony where the orchestra tuned its instruments. The footmen, wearing plaid kilts, carried trays of wine and whisky through the crowd.

Just a few short years before, wearing Highland dress had been a crime punishable by imprisonment or transportation. Now it was becoming a source of Scottish pride encouraged by Sir Walter Scott.

Eventually it was their turn and the Oxmont butler announced them, first Elspeth and then Mairi and Davina. They greeted the hosts, in this case, Elspeth's parents. Elspeth and Davina could hardly contain their excitement.

Mairi shook hands with Lord and Lady Oxmont.

'Are you watching over the girls?' Lady Oxmont asked her.

'I will certainly keep an eye on them, my lady,' Mairi

said. 'But I think they have been equally watching out for me. I understand that I have you to thank for this lovely gown.'

Lady Oxmont looked her up and down. 'It looks very well on you. And much different with the new lace and ribbon on it.'

'They did a wonderful job.' Mairi meant that.

'I hope you are enjoying the house party,' the older woman said.

'Indeed.' This time Mairi was less than truthful. 'It has been a very pleasant time. You were very kind to invite us.'

'Well, I knew I needed to entertain Elspeth and she and Davina have always rubbed along well together. And your brother and the Crawfurd boy were the right ages to give them their first dance.'

Mairi did not miss that the invitation for herself and her parents had been the price the Oxmonts had to pay in order to have Davina and Niven here.

'Mairi, come!' Davina cried. 'I see William and Niven.'

Her mother and father stopped them to ooh and aah over how lovely they looked. 'You are the prettiest girls in the room!' her father gushed. Which might have been true, because several of the men in the room seemed to be watching them wherever they went.

When they finally reached Niven and William, Mairi retreated to a corner where she could watch them, but where she hoped to be less conspicuous.

The first set was announced, and suddenly, out of nowhere, appeared Hargreave. He bowed. 'May I have the pleasure of the first dance, Miss Wallace?'

She hesitated. 'Very well,' she said finally, aware that she could not be rude. She wanted to be in the line to keep an eye on Davina and Elspeth.

He bowed and brought her a glass of wine, but then

left and did not return until the music began. But there he was, hand extended to escort her on to the dance floor. The music began and the dancers executed the figures. Davina had a jubilant skip to her step and a joyous smile on her face. She was rapturous and it was impossible not to gaze upon her. But some of the men's eyes were more than captivated. Including Hargreave's. When the dance brought him together with Mairi, though, his gaze was only for her, with a gleam that left her unsettled. He spoke to her only of the most mundane things. The food. The other guests. The weather.

When the set was over, Davina's expression was crestfallen, but William seemed to cajole a smile out of her. They said goodnight to Lord and Lady Oxmont and the four young people left the ball to go to their own entertainment.

Hargreave bowed to Mairi and left without a word. Mairi was alone, wishing she were anywhere else but in this ballroom. She took a glass of wine from a passing footman and drank it down too quickly. Now that Davina was safe, there was no reason for her to be there, but she did not wish to attract any attention by leaving through the main door and walking past half the people there.

The ballroom had floor-to-ceiling windows, though, and at one end, the window was open, even though it was cool outside. Mairi edged her way to that window. If she were outside, she could probably find an unlocked and unattended door that would allow her to sneak back in the house.

When it seemed like no one was looking at her, she stepped through the open window into the relative quiet of outside. She wrapped her arms around herself and worked her way around the house. Suddenly, a male figure appeared before her in the darkness and she froze in fear.

'Mairi?'

She breathed again. It was Lucas. She walked up to him. 'What are you doing out here?'

'I could ask you the same thing,' he said.

'I— There were too many people in there.' It was a poor excuse for climbing out of a window.

But he nodded as if it made perfect sense. 'I was visiting an old friend in the stables and walked back this way when I heard the music.'

The bagpipe began the second set.

'Oh, Davina would have loved to dance this! It is a Scottish reel.' She danced a few steps.

'I do not know the reel,' he said.

'You do not know the reel? It is a wonderful dance!' She took his hand. 'Come. I'll show you.' There was a small courtyard around the corner of the building. She led him there. 'I'll show you one simple step.' She lifted her skirts a little, showing her ankles as she kicked side to side and skipped from foot to foot. 'Try it.'

He tried it.

She laughed. 'Not too badly done.' She lifted her skirt again. 'Try it with me.'

They did the step together.

'Now just skip around me and take my hand, then skip around me again.'

He skipped around her and took her hand.

'If we were with the other dancers, we'd be weaving in and out and clasping hands with other partners.' She stopped and he dropped her hand. 'Now we'll do it all again, but after two times of clasping hands, take both my hands and we will spin around.'

He gave her an uncertain expression, then nodded in resolve.

She laughed. 'It is just a dance and no one can see.'

They began the sequence again and when they spun

around he laughed aloud. She did not think she had ever heard him laugh. The smile on his face made her heart swell with joy.

'Start again.' He released her and repeated the sequence without stopping.

They danced to the bagpipe's lively notes until Mairi felt breathless and free. How long had it been since she'd felt such abandon? How happy she was to share it with Lucas.

'This time, instead of spinning we skip towards each other and back.'

In a group of dancers they would hold hands and form a big circle for this part of the dance. Mairi and Lucas would only be an arm's length apart and when they came close their bodies touched.

They danced, apart and close, apart and close, and the third time, Lucas threw his arms around her, leaned down and placed his lips on hers. His lips were strong, but tender at the same time. She felt as if his kiss gave her life itself. She wrapped her arms around his neck and kissed him back with a hunger and need unlike any she'd experienced before.

'Mairi,' he murmured, and she felt her name on his breath.

He backed them against the house and held her so close their bodies were pressed against each other. He rested her on his thigh, her legs almost straddling him, and the ache inside her grew stronger. This was what she wanted—needed—from him. Not to be a friend. To be...like this with her.

She lost herself in him.

Lucas revelled in the sweet taste of her, in her soft curves pressed against him. He'd not meant to kiss her, but this time he had not been able to stop himself. She seemed to be the place he belonged. All his pain, loneliness and guilt fled in that moment and his empty spaces filled with the joy of her.

The air was chilly, but his senses were aflame with her. He wanted to touch every part of her, the soft skin of her arms, the swell of her breasts, the tenderness of her long graceful neck. Even though he'd left the castle without topcoat or gloves, he felt on fire.

He drew one hand down her arm and the other caressed her lovely face. The vision of her in her ball gown earlier had stunned him. It was as if she'd been a tight bud that had suddenly burst into an exotic blossom. His hand slid to her neck and his fingers pressed lightly into soft flesh there.

She made a strangled cry and suddenly she was thrashing and beating him with her fists like a wild animal.

'Mairi! Mairi!' He tried to break into this fit of hers. 'Stop. Be quiet!' If they were discovered, it would be the ruin of her to be caught with him.

He managed to pin her arms and put a hand over her mouth to silence her. Her eyes were panicked and she struggled against him.

'Mairi!' he whispered in her ear. 'Be still. I will not hurt you. You must be still and quiet.' What was happening here? 'It is Lucas, Mairi. I will not hurt you.'

She stilled and blinked as if waking from a reverie.

'Do not cry out,' he said. 'I will release you if you will be still.'

She nodded and he released her. She looked shaken.

'I will not touch you, I promise.' He stepped back, his hands raised with his palms facing her. A gesture of surrender.

'Lucas?' She looked at him as if unsure who he was and where they were.

'What happened, Mairi? I did not mean to hurt you—'

But what had he done? Nothing to hurt her, nothing to frighten her, he thought. She'd wanted the kiss; he'd been sure of that. What had happened?

'I thought you were—someone else.' She shivered.

He wanted to put an arm around her to warm her, but held back. 'Let us go inside and find a room where we may talk.'

They found an open door leading to the conservatory filled with lush, fragrant plants that belonged in some far-away land with more sun and heat than Scotland.

He removed his coat and placed it around her shoulders. 'Tell me,' he said. 'Who did you think I was?'

She glanced towards the door.

'Do not run,' he said in as mild a tone as he could manage. 'Tell me. Please.'

She shook her head. 'I cannot tell you. I cannot tell anyone.' She turned away from him. 'Nothing happened. Forget my…my panic. I am sorry. Please.'

He gently turned her back to face him. 'Mairi, you were some place else, thinking I was someone else. You cannot tell me nothing happened. You must tell me.'

Her eyes met his. 'You will hate me.'

He touched her arm gently and spoke words that would always be true. 'I will never hate you.'

What had so briefly passed between them proved that. He loved her. There was no denying it to himself. Everything he'd done for the family, he'd done for her.

There was a sofa in one corner of the room. He gestured towards it. 'Let us sit.'

She allowed him to lead her to the sofa and she sat, but he felt as if she were glass, about to shatter. She seemed half with him and half still in whatever memory had terrorised her.

'I promise it will be all right to tell me the whole.' He

sat next to her, careful not to come too close. He took her hand in his, though, needing to touch her. 'Who did you think I was?' he asked.

She gulped in air and her gaze darted anywhere but at him. 'I thought you were the Englishman.'

'*The* Englishman,' he repeated as calmly as he could. 'What Englishman?'

'The one I met on the road to the village. I was alone and he asked the way. He walked with me a little and I thought he was very gentlemanly. But then—' She stopped.

Lucas felt his body grow cold. 'He put his hand on your throat.'

She nodded. 'He—he would not let me go. He was stronger than I was.' She tried to pull away, but he held her hand tighter. 'He made me—made me—' She began to sob.

He wanted to hold her, but dared not. 'It is all right now,' he said in a low voice. 'He is not here. No one will hurt you here.'

She took in a ragged breath. 'You want to know what happened to me?' Her voice turned shrill. 'I will tell you. He pushed me to the ground and opened his trousers. He forced himself inside me.' She made a face of disgust. 'He forced himself inside me!'

Lucas felt his rage grow. He'd kill him. If the man were here now, he'd kill him with his bare hands. 'Who was he?'

'I do not know,' she cried. 'An Englishman. Like you. But not like you, not like you at all.'

Mairi felt herself back there again. She could smell the man. Taste him. Feel again the pain of him thrusting into her. And then—and then that explosion of feeling inside her. She could hear his laughter when he finished.

She heard his voice again.

'You liked that, did you? I knew you were a proper little harlot.'

And he'd done it again. And again.

He threatened to kill her family if she told anyone. Then he left her bleeding, sore and filled with shame.

Someone touched her face. 'Mairi? Come back.'

It was Lucas. And she'd told him what had happened. She finally said it out loud.

He still held her hand, but she pulled it away. 'Now you know,' she said mockingly, throwing up a new wall against feeling that pain and shame again. 'Now you know I am ruined. You see why I have no wish to marry. I am spoiled. Not fit for any decent man.'

But he looked on her with sympathy, not disgust. It rattled her.

'I acted the harlot with you, did I not?' She gave a dry laugh. 'Is that not proof enough?'

He took her hand again. 'No, Mairi. You did not act the harlot. You returned my kiss. That was all. You've felt it before, this attraction between us. I have felt it almost from the beginning. It is natural. It is how it should be.'

She did not know whether to believe him or not. She touched her lips, remembering the kiss.

'No.' She shook her head. 'He said I made it happen. It was my fault.'

He squeezed her hand. 'It was not your fault. You did not want him to attack you, did you? Did you want him to touch you?'

'I did not think so, but he told me I did.' She pulled her hand away. She did not deserve comfort.

'And you believed him?' Lucas said. 'He forced you.'

She could not think straight about this.

'When did this happen?' Lucas asked.

'Five years ago,' she said. 'When I was Davina's age—just a little older.'

'You have held this secret for five years?' He looked astounded.

She simply nodded, but could not meet his eye. What must he think of her! 'It comes back to me sometimes. Like I am there again. So very real. So I must be mad as well as shameful.'

He gripped her upper arms and made her look at him. 'You are not mad. You are not shameful.'

She wrenched away and stood up. 'What do you know of such a thing, Lucas?' she snapped. 'You cannot know what it is like. The shame. The guilt.'

Lucas rose, too, and faced her. 'I know shame. Guilt. Regret.'

'Guilt? What did you do? Commit some infraction of the law?' Her tone was mocking, but he knew what she was doing, trying to push him away by using anger. He'd used that tactic himself. 'Something you must keep secret?'

'Something I do not speak of,' he admitted. Findlay knew, but Findlay had been there to scrape Lucas off the floor in his despair.

Her eyes still held her pain. 'Then you must tell me, Lucas, since I have told you my terrible secret.'

He would tell her. He wanted to tell her. Because it might help her. 'I do not pretend my experience in any way compares to yours.'

She glanced away, as if to hide her pain, but she turned back to him, armour erected, arms crossed, waiting for him to speak.

'I had an older brother—' he said.

'You told me you had a brother,' she said. 'You called for him in your delirium.'

He remembered the fevered dreams. Reliving Bradleigh's death over and over.

He nodded. 'Bradleigh was everything to my parents, especially my father, but he was also as impulsive and reckless as he was charming. He was impractical, prone to romanticism and mad for the cavalry. For the glory of war. Against my father's wishes, he purchased a commission. My father purchased a commission for me, too, in the same cavalry regiment, with the charge to keep my brother out of harm's way.'

She lifted a hand. 'Wait. Surely that was impossible.'

He felt it all again. 'But it wasn't! We were outnumbered at Fuentes de Oñoro and the fighting was fierce, but I managed to block the blows intended for my brother.'

'The scars on your chest,' she went on. 'You were injured keeping your brother safe?'

He had not realised she'd seen his scars. 'I protected him. At Villagarcia. And at Maguilla.' The confusion of that battle rested in his gut again, as did the shame of his Royals bolting like scared rabbits. 'But the night before Waterloo, we quarrelled. He accused me of being jealous. Of wishing I *were* him. It was a foolish argument, but I resented him for it, so the next day, when we were in formation for the charge, I made no effort to be near him. When we were in the thick of it, I did not think of him. It was only when I heard the signal to withdraw that I looked for him. I tried to reach him.' His throat went dry and it took a moment before he could speak again. 'I saw him impaled through the neck.' He felt the pain all over again. 'I was too late. It was my fault. I should have been at his side. I should have done what I promised my father. If I had, my brother would be alive.'

She closed the distance between them and put her arms around him. 'Do not torture yourself! You could not keep such a promise. Men die in battle, do they not? How could it be your fault?'

He held on to her and the feel of her arms and the warmth of her body seemed to draw some of the pain away.

'Mairi, it was not your fault either,' he murmured to her.

Her muscles tensed. 'I am not sure. I am not sure.'

He drew away so she could look at him directly. 'I have known men like that Englishman. And I know that what happened was because he forced you against your will and there was nothing you could have done about it.'

She blinked and her gaze pierced him before she glanced away again.

Here was the opportunity to tell her who he was. He'd already disclosed that he came from a family of means, a family wealthy enough to purchase lieutenant's commissions for two sons.

But she was still raw from disclosing how some blackguard had forced himself on her. This was not the time to burden her with the knowledge that he'd deceived her and her family.

The bagpipes were silent, he realised. He wiped the tears from her cheeks with the tips of his fingers. 'You should return to the ball.'

She shook her head. 'I was fleeing it.'

'Will not someone question where you have been?' This moment between them must not bring her any more harm.

'Perhaps.' She leaned against him and he put an arm around her. 'But I would rather stay with you.'

He wished he could hold her for ever. 'It would be the ruin of you if you were found alone with a man, especially with me.'

She laughed drily. 'I am already ruined, Lucas.'

'No, you are not.' He pulled away, facing her to make

sure she heeded him. 'As long as no one knows, you are not ruined.'

'But—but a man will be able to tell.'

He could reassure her on that score. 'No, Mairi, I know this. No matter what anyone tells you, a man cannot tell.' He'd seen his soldiers fooled over and over, believing they were bedding a virgin until they realised they'd all bedded the same one. 'So, go. Live the life a daughter of a Scottish baron was meant to live and enjoy it without guilt or shame.'

She pressed her fingers against her temples. The music started again and she glanced towards the sound. 'I do not want to go back in there, but I will, if you tell me to, Lucas.'

'No, not because I tell you. You decide, Mairi.' Too many people discounted what she wanted. Her parents. Hargreave. That debaucher who'd so wounded her.

She sighed. 'I'll go back.' She straightened her dress and patted her hair. 'Am I presentable?'

She looked beautiful in his eyes—but also quite well kissed. 'Perhaps you ought to freshen up.'

'I'll find Nellie and have her put me back together.'

'And I will wait, then, until I am certain no one will connect your absence with me.'

She turned to leave, but spun back around and put her arms around him again. She kissed him on the lips, very lightly, but he felt it long after she had fled the room.

Chapter Twenty

Lucas sat back on the sofa and waited. He lowered his head in his hands. It all made sense now. Why she always seemed so on guard, why she always seemed so sad. He wished he could get his hands on the scoundrel who'd stolen her innocence, who'd left her body and emotions with a pain that would never leave her.

But he couldn't, any more than he could bring Bradleigh back.

No matter what she said, he should have stopped the cuirassier. He should have been with Bradleigh.

Lucas took some solace in having helped save Mairi's family from losing their home, their land and their pride. Perhaps some day she would believe the assault was not her fault. He was not certain he'd convinced her.

He rubbed his face. He should not have kissed her, though. Not that he regretted it. He did not. But it had cracked open his emotional armour in a way that he could never again repair. He again felt the pain of losing Bradleigh, but now it was alongside Mairi's pain, which he felt on her behalf as well. He faced the fact that he loved her and that it was she, and not his cowardly attempt to run away from his responsibilities, that could make him whole again.

But how could he stay with her, desiring her as he did?

These thoughts tumbled through his head until he had no idea how much time had passed. The music had stopped and started again. He rose. He would not return to Dunburn's room yet, though, in order to be absolutely certain no one would realise they'd been together. That Scots Grey had appeared briefly in the hallway when he was talking with Mairi and Davina and the Oxmonts' daughter. Lucas was certain that little scene had not looked like three young ladies conversing with a servant.

He left the conservatory and used the nearest servants' door to go down to the servants' hall, where several of the servants were passing the time. He nodded to them and picked up a newspaper someone had left on the table. He sat and pretended to read, his mind still filled with Mairi and his body now aching for her.

Hargreave's valet came up and sat in the chair beside him.

'I have something to tell you,' the man said in a quiet voice.

Lucas nodded.

He leaned a bit closer. 'There is someone here who knows you from before. Not the coachman. One of the guests.'

Lucas's stomach clenched. 'I know. He spoke to me.'

'He came to Hargreave's room before the ball. I was there, of course.'

This could not be good.

The valet went on. 'The man told Hargreave that you are the son of an English earl, that your real name is Johns-Ives, and he speculated that you must have done something quite awful to be reduced to working as a servant.'

It could not be worse. Of all people, Hargreave had

learned the truth about him. 'I am indebted to you for telling me.'

The valet shrugged. 'I have no need to keep Hargreave's confidences.' He peered at Lucas. 'Is it true?'

'Yes,' Lucas admitted. 'The family I serve know that I am not really a butler or a valet, but they do not know the rest of it.'

'Then why are you acting the valet for Dunburn?' he asked.

'As a favour. I was recovering in their house and—' He did not wish to explain more. 'I tell you, it gives me a new appreciation for you men who do this work.'

The man's expression turned bleak, but he seemed to recover. 'I won't say anything to anyone. But I thought you should know.'

'There is something I wish to tell you,' Lucas said. 'Dunburn's valet is quite old and deserves to be pensioned off. I will ensure Dunburn is given your name and my highest recommendations, if you should wish to seek employment there.'

The valet's eyes widened. 'You would do that?'

'I would do more if I could,' Lucas said.

The man rose and moved away.

Lucas took in a deep breath. Hargreave would undoubtedly use this information, but Lucas was uncertain how. In any event, Hargreave would certainly tell Mairi. And Lucas did not know how he could speak with her before Hargreave got to her.

Mairi found an inconspicuous corner of the ballroom in which to sit while she waited for the ball to end. Two or three gentlemen of her acquaintance asked her to dance, but she declined them all. She had no wish to be touched by any man. Except Lucas.

Their dance, that breathtaking kiss, had lifted her to heights she had never dreamed possible, until her memory stole it all from her, bringing her back to the terror of the Englishman's assault. She could not believe Lucas had convinced her to tell him what had happened to her, but she knew without a doubt that she could trust him with it. He had even tried to comfort her over it, saying it was not her fault and that no man would know she'd been ruined.

She was not sure she could believe that, but it endeared him to her even more. Her heart bled for him when he spoke of feeling guilty for his brother's death. Could he not see how nonsensical it would be to promise to keep someone alive in a war?

The dancing continued and she watched the guests perform the figures, their patterns and symmetry pleasing to the eye as well as bringing pleasure to the dancers. The pleasant music filled Mairi's ears as her thoughts drifted to Lucas.

How could she make him stay? Was there any path to a future together? It all seemed so far-fetched, but he must have come from a family with wealth enough to purchase commissions for two sons. Surely his birth was respectable enough to make something possible between them, no matter what circumstances he had been reduced to since returning from Waterloo. But if he came from some wealth, why had he agreed to act as a servant? What could have happened to his family so that he'd had nothing to return home to? What had he been doing in Scotland?

She watched her father emerge from the card room and stride across the ballroom to the door to the corridor. He looked upset. Had he lost? Mairi would be furious at him if he had lost. He should not have been playing cards in the first place.

She also spied Hargreave across the room, talking to a

gentleman she did not know. The man wore the red coat with gold braid of the Scots Greys. She wondered if her father had met him. If so, poor man, he'd be forced to recount the battle.

The same battle in which Lucas's brother had died. How painful it must have been for Lucas to be asked by Niven and their father to tell stories of that day, over and over.

Hargreave and this Scots Grey circled around the dancers just as the music stopped. The lovely patterns broke into gentlemen and ladies eager for something to drink.

One of the footmen circulating the room with trays of wine glasses approached her. 'Wine, miss?'

She smiled and shook her head. At that moment, Hargreave and his companion appeared before her.

How could she rid herself of this man for good?

'Miss Wallace, may I present Lieutenant Urquhart?' Hargreave asked, looming above her.

'How do you do, sir?' She inclined her head to the gentleman who exchanged a quick glance with Hargreave. She looked from one to the other. There was more to this.

'The lieutenant is a Scots Grey,' Hargreave added.

She turned politely to the gentleman. 'My father will be pleased to meet you. He is very proud of the Scots Greys.'

Hargreave had managed to trap her in her chair. She could not leave without causing a scene.

'Urquhart is acquainted with someone you know,' Hargreave said.

She looked away from Hargreave and addressed Urquhart. 'Are you, sir?'

'You might wonder who,' Hargreave persisted.

She stared at Urquhart as if willing him to answer.

Hargreave nudged the man to make him speak. 'I knew

him as Captain Johns-Ives, but I understand he goes by an-other name here.'

Hargreave grinned. 'He is your butler, Lucas!'

Mairi felt the room spin. Lucas? She fought for compo-sure. So Lucas was using a different name. That was not so bad, was it?

'And there is more,' Hargreave said gleefully. 'Johns-Ives is the son of an English earl. Is that not a good joke? An earl's son reduced to service.'

'He was wealthy, too, I believe,' Urquhart added. 'He and his brother were well equipped.'

She faced the man. 'Did you speak with him here?'

'I did,' Urquhart admitted. 'But he did not explain. All he asked was that I not tell anyone of it.'

She gaped at him with disdain. 'So you gave your word not to speak of this?'

The man had the grace to look shamefaced.

She averted her gaze from both of them, her emotions swirling inside her. Why had Lucas—Johns-Ives—or who-ever he was not confided in her? Why hide this? Surely being the son of an earl was not something to hide.

Hargreave snorted. 'Can you imagine what scandal must be attached to his name if he is reduced to working as a mere servant? How low a man can fall? A veritable plummet.'

Near her, the footman who'd offered her refreshment rattled the glasses on his tray.

Was there something worse Lucas had done? All that kindness, that helpfulness, that comfort. Was that all hid-ing something truly dark in his past? Why else come to Scotland and keep his identity a secret?

She did not want to believe it.

Her throat tightened. 'Have you told Papa this?'

Hargreave's expression turned serious. 'Not yet. Your father and I had other business together.'

Was that why her father had looked upset?

Urquhart cleared his throat. 'I—I must take my leave. Urgent matter to attend to...' He bowed curtly and strode off.

Hargreave put on one of his charming smiles. 'What a surprise, is it not, Miss Wallace?'

She felt sick. She wanted to run from the room and search for Lucas and confront him with his deception. Make him explain.

The footman cleared away some empty glasses. Mairi supposed he'd heard the whole tale. Soon everyone would know and her father—their whole family—would be a laughing stock.

Hargreave grinned down at Miss Wallace. What a triumph, being able to tell her that her fancy English butler, the Waterloo hero, was the ruined son of an earl. Here the man fancied himself her younger sister's protector and all the while he was engaging in deception.

Hargreave would give anything to know what had sunk Johns-Ives so low he'd had no recourse but to flee to Scotland and become a butler.

Let's see if he acts all hoity-toity now.

'What say you to this, Miss Wallace?' he asked. 'This must take you aback.'

The chit merely glared up at him. 'That was your intention, was it not, sir? I wonder you would propose marriage to me one day and the next strive to so purposefully unsettle me.'

He felt his anger rouse. 'I wonder you would speak so to me. I dare say you will regret it.'

Wait until she learns what else I have planned for her.

This was one triumphant night for him! His plans were unfolding even better than he'd expected.

Her gaze did not falter. 'Please step back. I wish to walk away from you.'

Perhaps she had a bit of her younger sister's spunk after all. That only made winning her into better sport.

'I will meet with your father in the morning. Perhaps you will care to join us?' He bowed, but stepped back and extended his hand with a flourish.

She rose, tossing him one more glare, and swept past him. His laughter followed her.

Lucas watched for Mairi to appear in the hallway after the ball, but, to his dismay, Dunburn returned to his bed-chamber first.

The man looked ill. Each night he returned to the room full in his cups, but mostly jovial. This night his demeanour was quite different.

'Are you unwell, Baron?' Lucas asked him.

'Never better,' barked Dunburn, his tone angry. 'I'd be a deal better still if you would get me a bottle of whisky.' He waved his hand dismissively. 'And be quick about it.'

Something was amiss. 'What is wrong, Baron?'

'Nothing!' Dunburn snapped. 'None of your business anyway. Damned sick of everyone wanting to know my business.'

Obviously something had happened to turn his perennially cheerful mood so sour. Could Hargreave have disclosed Lucas's true identity? Wouldn't Dunburn simply say so, though? The man was downright defensive.

'I'll get your whisky.' Lucas left the room.

He went below stairs and found the butler, who gave him a bottle of whisky for Dunburn.

* * *

Mairi walked as quickly as she could to escape Hargreave's presence. She needed to speak to Lucas. To ask him why he had not told her the truth.

The story of his deception would undoubtedly spread throughout the house party. *That Baron and Lady Dunburn couldn't even tell the difference between an English earl's son and a butler,* they'd say. Mairi could imagine all the stories that would be spun to make them appear foolish.

She wanted the real story.

As she reached the hallway leading to her bedchamber, she glimpsed him at the other end, just entering the servants' stairway. Good. She would await his return. She stood by the door to the stairway. It was all she could do to keep from pacing in front of it. Two servants came up the stairs and eyed her curiously. When the gossip started, she supposed they'd add how odd Miss Wallace was, loitering in the hallway for no good reason.

She had a good reason. A man she'd trusted, a man she *loved,* had been deceiving her.

After about a quarter of an hour had passed, she heard more footsteps on the stairs. The door opened. It was Lucas carrying a whisky bottle.

'Mairi!' He looked surprised but pleased. 'There is something I must—'

She did not let him finish. 'There is a man here who knows you by a different name.'

He blanched. 'That is what I—'

She glared at him. 'Your name is Johns-Ives and you are the son of an English earl. Not a servant.'

'I never said I was a servant—'

'You never wanted us to know!' she accused. 'Son of an

earl! Why deceive us so? What did you do that you had to hide who you were?'

He looked away.

She waited for his answer.

Lucas turned away from her wounded, accusing eyes. This was precisely what he had not wanted to happen. How could he explain that he'd wished his life to be at an end, that he'd wished to be someone else—anyone but the man who let his brother die and then had taken everything that should have been his?

He faced her again. 'I never meant to deceive you. I never even meant to stay—'

She interrupted him again. 'Hargreave will waste no time spreading the story. About how the Wallaces were duped by the fallen son of an earl. My poor parents will be humiliated. I know these people. I know they will relish this piece of gossip.'

'Hargreave.' Lucas spat out the name. Just as he'd feared. 'Did he tell your father, as well?'

'He said not, but I suspect he will do so in the morning. Hargreave says they are to meet.'

There was no use telling her father tonight, not foxed as he was. 'I will tell him in the morning.'

She looked hurt. 'What happened to you? Why did you not tell me?'

She thought him ruined in some way. The truth suddenly seemed more unbelievable.

'Nothing happened. I am not fallen. I simply did not wish to be my father's heir and I had no reason to think I would encounter anyone in Scotland who would know otherwise.' Instead he had met two people who knew him. Findlay, whom he'd known he could trust, and Urquhart, who had proved he could not.

'That is not an explanation, Lucas—my lord, I mean. Did your parents disown you?'

'No.' She still did not comprehend. They could not disown him, although he had no doubt they'd wished they could. He was the heir whether they wanted him to be or not. He would inherit everything that had been due his brother. Wishing him dead had not changed that fact.

Although he might have granted them that wish, had it not been for her.

She expelled a frustrated breath. 'Then why give a false name?'

'I did not want to be Lucas Johns-Ives,' he responded. 'I thought no harm could come of it. I wanted to be thought of as a person of no consequence.'

'Why?' she pressed. 'The name Johns-Ives would have meant nothing to us.'

But it meant something to him. He'd wanted to erase himself completely and rescuing her family had given him the opportunity. He'd been happy being John Lucas.

She threw up her arms. 'You are not going to explain, are you? You still hide yourself from me.' Tears glistened in her eyes. 'After all I have told you.'

Before he could say another word, she spun around and almost ran down the hallway to her room. Lucas heard the voices of some other guests coming up the stairs, so he did not dare go after her.

He walked to her father's room instead and went back inside.

Dunburn sat sullenly in a chair. He'd removed his coat and waistcoat and thrown them on the floor.

'It's about time.' Dunburn waved his hand. 'Pour me some whisky and be off with you! I'll summon you when I need you.'

Something else must have happened.

Lucas thought he knew what. 'Sir, you had better tell me what is the matter. Did you lose at cards tonight?'

Dunburn rose from the chair and started shouting. 'I do not have to tell you what I did or did not do! Leave me be! Leave me be!' He was loud enough to be heard outside the room.

In the man's state he could rouse the whole hallway. Lucas could not pursue this now. How much had he lost?

'Get out!' Dunburn shouted again. 'Out of my sight!'

Lucas withdrew to the dressing room. He stripped down to his shirtsleeves and trousers and sat on his cot.

When he closed his eyes, all he could see was Mairi's wounded, accusing face. He'd done a poor job of explaining himself to her, he had to admit. Although, perhaps nothing he said could have changed anything. The damage had already been done by Hargreave, who must have been delighted in the task. And the Scots Grey. Urquhart. Urquhart had broken his word.

Lucas felt the familiar darkness of despair enveloping him. None of it could be undone. Like the quarrel with his brother, like the battle and his failure to be at his brother's side, it could not be undone.

The clock struck the next hour. He took a deep breath and stood. There were still his duties of a valet to perform. Lucas would not miss having to take such personal care of another man, but feeling like he'd been of use to someone had restored his spirits for a while. Now he was sinking back into the depths. Too bad Mairi had pulled him away from death. They'd all have been better off if he'd simply died. *No!* He shook himself. He was past that now. Mairi had brought him through the worst. Now he must do what he could to repay the family who had inadvertently saved his miserable life.

Surely Dunburn had not gambled away the money from

the sale of the jewels and furniture? Even he could not be such a fool.

Lucas left the dressing room. Dunburn was slumped in the chair, asleep and snoring and stinking of drink. Lucas held up the whisky bottle. Empty. No drinking this despair away.

'Dunburn?' Lucas shook him.

Dunburn mumbled, but did not wake. Lucas removed Dunburn's shoes and lifted him out of the chair. Dunburn made a feeble attempt to walk with Lucas dragging him to the bed. He managed to lift the man on to the mattress. No use trying to remove the rest of his clothes.

Like a valet ought to do, he laid out a fresh set of clothes and picked up the ones on the floor.

Dunburn would be more rational in the morning. Lucas could deal with him then. Find out how much he had lost at cards. Tell him of his deception and that everyone else at the house party would likely know before the end of the day.

And try to contrive something to say to Mairi.

Chapter Twenty-One

The next morning, Mairi rose early. In truth, she had not slept much. She'd had too much to think about, but she could not afford to think about Lucas now. Her father was meeting with Hargreave and she wanted to be certain she was present. Her father was no match for Hargreave, Mairi feared, and would sign her life away given the chance. Whatever the man had to say to her father, it could not be good.

She glanced out of the window at the grey dawn. The day seemed to reflect her mood and it had started to rain. No outdoor activities for the men this day, unless they wished to risk being caught in a downpour.

She rose from bed, washed and dressed herself as much as she could, then sat in her corset and shift and combed out her hair, strand by strand.

Davina rustled the bedcovers. 'You are awake?' Her sister rubbed her eyes and stretched. 'What time is it?'

She turned around and faced the bed. 'A little past six o'clock.'

Davina groaned. 'Why are you up so early?'

For so many reasons, Mairi thought, but mostly so she would not miss her father and Hargreave. 'I just woke up and I could not get back to sleep.'

Davina sat up and looked out of the window. 'Ugh. It is raining.'

'Yes. No walks today.' Mairi rose from the chair and walked over to the bed. 'Will you help me tie my stays?'

Davina pulled the strings and tied them. Mairi donned her dress and returned to the bedside so Davina could do up the buttons. She sat at the dressing table again and hurriedly pinned up her hair, taming the curls from the night before.

'I don't want to wake up,' groaned Davina, who burrowed under the covers.

Mairi walked over to the bed and gave her sister a kiss on the head. 'Sleep, then. No reason not to.' Sleep peacefully while you can, she thought.

When Mairi left the bedchamber the hallway was empty. Perhaps she would be the first person in the breakfast room. No matter, as long as she did not miss her father and Hargreave.

When she entered the breakfast room, though, her father and Hargreave were already there and the footmen were still bringing up the food.

'Miss Wallace, what a delight to see you this morning,' Hargreave said with great cheer.

Mairi's father looked pale and shrunken.

'Good morning,' she responded coolly. She kissed her father on his cheek. 'Good morning, Papa.'

He did not return her greeting.

Besides the footmen, they were the only three guests in the room. Although she had no appetite, she selected toasted bread and jam from the sideboard and the footman carried her plate to the round table that was large enough for at least eight people. She sat next to her father, who had a plate of food that looked untouched. Hargreave, on the other hand, ate with gusto and signalled to the footman attending them to bring him more. He kept up a steady stream of conversation about the weather, the activities of the house party, the ball. His card playing.

When he spoke of his great luck at cards the night before, Mairi's father's hands started to shake. She began to feel even more alarmed.

When Hargreave finally finished his second plate of food, he placed both palms on the table. 'Well. Shall we have our little meeting, Dunburn?' He turned to Mairi. 'Does your presence here so early mean you wish to join us, my dear?'

She was *not* his dear. 'Yes.'

She rose first. Hargreave wiped his mouth with his napkin before getting to his feet. She had to tug at her father's arm to get him to rise.

Hargreave turned to the footman. 'We will use the green drawing room and would appreciate it if you would see that we are not disturbed there.'

The footman's eyes flickered, but he bowed. 'As you wish, sir.'

Hargreave offered Mairi his arm, but she took her father's instead, which made Hargreave laugh. He led them to a small sitting room tucked away in one of the corridors of the castle, continuing all the while to chat about mundane matters with hints at more serious things. Like Lucas's deception. Mairi thought Hargreave must have scouted out this room for its remote location. They were not likely to be disturbed.

It also occurred to her that if she screamed, no one would hear her.

He extended his hand grandly. 'Do sit wherever you will be most comfortable, Miss Wallace.'

She led her father to a sofa and sat next to him. 'What is this about, Hargreave?'

He sat in a chair adjacent to her, stretching out his legs

as if simply at leisure. 'Well, your father knows some of it, do you not, Dunburn?'

Her father actually replied to him. 'I do,' he rasped in a tone of despondency. He turned to Mairi. 'I am sorry, Mairi. I am so sorry.'

Hargreave addressed her as well. 'Perhaps you know that your father and I have enjoyed several evenings of card play. I must say, there were many moments I was losing badly, were there not, Dunburn?'

Her father replied, 'Yes.'

Hargreave continued. 'Last night, however, my luck changed.' He laughed. 'It seemed I could not lose. Your father believed his luck would turn again, so he insisted— against my urgings, I might add—that he be given a chance to recoup his losses, so we played on.'

Her father moaned and dropped his head in his hands.

Hargreave smiled. 'It seems, Miss Wallace, that I have won a great deal of money from your father.'

Mairi turned to him. 'Papa, is this true?'

Her father nodded.

Her heart pounded painfully in her chest. 'How much?'

'All of it!' her father wailed.

She felt the blood drain from her face. 'Do you mean, everything we raised to pay off your debts?'

He nodded.

Hargreave sat up straighter and leaned towards them. 'But do not fear. I will rescue you. I will give you enough money to pay off all your debts. All you have to do is sell me your title and property.'

'No!' she cried.

He smiled at her. 'You might as well sell it to me. When you are thrown in debtors' prison, I shall purchase the *caput* anyway. At less cost, I am certain.'

Mairi felt sick.

He reached over and clasped her hand. 'Believe me, my dear. I wish only to help your family. I do not wish to see your father in debtors' prison. Or you and your sister forced to earn a living yourselves. How would you do that?'

Perhaps there were worse things than losing their home after all.

'But,' he went on, 'I do ask something of you in return and, if you agree, you and your family may continue to live at Dunburn House. I will see Niven gets a Grand Tour or goes to university. Davina may attend a finishing school and have a regular come-out. I'll even provide her a dowry. But you must do something for me in return.'

She stiffened. 'What must I do?'

He grinned and squeezed her hand. Painfully. 'You must marry me.'

Her father shook his head. 'Forgive me, Mairi.'

She glared at Hargreave. 'You planned this!' she cried. 'You manipulated my father! Tricked him into playing cards with you!'

He laughed. 'Isn't it grand when things work out the way we want them to?' Without a break, he turned to her father. 'Dunburn, let me tell you the most interesting gossip I heard last night. It is about your butler, the Waterloo hero, I believe you call him—'

Lucas woke to the clock striking seven. He rose from his cot, dressed himself hurriedly and opened the door.

Dunburn was gone.

Except for the day of the hunt, Dunburn had never risen before eight in the morning, and on the hunting days, it had been Lucas who had woken him.

Dunburn's shirt and breeches from the night before lay in a heap on the floor and the fresh clothes Lucas had set out were gone. The man had dressed himself. He must have moved quietly so as not to wake Lucas. Purposely avoiding him? That was not a good sign.

Lucas washed, shaved and dressed himself as quickly as he could.

Mairi had said that Hargreave meant to meet with her father this morning. Lucas wanted to find him first. He rushed out of the door.

He could check first in the breakfast room. Although it was early, others might be eating there, but he could invent a pretence of having a message for Dunburn.

He ran down the servants' stairs and made his way to the breakfast room. He knocked on the door.

The footman Anderson opened it. 'Lucas!'

'I have a message for Dunburn,' Lucas said, nearly out of breath. 'Is he there?'

Anderson stepped out of the room and closed the door. 'I was thinking I would have to search for you. Something is afoot with Hargreave. He made a big show of having a meeting with the Baron and his daughter.'

'Miss Wallace?' She was to be there, too?

'It doesn't look good,' Anderson went on. 'The Baron looked pale and sick. Hargreave was jubilant.'

'Are they still in the breakfast room?' Lucas asked.

'No,' the footman replied. 'They went to the green sitting room.'

'Where is the green sitting room?' Lucas had no idea.

'I'll show you.' Anderson led the way. Before they reached the door, Anderson stopped Lucas. 'Two things you should know. I was working in the card room last night. The Baron lost a great deal of money to Mr Hargreave and left very upset.'

As Lucas had feared.

The footman smiled. 'And I also heard Hargreave tell

Miss Wallace that you are the son of an earl. Can that be true?'

There was no use denying it. 'Yes. It is a long story that perhaps I can tell you later. I would appreciate it if you would not say anything to anyone about it.'

'My lips are sealed,' the footman said.

Lucas did not doubt that Anderson could be trusted. As could Hargreave's valet. Honourable men, both.

'Thank you, Anderson,' Lucas said. 'Decent of you to help me.'

Anderson shrugged. 'I do not like Hargreave much.'

They reached a door at the end of a labyrinth of corridors. Anderson gestured to it and backed away.

Lucas opened the door without knocking.

All three heads turned to him.

Mairi sat on a sofa looking deathly pale. Her father sat next to her, his expression bleak.

Hargreave stood. 'Lucas! Or shall I call you Johns-Ives? How fortunate you have found us. I wanted you to hear this.'

Dunburn averted his gaze, but Mairi continued to look at him with aching eyes.

'Shall I explain what we have been discussing?' Hargreave directed his question to Mairi and her father. Neither responded. Hargreave continued as if they had. 'We have been discussing what to do since Dunburn lost a vast amount of money to me in cards—'

As Lucas had feared. 'How much, Baron?'

'All of it.' The older man almost choked on his words.

Hargreave continued, his tone deceptively solemn. 'I told Dunburn that I would pay off all his debts and, in return, he will sell me his title and *caput*. But I am a generous man.' He smiled. 'I will also marry Miss Wallace. Her parents will live with us at Dunburn House for the rest of their lives. I will fund Niven's future and provide a coming out and a dowry for Davina. Will not our friends praise me for such generosity?'

Everything Mairi wished for. All she had to do was marry him.

Lucas turned to her. 'Do you want this, Mairi?'

Her voice trembled. 'What other choice do I have?'

Lucas felt as if he were watching the cuirassier impale Mairi and her whole family. He'd failed them. He'd thought helping them would atone for the death of his brother, but he had utterly failed. Perhaps he'd even helped deliver them to this end by making an enemy of Hargreave.

Hargreave smirked. 'You might wonder when all this will be accomplished,' he said to Lucas. 'I told Miss Wallace that I would like nothing more than an irregular marriage. Find the village blacksmith and declare ourselves husband and wife—'

'No.' Mairi spoke up. 'I will marry in a church, with banns read and everything proper. I insist on it.'

A small battle for her to win, Lucas thought.

'And I will do what my intended bride desires,' Hargreave said. 'Her happiness is my greatest desire.' He added, 'On another note, I will, of course, hire my own servants, the butler and footmen, especially. I'll pension off the old ones.' He turned to Dunburn. 'You have so many ancient servants. It won't do to have such feeble people around me.' He smiled at Lucas again. 'However, if you would like to continue as Dunburn's valet...?'

'Won't have him!' Dunburn muttered.

Hargreave raised his hands in a helpless gesture. 'There you have it, then. You will need to seek employment elsewhere.'

Lucas's anger burned red hot. Would it help matters if he beat Hargreave to a pulp? How much scandal was he willing to bring to Mairi and her family? Could he fail any more completely?

Hargreave continued to make the most of his moment. 'Did you wish to explain to these good people why you deceived them? Why an earl's son would need to pretend to be a servant?'

There was nothing he could say that would ease matters. He feared for Mairi. At this moment she looked as fragile as glass. One more tap and she might shatter.

'I would like to ask why you would do this to this good family,' Lucas said instead.

Hargreave's brows rose. 'You act as if I am the villain when I am doing something heroic in rescuing them all from their own follies.' He paused. 'But to answer your question, I want a title and land and this way it is easily accomplished. Or it will be soon.'

A title? He'd destroy the happiness of all of them for a title?

Hargreave continued. 'We will finish out our time at the house party and travel back to Dunburn. I suspect the sale of the *caput* and the title will take a while, but there is no reason we cannot be married after the banns are read. In the end, I will be the Baron of Dunburn.'

Lucas looked him directly in the eye. 'There is more to being a gentleman than having a title, Hargreave.'

Hargreave's nostrils flared. 'You will leave us, immediately.'

Lucas crossed the room and seized Hargreave by the lapels of his coat, lifting him completely out of the chair.

'Put me down!' cried Hargreave. 'Put me down this instant or I swear this time I will see you sent to the gallows for assaulting me.'

'Put him down, Lucas,' Mairi said. 'I've no doubt he'll do as he says. We are not worth your life.'

But he'd gladly sacrifice his life for hers.

'Please put him down,' she said more quietly.

Lucas cast a glance at Mairi—perhaps his last one. He shoved Hargreave back into the chair so forcefully it tipped backwards. While Hargreave was scrambling to get up, Lucas bowed to Mairi and her father and walked out of the room.

It was over. He'd failed and it was all over. In about four weeks' time she would marry Hargreave and soon after Hargreave would take her father's title and lands. And she would be his wife. His *wife*!

How could he bear it?

Mairi felt her heart shattering as Lucas closed the door behind him. Had she been expecting him to rescue her? What could he do? Hargreave had backed them all into a corner and the only way out was through him. Clever man. Clever, hateful man.

What a fool she'd been to hope for any other outcome. She'd loved Lucas, but he had deceived her, used her, like any other man in her life.

She rose from her chair and strode across the sitting room past Hargreave.

He caught her arm. 'Where are you going?'

'Out of this room,' she said.

'No,' he said. 'You will stay here with me and we will leave together.'

She pulled her arm away. 'You cannot command me yet and I do not wish to be in your presence another second of this day.'

She feared he would follow her, but he did not. She hurried up the stairs to her father's room. She entered the room and found Lucas in the dressing room, packing his satchel.

She entered and closed the door.

He turned and saw her there. 'Mairi.' His voice had a hint of longing that she could no longer believe.

'You are leaving.' It was a statement.

'I must. I fear I will kill him if I stay.'

She forgot her anger at him. 'Where will you go?'

He faced her. 'I do not know.'

They stared at each other without speaking for a time. He returned to packing.

'I am sorry,' Lucas finally said. 'I am sorry I failed you.' He buckled the satchel.

She stepped into his arms. 'It was not your fault.'

Is that not what he had told her? It was not her fault? Perhaps bad things just happened and were not able to be stopped.

Like his leaving.

His embrace lasted all too brief a moment until he released her and walked out.

Chapter Twenty-Two

It had been a little over three weeks since Lucas left Oxmont Castle, but now he was on horseback, returning to Scotland.

After he'd left Mairi, he had come to a crossroad and had known this was the moment to decide what direction he should take. Finally, he had realised what he must do. He returned to Kent, to his family, to the great relief of his mother and father. He returned to the life he'd fled. To save Mairi, he needed to again become Lucas Johns-Ives, heir to the Earl of Foxgrove—Viscount Bradleigh. He needed to accept everything that should have been his brother's.

His father had been so grateful for Lucas's return that he readily agreed to the plan Lucas presented to him. He willingly tapped into his considerable resources to help make it happen. With his father's help and influence, Lucas had been able to prevent Hargreave from gaining the *caput*, but the only way to stop the marriage was to reach Dunburn in time.

Nothing seemed to co-operate, least of all the weather. Lucas rode hard to Scotland, changing horses often at the coaching inns. He rode as long as daylight allowed him, but these last days were the most difficult. He'd had to ride through snow.

He'd carefully calculated the likely time of Mairi's wedding, three Sundays after the end of the house party, and figured Hargreave would insist on marrying as soon as possible. But the cold and snow made for slow progress. He pushed on.

Mairi was dressed in the ball gown she'd worn when Lucas kissed her, but this day it was to be her wedding dress. She'd refused to allow Hargreave to purchase a new wardrobe. She wanted to wear the dress she'd worn when she'd last been happy—in Lucas's arms.

How foolish she was. He'd left her, hadn't he?

She'd half-hoped he would rescue her somehow, the way he'd rescued her family over and over again. But perhaps he'd only been playing a game with them. The earl's son playing at being a manservant.

She glanced in the mirror in her bedchamber in Dunburn House, her grandmother's mirror, the one Lucas had refused to allow her to sell, but she got no pleasure in seeing her image in it today.

Davina stood behind her. 'You look nice. Why do you look so unhappy?'

Mairi turned and hugged her sister. 'Never mind me. Everything will work out, I am certain.'

At least for Davina and Niven it would, Mairi was determined. And her parents would be comfortable in their familiar surroundings.

Hargreave had been increasingly unpleasant these past couple of weeks. He was angry at how much time it was taking to arrange his purchase of the title and land, which he wanted much more than to marry her. There was some delay with her father's debts being paid and the Prince Regent had yet to approve confirmation of the title. Mairi wished she could delay the wedding as well.

She'd insisted the wedding be conducted with the least amount of fuss possible. It was no cause of celebration in her eyes. Everyone thought she was being frugal, when she really felt the day should be one of mourning, at least for her.

Davina, on the other hand, was all starry-eyed at the idea of her marrying Hargreave. Hargreave hid his foul mood around Davina and made a point of charming her. That in itself made Mairi uneasy. Niven was rightfully upset at the loss of the title and lands that he'd always expected to be his some day. What would become of him now there was nothing to inherit? Her mother's eyes had opened wide enough to recognise Hargreave's treachery and to appreciate the sacrifice her daughter was forced to make for the family. Her father was a ghost of his former self. Mairi prayed they would get used to the changes Hargreave had forced upon them. At least they would not be impoverished.

Her mother opened the bedroom door. 'It is time to go to the church.'

Before they wrapped up in their warmest cloaks and climbed into the carriage for the short ride to the church, her mother embraced her. 'My poor daughter.'

Mairi's eyes pricked with tears. 'We will manage, Mama.'

Perhaps the carriage would become stuck in the snow or one of the wheels would fall off, anything to delay this hated event. At least Hargreave travelled to the church separately, in his own carriage, and they did not have to suffer his presence. Because of the bad weather, his family declined making the trip over from their estate.

Their carriage pulled up to the church where her family had always sat in the pews reserved for the Baron of Dunburn. They would still, but Hargreave would be there.

They entered the church, which was chilly and empty except for Hargreave, Reverend Hill and his wife.

Mairi kept her cloak on as she walked up the aisle on her father's arm. Her mother, Niven and Davina walked behind.

Mrs Hill played a hymn on the organ. Hargreave eyed Mairi with a smug expression.

Reverend Hill intoned, 'Dearly Beloved, we are gathered here…'

Lucas galloped through the gate at Dunburn House and, upon reaching the house, jumped from his horse and pounded on the door with his fist.

Robert opened it. 'Mr Lucas!'

'Where is Mairi?' Lucas demanded. 'Am I too late?' He didn't need to explain late for what.

'They will already be at the church!' Robert cried. 'Hurry!'

Lucas remounted the horse and sped off to the church. As he neared it he dismounted.

Through the door he heard the Reverend's voice. 'Therefore if any man can show any just cause, why they may not lawfully be joined together, let him now speak, or else hereafter for ever hold his peace—'

Lucas flung open the door and charged in. He must have looked like a creature from beyond the grave, an apparition, his topcoat and hat all caked with snow.

'Stop!' he cried.

A collective gasp came from those present.

Mairi took several steps forward. 'Lucas?'

He removed his hat. 'Do not do this, Mairi! You do not need to—'

'See here,' Hargreave cried, shoving his way past Mairi to face Lucas. His face was menacing, but a threat from Hargreave was a mere trifle to Lucas.

Lucas glared at him. 'It is over, Hargreave. Over.' He turned to Dunburn. 'Your debts are paid, sir. In full. All of them.'

'You cannot do this—' Hargreave sputtered.

Lucas swung back to him. 'Your money is returned to you, Hargreave. See your man of business if you do not believe me. The Prince Regent will not approve you as the holder of the *caput*. It is over.'

Mairi walked up to him. 'Lucas, is it true? Was it you? You paid Papa's debts?'

He held her arms. 'You are under no obligation to me for it,' he told her. 'Nor your father. But you are free of Hargreave, if you wish to be. You may choose what is best for you. I paid the money to free you, Mairi.'

Dunburn collapsed in the pew. His wife held him and they both wept. The Reverend and the Reverend's wife came to their side.

Davina and Niven ran up to Lucas. 'What does this mean?' Davina asked.

Lucas answered, 'Hargreave was forcing Mairi to marry him. I have made it her choice.'

'Forcing you?' Davina looked confused. 'I thought he was saving us.'

'I thought so, too,' Niven said.

Lucas responded, 'He tricked your father into playing cards with him, first letting him win, then cheating him out of all the money. He wanted the title and land. And Mairi.'

Hargreave grabbed Mairi's arm and started to pull her away. 'Come on, Mairi. You made your promise to marry me. That is the same as marrying me.'

'I never promised,' she told him. 'All I said was that when I married I wanted the banns read.'

Lucas seized Hargreave by the lapels of his coat and

lifted him off the ground as he had done the last time he'd seen him. 'Do not touch her!'

'Let me go! Let me go!' Hargreave cried, his eyes panicked.

This time he had nothing over any of them.

Lucas dropped him and he fell to the floor. 'You may consider yourself lucky you are in church.'

The Reverend spoke up. 'I think you should all go back to Dunburn House. The Baron and Lady Dunburn are quite undone.'

'Mama! Papa!' Davina cried and ran to them.

'She does not have to marry him,' their mother cried. 'She does not have to marry him.'

'Hargreave,' the vicar said. 'Get in your carriage and be on your way. I suggest you do not bother these good people ever again.'

Lucas picked up his hat. 'Come with me, Mairi.'

Together they ran down the aisle and out of the door to where his horse waited. He mounted the horse and reached down to lift her into the saddle in front of him. He headed in the opposite direction from the house.

'Where are we going?' she asked.

'You will see.'

They rode up into the hills until they reached the stone circle. The snow had stopped and the horse pawed at the ground until he found a patch of grass to nibble on.

Lucas and Mairi stood among the standing stones. 'This is where you found me.'

'Where Davina and Niven found you,' she corrected.

'Where you all saved my life,' he added.

She held on to the front of his topcoat. 'We are even, then, because you have saved my life.'

He put his arms around her. 'Mairi,' he murmured. 'I stand before you now as an equal. No more secrets. I could not find the words to tell you that I am my father's heir. I will some day have everything that was due my brother. That was what I could not bear. He died because of me and I profited. I wished to die as well. Without you, I would have achieved that.'

'You could not tell me this?' She still sounded hurt by it.

He shook his head. 'I know I should have told you right away. So I will not hesitate to say what I wish to say to you now—to ask you—if—if you would be willing to become an English viscountess?'

She looked puzzled for a moment. Then her brow cleared.

He released her. 'I know I have made a shambles of things. I know I hurt you by not telling you my real name, my real situation. But I have loved you almost from the first. I just could not admit it to myself, much less to you.'

'You love me?' she asked.

'I love you,' he repeated. 'But, because I love you, I desire your happiness above all things. If I cannot make you happy, then I will let you go.'

The wind gusted, making her shiver. 'Let us leave here.'

They got on the horse again and slowly made their way to the house. Lucas was losing hope, but he meant what he'd said to her. He wanted her to be happy. She was free to make her choice.

Robert opened the door to them with a grin on his face. 'I'll see to the horse.' He walked outside when they entered the hall.

'Would you like my answer?' Mairi asked while Lucas helped her off with her cloak.

He nodded and braced for it, removing his topcoat and hat and laying them over a chair.

She threw her arms around him. 'Yes, Lucas. Yes. I will be your English viscountess.'

He laughed aloud with relief and swung her around

with joy. When they stopped she was in his arms. Like the night of the Scottish reel, Lucas once again placed his lips against hers.

And felt content.

Epilogue

Scotland—May 1818

It had been a year and a half since Lucas had last been in Scotland to stop Mairi's wedding to Hargreave. He'd forgotten the beauty of the country. In fact, he'd never seen it in the glory of spring. The mountains were an even more intense green and teeming with not only deer, but grazing sheep, whimsical rabbits and other wildlife. Under impossibly blue skies could be found carpets of bluebells, their blooms so fanciful they were often called fairy flowers.

Lucas's pleasure in the countryside, though, was multiplied tenfold by the woman riding at his side. His wife, joyous at being back in the land of her birth.

He and Mairi had endured so much since last she'd been home. They'd married as soon as the banns had been read. What the people of Dunburn thought of these new banns being read right after the ones with Hargreave, Lucas did not know. He suspected not everyone was happy that the Baron of Dunburn's daughter had married the son of an English earl. Luckily, his English counterparts had been easily charmed by Mairi, who, as she had in Scotland, treated everyone she encountered with kindness and respect. His parents rightfully credited her with lifting him out of his debauchery and despair, so she could do no wrong in their eyes. But she'd often pined for her mother and father, sister and brother, the people she loved fiercely.

The past year had not been without challenges. As Lucas's father had shown him what duties would be expected of him, Lucas continued to battle the feeling that he was stealing what should have been his brother's. He was not certain he could ever accept it.

The biggest challenge, though, for both him and Mairi had been the physical side of marriage. The assault she'd endured reared its ugly head all too often when they attempted lovemaking. Together they learned how to overcome this, and when they did, he could not describe the elation he experienced. To be so united in love with Mairi made Lucas into a better man. Certainly a happier man.

Their lovemaking blessed them with a robust baby boy, a fine prize for finding their way through the maze of past trauma.

This day, their son was happily being spoiled by Lady Dunburn, his doting grandmother, and his aunt Davina, who was eager to show the baby all sorts of adventures. Dunburn House was filled with happy, well-paid servants, equally as willing to spoil the child. Hargreave's former valet had come to work for Dunburn. Both the Baron and Lady Dunburn were gratefully accepting the efforts of a very efficient estate manager and man of business, who controlled their spending and ran the property at a nice profit. Lucas was perhaps most pleased with the devotion the Baron and Lady Dunburn showed to Mairi now, eager to make up for their neglect in the past. All in all, Dunburn House had become a happy place.

And a beautiful one. As Lucas and Mairi rode over the lush land of the Dunburn estate, he could not help but marvel at the sight. He understood completely the Scotsman's attachment to his country.

He and Mairi wound up at the standing stones, a place that had figured so prominently in their lives. He'd been saved here in more ways than one. By his rescue from death. By Mairi accepting his proposal of marriage.

They dismounted.

'There are tales that the Druids worshipped here and that they still come and defend their sacred ground against anyone who trespasses at night,' Mairi told him.

'I spent the night here, did I not?' Lucas walked around the stones, remembering nothing real of that day.

'Perhaps you were attacked,' she said, leaning against the tallest stone. 'Perhaps they gave you the fever.'

'Nay,' he said, speaking like a Scot. 'I think the Druids rather liked me.'

She laughed. 'Why? You were near death when Niven and Davina found you.'

He came close to her, but was careful not to make her feel caged in his arms. He did lean close and as though to touch his lips to hers. With his lips only inches away, he murmured, 'The Druids brought me you.'

He kissed her again.

* * * * *